I, Ada

I, Ada

JULIA GRAY

ANDERSEN PRESS
LONDON

First published in 2020 by
Andersen Press Limited
20 Vauxhall Bridge Road, London, SW1V 2SA, UK
Vijverlaan 48, 3062 HL Rotterdam, Nederland
www.andersenpress.co.uk

2 4 6 8 10 9 7 5 3

Cover image: *Ada King, Countess of Lovelace*, 1840 © Science
Museum / Science & Society Picture Library
Interior images: GAC 2172, Margaret Sarah Carpenter, *(Augusta)*
Ada King, Countess of Lovelace (1815–1852), GAC 1976, Thomas Phillips,
George Gordon Noel Byron, 6th Baron Byron (1788–1824) © Crown Copyright,
UK Government Art Collection

Preface and quote on page 320 are reproduced by permission of
Paper Lion Ltd and the proprietor of the Lovelace Byron Papers.

British Library Cataloguing in Publication Data available.

ISBN 978 1 83913 007 6

Printed and bound in Great Britain by Clays Ltd, Elcograf S.p.A.

For my parents, Stanley and Jennifer,
and in memory of Ada

We talk much of Imagination. We talk of the Imagination of Poets, the Imagination of Artists, &c; I am inclined to think that in general we don't know very exactly what we are talking about . . . Imagination . . . is the Combining Faculty. It brings together things, facts, ideas, conceptions, in new, original, endless, ever varying, Combinations . . . Imagination is the Discovering Faculty, pre-eminently. It is that which penetrates into the unseen worlds around us, the worlds of Science. It is that which feels & discovers what is, the real which we see not, which exists not for our senses.

From 'Essay on Imagination',
by Ada, Countess of Lovelace, in 1841

(Augusta) Ada King, Countess of Lovelace (1815–1852)
by Margaret Sarah Carpenter (1793–1872)

Prologue

London
August 1836

The summer rain covers our faces like a fine gauze as we step down from the carriage. It's a long time since I've been in London, and I'd forgotten how loud it is here: rattling coal-wagons, hurtling omnibuses; street sellers advertising their wares with guttural yells on either side of the Strand. I stand, a little hesitant, before the entrance of New Somerset House, not wanting to enter until I am ready.

'Ada, are you feeling quite well?' comes a voice from beside me.

'Yes,' I reply, for the sake of brevity.

'Well then, let us not waste any more time on the pavement,' says my mother.

A small hand presses between my shoulders, urging me on. Short in stature, quick-footed, utterly formidable, Mamma is, today, in her element, as she leads me into the Annual Exhibition.

'All the world and his wife seem to be here, don't they?' she says, surveying the scrabbling throng on the marble staircase: fine-feathered ladies calling out to each other, gentlemen in coal-black top hats, their tailcoats flurrying like ravens' wings. We make our way slowly, Mamma stepping nimbly into vacant spaces, never letting go of my arm. (I am not as strong as I would like to be, and at the moment have difficulty walking, much to my irritation.)

Mamma used to despise places like this one. When I was a little girl, we avoided them; she never wanted anyone to notice us, to point and stare and call attention to who we were, and gradually I came to despise them too. But there's no evidence of that avoidance today on her part. 'Oh, *where* have they put it?' she mutters, as we reach the top of the stairs. A sequence of high-ceilinged rooms now opens out in several directions. The walls are a rich, forest-like green – not that much of them can be seen, for every inch, right up to the top, is covered in paintings. I am reminded of a magnified mosaic, or a patchwork quilt of extraordinary variegation – overwhelming at first glance, but quite wonderful too. It's a shame, really, that there are so many people. The crush of bodies obscures so much that one might want to see. And the noise: I cannot hear myself think above the bellowing laughter, the shrill screeches of praise and recognition.

'It is so *nice*,' cries one woman, passing us, 'to see which of one's friends have been immortalised in the exhibition.'

I am just admiring one of Mr Turner's paintings; it's a view of Venice – a place I have never visited, although I would like to – when Mamma comes hurrying over with a programme and beckons for me to follow. Through crowds we thread, until we reach a room with a domed

2

ceiling, on which the rain pounds ominously. It is as though we are in the middle of a huge drum.

'I still can't see it,' Mamma says crossly, as though the entire exhibition should really have been planned with her involvement. (Very Mamma, this: she likes to be in control of everything.)

'Oh well,' I say. 'I never much liked it anyway.'

'Don't say that, Ada; Mrs Carpenter might be here somewhere.'

'I never liked her much either.'

Wisely, Mamma decides to ignore me. I am sorry I was rude; there's just something about being with Mamma sometimes – even though I am a woman of twenty, I still want to behave like a petulant child when I'm with her. Mamma cranes her neck upwards, to those sorry paintings that have been squashed unceremoniously close to the cornice. 'I fully expect the painting to be in a position of prominence,' she says. 'Not, for example, near a doorway, or placed too high.'

'It's called being "skyed",' says a kindly, grey-haired gentleman standing nearby. 'The painters hate it, especially the well-known ones.'

Mamma turns to him eagerly. 'Have *you* seen my daughter's portrait, sir?'

He studies me curiously, not quite with an eyebrow raised, but with a certain amount of surprise. I have not, I admit, taken any particular care with my clothing today; why should I, when there are more interesting things to think about? Just this morning, for example, I reminded myself of the

3

correct way in which to approach biquadratic equations, and lost myself quite blissfully in the process, at least for a while. Then, I think, the gentleman does recognise me, as people tend to do; he is just opening his mouth to speak, when Mamma gives a squeak of delight.

'Oh, look! *There*.'

As she says the words, the crowd parts, with appropriately dramatic timing, and – for the first time since it was painted, last year – I come face to face with another Ada, in three-quarter profile, dressed in oyster-coloured silk. A rising staircase in the background is illuminated by a tempting square of daylight. That staircase promises far more interest, far more excitement, than dull, staid, pale-skinned Ada, who stands with a hand to her middle as though she is wrestling with the pains of indigestion. One foot pokes out from beneath my skirt, hinting at a step that I will not take.

Oh, how incredibly I dislike it.

Looking at it now, I have a brief, intense recollection of being painted by Mrs Carpenter late last summer, in Surrey. Margaret Carpenter was forthright and eccentric; she had a habit, when tired, of flinging down her brushes with a dramatic clatter, and of making me hold my position for far longer than was comfortable, even though she knew I was suffering from debilitating sickness. But I'd agreed willingly enough to the portrait. Mamma had commissioned it in a state of great excitement, pride and (I suppose) relief, and I couldn't bear to deprive her of any of those emotions.

'What a handsome thing it is,' says Mamma, still staring

with the fond-eyed indulgence of nursemaid to newborn. 'It is quite – *quite* – perfect.'

Is she referring to the skill of the artist, the composition of the painting, or the appearance of the sitter? Is she referring to perfections that I myself have never personified?

Is this the Ideal Ada – a person whom neither of us has ever met?

'Well, Ada, and what do you think?' she says.

'I believe, Mamma,' I say, with deliberate slowness, 'that you told Mrs Carpenter to exaggerate my jaw.'

'I . . . well, I . . . No. Not exactly . . .'

She cannot lie – she is terrible at it – and so she does not quite know how to respond. But I can imagine the conversation so easily, knowing my mother and the way she works, and it would have gone something like this:

'*But of course, Mrs Carpenter, you're acquainted with Mr Phillips' renowned portrait of Ada's father? Well, I hardly think it would be a mistake to, perhaps,* heighten *the resemblance to him a touch.*'

'*Why, yes, certainly, milady.*'

'*For example, around the . . . hmm. Around the jawline. Yes.*'

So there we stand, one Ada facing another, and I see myself, familiar and yet unfamiliar: wide of jaw, and strangely dumb-looking, as though a clever thought never so much as skated around the periphery of my head. When I was a child, I longed to look more like my father than I actually did; now, Mrs Carpenter has deliberately enhanced my features to resemble his. It's not the resemblance that I object to; it's the fact that it is an artificial one. My jaw *is* wide, yes: so wide that you could write the word MATHEMATICS across it, if you so desired. As a friend of Mamma's once told me, I really am not beautiful. But Mrs Carpenter has made it as broad as a boat's hull; I loom, moon-faced, in my silks, and do not look like me in the slightest. Suddenly I long to be anywhere else but here, in the presence of this painted stranger.

'I'm going for a walk,' I say to my mother. 'I won't be long.'

Out in the street, I find that the rain has stopped. I walk along the Strand before turning left towards Waterloo Bridge, where I feel in my pocket for a couple of pennies for the toll. The bridge isn't as busy as it normally is, and I make my way slowly to its midpoint. I feel unusual. The portrait has done something strange to me; it has reflected me to a gallery full of strangers with all the force of some darkly enchanted mirror. Captured in space and time, *that* Ada lays claim to every identity that I might hope to possess, leaving no room for anything else, or anything more. She is proud, bold, declarative . . . and yet, I do not know her. But if I do not know *that* Ada, do I know *this* Ada – the one who is, just now, walking over a bridge, unsure of her destination? And is *this* Ada different to *those* Adas who have gone before – I think of myself aged four, eight, twelve, sixteen, and reflect that in some ways there have indeed been many Adas – and, if so, then how different is she?

It's a thought of intriguing, almost mathematical complexity: I imagine a line of Adas, like dolls cut from card, each ever so slightly bigger than the last, stretched out alongside me.

Do they form a progression, a pattern? Is it a pattern that must perpetuate, or might the pattern possibly ... be changed?

In short: who is the Actual Ada, and what does she intend to do with herself?

In the absence of company; in the relative tranquillity afforded to me now by solitude, and the prospect of water, I stand perfectly still, and think about it. The sun comes out, faint behind the ever-present veil of yellowy smog, and I look – as I always do – for a rainbow. Sure enough (even as a small child, I used to believe, sometimes, that I was quite able to *will* rainbows into existence) that band of brilliant light spans the heavens like a pale smile. I lean for support against the stone wall, staring at the rainbow all the while. Then, briefly, I feel my eyes close, and – almost without any impulse, any intention on my part – an Ada comes to me ... There she is: round-faced, snub-nosed, and quite innocent. Fittingly, she is by the sea – from the looks of it, Brighton beach. No – it's Hastings. I remember now. Our hotel is not far away. How old is this Ada, who has appeared out of almost nowhere? I think, perhaps, she is five. She is building something out of stones and shells, examining each item with delicate care. It looks like a fortress of some kind, or a house. She is intent on her work. I watch her, breathing in the sweet-salt air, and suddenly I *am* her; I am her entirely, my own body forgotten. Her thoughts are mine.

I am not alone. Mamma is somewhere not far away – I know this, somehow, although she cannot be seen; and

7

perhaps my nurse, Nanny Briggs, is also keeping watch, somewhere in the shade, worrying that I may wet my feet. But there are others here too, a pair of women, as comfortable and gossipy as nesting hens. They are sitting perhaps ten feet away, and they are talking, and their voices carry.

'My dear, do you know who that is? Why, she's quite famous, you know. It's little Ada Byron. Lord Byron's daughter.'

Part One: 1821–1829
Age five to thirteen

Kirkby Mallory, Leicestershire
May 1821

I am in the vegetable garden of my grandparents' estate, hunting for fairies. *Hunting* is the wrong word, because I do not intend to kill and eat the fairies – I would simply like to observe their gossamer-winged ways, and perhaps, if I can, to be friends with them. My suspicion is that these particular fairies live beneath cabbage leaves, and so that is where I am looking when I see the spider's web. Strung like a silvery scarf between the plants, it could have been wrought by the fairies themselves. I've never seen one so close. I stretch out one finger – not to touch, just to get a better *sense* of it, so intricately woven, so slight and yet so strong – when I hear Mamma.

'Ada, where are you? Ada!'

Obeying the summons, I scramble up via a wheelbarrow onto the low garden wall. I intend to jump off the wall in one neat movement, but the hem of my dress catches on something, and I end up tumbling off it like Humpty Dumpty and into the arms of my mother.

'What in heaven's name were you *doing*, Ada?' she says, as she sets me down upright and pats the earth from my skirts.

'Looking for fairies. They're quick, you know – so quick that I can't quite catch them. But I mean to, one day—'

She makes a loud, impatient sound with her teeth as she drags me back along the path towards the house. 'Fairies! I never heard such foolishness. Why must you tear about so?'

'Stillness is for statues,' I protest. 'You wouldn't want me to be motionless all the time, would you, as though I were a horrid, sad, dead thing?'

'Really, Ada,' she mutters. 'Your father asks for evidence of your development. I've no intention of reporting that you spend your time haring about the grounds like a wild creature.'

In mentioning my father, she has won the point. I am mindful of what she writes to him – she is a prolific, passionate letter-writer – and I want her to tell him good things. (She does not write to him directly, but through someone else, for reasons that I do not quite understand.) I think of him often, this Lord Byron whose name I bear. I would like to see him, but I know that he doesn't live in this country. I do not know why. He sends me gifts – a locket, a ring; items that I treasure – and writes letters to Mamma, in which he demands news of my progress. I have, of course, read nothing of his work. But I know that he writes poems. He is famous for them. I know that he is somewhere in Europe, a place I have never been. I imagine that he lives in a castle on a high cliff overlooking a vast, grey-green sea. He sits at a desk from where the waves are visible, and he dips his pen with a flourish, words of great beauty on his lips as he writes. Servants wait at a respectful distance in case he should have need of anything. It's a hot

12

place, populated by strange insects, unfamiliar scents; these things weave themselves into his poems, adding colour and light. Just sometimes, they weave themselves into my dreams as well.

I am occasionally so spellbound by this vision that I struggle to detach myself from it, earning myself a sharp telling-off from Mamma, or from Nanny Briggs. 'Don't daydream, Ada,' they say, in the same urgent tone of voice that they might use to warn me of an incoming tide or unfriendly dog. But I can't help myself. Other people don't understand how easy it is for me to slip into the unbordered realms of the imagination.

For perhaps four months of each year, we live here in Leicestershire, at a place called Kirkby Mallory Hall. Not far from the market town of Hinckley, Kirkby Mallory is a beautiful, broad, cream-coloured house, whose front windows I love to count (there are seventeen) each time I approach it. Inside, there are cool, high-ceilinged rooms, and secret passageways that I explore with all the vigour of an intrepid voyager, scuffing my knees as I crawl alongside skirting boards with my cat Puff in search of mouse-trails or hiding places for my dolls. There are outbuildings full of promise and delight: a bakehouse, a cheese house, a beer cellar. The parkland is populated with deer, creatures of magic and myth; I tell myself that Hercules' hind is among them, and spend long hours looking for a telltale flash of gold.

I am not supposed to run around so freely and with such abandon, as the gardener's sons are wont to do. I know this, but it's not enough to stop me from doing it.

13

We enter Kirkby through the kitchen door. Mamma strides down the passage – she is short, but able to propel herself forwards with tremendous speed – and I hasten after her. Just ahead of us, the parlourmaid, Lotty, is carrying a tray into the drawing room. Under the chandelier in the hall, Mamma pauses and takes hold of my hands, scanning them for vestiges of dirt. 'Hmm,' she says. 'You'll do, I suppose.'

The drawing room door stands ajar: I can see Grandmama in her reading-chair, head bent in pleasant silence over a little book. Grandpapa is out of sight, but he may well be at his desk, looking over some correspondence to do with the estate. I am very fond of my grandparents.

'Your new governess has arrived,' says Mamma, interrupting my thoughts. 'I want you to be a good, diligent, obedient child – when she's teaching you, and at all other times as well. Will you, Ada?'

She looks down at me, her expression conveying exasperation and affection in equal measure, as it so often does. I look back at her in contemplation. I *do* want Mamma to be pleased with me. I want it so much that I can feel it in my very veins; if you opened me up, you'd find it written large inside of me, I'm sure.

But then there's the other thing that I want, and it's to do things my own way. I wish those things were reconcilable. It seems, so much of the time, that they are not; that I am not one person, but two people, who want different things.

'Well, Ada?'

She is waiting for a reply, and I give it to her. 'Yes, Mamma,' I say.

A governess! I hadn't realised that I was to have such a thing. What will she be like? I perch on the sofa, laughing at Grandpapa as he makes amusing animal-noises for my benefit, and keep a close eye on the door. Will she be strict? Serious? Young or old? What will she teach me?

Soon enough, the door opens, and Miss Lamont is shown in. Her face has the appearance of being freshly scrubbed, but she still seems a little hot and dishevelled from her journey. She is small and neat, with fairish hair combed strictly away from a central parting, and cheeks as round and rosy as apricots. Miss Lamont takes my hand with solemnity, but a smile lurks at the corners of her mouth, hinting at a sense of humour.

'Ada is in great need of intellectual discipline,' Mamma says, pouring tea. 'You must take a rigorous approach.'

'Yes, milady,' says Miss Lamont respectfully. Her Irish accent is soft and pleasant to hear. She darts a look in my direction, a questioning sort of look, as though she is testing the validity of Mamma's request. I nibble at a piece of sugared fruit and listen as they organise my education: we are to do French and music and geography, and drawing too, and reading and grammar and spelling . . . the list seems almost endless.

My grandmother says to my mother: 'A fine range of subjects, Annabella.' Turning to my new governess, she adds: 'We made sure our daughter was just as well-educated at a similar age. It was of great importance to us.'

'But we must *also* make sure,' says Grandpapa, giving me

a wink of solidarity, 'that little Ada has time enough for amusements.'

'Arithmetic,' says Mamma, as though she has not heard this. 'It is through mathematics, Miss Lamont, that I feel sure that the wildness of Ada's nature will be successfully trammelled.'

I do not know the meaning of the word *trammelled* but it sounds like the sort of thing my mother would want my nature to be: a mixture of trained and pummelled. Something meaningful and intense, like a basin full of shockingly cold water into which one must plunge one's face.

'This is a beautiful house,' says Miss Lamont, rather hesitantly, looking out through the great bay windows. 'And what woodland!'

'I prefer my own childhood home,' Mamma says, 'at Seaham.' She sighs. 'But this place is not without its attractions. There is a tree in the park – a Lebanon cedar – that Lord Byron particularly loved. He accompanied me here – only once, before my parents inherited the estate from my uncle, but I recall he spent a full afternoon in the shade of its branches, writing verses. Alas, I cannot remember which ones.'

Miss Lamont expresses surprise and interest. I too am fascinated. A tree that my father loved – here at Kirkby Mallory? It is news to me, and exciting news. It is very unlike her to mention my father at teatime; perhaps it is for the benefit of my new governess.

'Where is the tree, Mamma?' I say.

But my mother is asking the parlourmaid for more milk and does not, I think, hear me.

Kirkby Mallory, Leicestershire
May 1821

My lessons begin the following day. Each lesson is to last fifteen minutes precisely; we are to do four or five lessons before we have lunch at one o'clock, and then the same quantity of lessons in the afternoon. Miss Lamont is full of energy and enthusiasm, which in turn affects me, and the first morning passes quite quickly. I follow the motion of her hand as she writes; I nod my head, showing my understanding; I trace letters in a hand that barely wobbles. I write my name: ADA.

Miss Lamont leans over my work with approval. 'That's very good, Miss Byron; very precise.' She rewards me with a ticket; I cradle it on my lap, pleased to have been given it, although I realise that it is a meaningless square of paper. Mistress Puff appears at my ankles, oozing warmth and companionship; surreptitiously, I reach down to stroke the ridge of fur that runs vertically down her head. She mews in pleasure; Miss Lamont sees her, and smiles. 'That's a lovely cat.'

'She's Persian,' I say, with importance. I do not expect that Miss Lamont has ever seen a nobler creature than mine.

We move on to arithmetic: my governess sets me some sums – addition and subtraction, nothing that I can't do with ease. I complete my tasks, and am given another ticket.

Time passes. The sun swells, beating hotly through the curtains. A fly presses its wings with urgency against the window. A familiar restlessness in my limbs begins to take hold. The nursery becomes an airless prison, a trap. I wriggle and fidget; the sums don't come out right; I know I am not taking as much care as I should, but there's nothing I can do about it. Miss Lamont reminds me repeatedly to sit still.

'Will I have to lie on the board if I cannot keep still?' I ask her.

Miss Lamont looks perplexed. 'I believe you, ah, *ought* to,' she says, and I hear in her tone of voice that she herself would prefer not to make me do such a thing. There is a long, wide floorboard in the centre of the nursery floor, and there have been occasions when Mamma has insisted that I lie upon it, still as a gravestone, as punishment for fidgeting. To a body that loves to exist in motion, nothing is harder to bear than forced stillness and I have always dreaded that particular penance, worse even than being shut in a cupboard – another of Mamma's occasionally prescribed punishments.

'Now, please take out your French grammar,' says Miss Lamont, banishing the subject of the board from our conversation. She begins to talk about irregular verbs. I quite like verbs: they are learned in patterns, and I love patterns of all kinds. There are rules that you can learn, and exceptions to those rules. And then, if you try hard, you can talk in another language – a concept that I find quite thrilling.

At first, I listen carefully to Miss Lamont. Then, after a while, my attention drifts, as it is wont to do. I can't help but look out of the window, which gives onto the wide lawns at the back of Kirkby, with the dark smudge of woodland beyond. Did my father really come here and walk amongst those trees? How could I have never known this? There is, I suppose, so much that I do not know about him. I wish Miss Lamont were telling me fairy stories – her voice would be well-suited to it, I think – or else about volcanoes, for which I have lately developed a passion. There is so much to find out, not all of it on the pages of books, but in . . . well, in everything.

'I fancy that you are not quite paying attention, Ada. What are you thinking about?'

'The tree in the park that was my father's favourite,' I reply truthfully.

Miss Lamont smiles. 'Now, the verb *savoir*, again, from the first person singular, if you please—'

'*Je save*,' I say, faltering.

She stops me. '*Je sais.*'

'*Je sais, tu sais* . . .'

Rather laboriously, I stumble and garble my way to the end of the paradigm. I wait for another ticket to be bestowed. Instead, Miss Lamont says: 'I think perhaps we have done enough for the morning. Would you like to go outside?'

I fairly fall over myself in my haste to get out of my chair. 'Oh, yes, Miss Lamont. Yes *please*.'

'Good: then we shall go. I have not yet explored the grounds, and they seem quite magnificent.'

We have no need of outer garments, the morning being dry and fine, but we put on sturdier shoes outside the scullery before taking the back door out into the kitchen gardens. I make a point of showing Miss Lamont everything – the leafy dell where I suspect the cabbage-fairies hide; the miniature strawberry plants, whose fruits are blissfully tart and will soon be in season.

'Miss Lamont,' I say. 'Do you know what a Lebanon cedar looks like?'

'Why, yes,' she replies, after some thought. 'I believe I do.'

'I would like to find the tree that Mamma says my father loved so much. I want to know where it is. I want to see it for myself.'

'If that is what you want to do, Miss Byron, then that is what we shall do.'

It is at this moment that I decide that I very much like my new governess.

Now we are making our way through the park. My governess exclaims with delight as two deer – a mother and her fawn – lope gracefully across our path, not seeing us. It's a beautiful morning; birds call to each other above our heads, and twigs rattle under our feet as we pass. We are not quite sure where we are going, but Miss Lamont promises me that she will know a Lebanon cedar when she sees it, and I am bound to believe her.

'Do you know much of my father's work, Miss Lamont?'

There comes a pause. 'I know a little; perhaps not as much as I ought.'

We have come to a clearing, beyond which the ground rises up into a soft slope. There, at the edge of the clearing, is a tree, quite immense in stature. It crowns its peers by a good ten feet, like a watchful and kindly god, looking down from a great height. Its leaves burst from its branches in a kind of cloud-formation, as though they are desperate to fly away. At the base of the tree is a little hollow, where a person could lie and look up, content.

'It is a Lebanon cedar, Miss Lamont?'

My governess assures me of her certainty in this regard.

'Then—' I am so delighted that I can barely articulate the words. 'Then this is the tree!'

Stumbling in my excitement, I race through the swathes of grass. Oh, I can picture him now (even though I do not actually know what he looks like) – my father, long legs carelessly crossed and arms spread out towards the canopy above, head tilted back against the leathery bark. He is deep in thought: verses come to him, swimming through silence, syllables jostling for position like washing on a line . . . He is calm. He lets the words shuffle and reform. The poem grows like the tree itself: branches sprout from the trunk; shoots and buds bloom brightly, each greener and more alive than the last . . .

Reaching the hollow, I throw myself down, with a little more force than perhaps was necessary, because I tear a stocking quite badly. I curl, wriggle, uncurl, the way Puff might do when she wants to make herself comfortable in a chair. Miss Lamont is keeping a tactful distance. Never, never for a minute do I think that this might be the wrong tree. Some knowledge cannot be known, only felt, but it is none the weaker for it. The opposite, in fact. The cedar exudes a smell of impossible richness – a dark-green, smoky perfume, so powerful that one might almost be able to see it wreathing the leaves.

'Do mind your clothes,' says my governess.

'I shall now compose a poem,' I tell her, feeling quite giddy at the thought.

'Very well, Ada. Have you need of a pencil?'

'I shall compose it in my head, and we shall write it down later.'

It must be something fittingly grand: something my father might have thought of writing. Oh, I wish that I knew his work! His books – Mamma has everything he has written to date, I believe – are kept on a shelf in the library that I have not been able to reach. I know that he wrote a good deal about love. Well, I too can write about love. Immediately, I think of Puff, who is very much an object of my affection, although I was very cross with her earlier today on account of her vomiting up something grey and distasteful all over my coverlet. But we won't worry about her minor indiscretions now. Carefully, eyes tight shut, I begin:

'A sweeter cat there never was
And nevermore will be.
All silky ears and spiky claws
And . . .'

It is actually harder than I thought. Perhaps I have started wrong. I am just thinking about what I might reasonably change in my composition in order that the final line might hold a satisfying resolution, when a rather unwelcome sound breaks the peace of my thoughts.

'Ada! Miss Lamont! What is the meaning of this?'

I open my eyes, Puff and her associated verses dispersed. Wheezing, puce-cheeked, and quite furious-looking, my mother is pacing through the clearing towards us. I hasten to my feet. Miss Lamont brushes the twists of moss from my dress. I have a sense that she is just as trepidatious at this moment as I am, of what is to come.

'Did she run away from you, Miss Lamont?'

'No, Lady Byron. No, she – we—'

'Yes, I did,' I say, determined that my new governess should not be thought badly of so early on in her employment.

My mother turns towards me, her eyes full of wrathful perplexity. (She has a rather round face, like a doll's, but you should not for a moment imagine that her expression is doll-like. Dolls are placid and unquestioning. Mamma is not.)

'I wanted to see my father's tree,' I tell her.

At this, Mamma blinks, looks doubtful, and then casts the sort of glance at the cedar as, perhaps, the King might do to an unwanted subject that he wishes to dismiss hastily from Court.

Then she says: 'Arithmetic, and French, and letters, and geography.' She speaks with such loudness, such deliberate clarity that I fancy any deer who have not been scared away by her appearance will surely remember those words for evermore. 'At no point in the morning's schedule were you supposed to go gallivanting off into the woodland. Remember that, please, in the future, Miss Lamont. Ada is a woefully headstrong girl whose passions are difficult to tame. That, however, is your charge. When you return to the nursery, Ada, you will lie quite still on the board in penance. Miss Lamont, you will see to it that she does not move.'

The sad, shamed procession begins to weave its way joylessly back to the house. Mamma leads, as stiff as the board on which I am to lie. Miss Lamont is looking quite woeful – as though it is she, not I, who will be punished. At the edge of the lawn, I cast a final look back at the Lebanon cedar, and promise that I shall return – one day when Mamma is far out of reach, perhaps at Leamington Spa, a place to which she is fond of going – and finish my poem. And just as I am doing this, I realise that my mother is doing the same. She stares at the tree, love and longing written all over her face. There is a tenderness in her expression now that was not there before.

I am only five, but I know that it is a tenderness that she wishes to keep a secret, for reasons best known to herself.

Branch Lodge, Hampstead
May 1824

Mistress Puff undulates down the stairs, one leg at a time, and I am trying my hardest to copy her; to become a cat as best I can, with all the feline grace that an eight-year-old can summon on a dull May afternoon.

We are living in Hampstead, in a mansion that my mother has rented called Branch Lodge. We came here after my grandmother died – Mamma and Nanny Briggs and Puff and Grandpapa and I. I like it well enough, especially our vantage point, perched as we are over London. But I miss the wide-open spaces of Kirkby Mallory; the garden here is nothing in comparison to the deer-filled park. I miss my grandmother more than I can say. When I was very young, Mamma would go away quite a lot – for rest cures, usually – and it was Grandmama who looked after me. She was almost a second mother. It's hard to imagine that I will never see her again.

I also miss having a governess. For all her good intentions, Miss Lamont did not stay long – after a few months, she was gone. Mamma concluded, on the basis of a number of misdemeanours on my part (one episode in particular stands out, in which I bit the housemaid), that my young governess was not able to control me in the manner she had hoped for. I was sad when Miss Lamont left, for I liked her, and I believe that she liked me.

'Why is it, Mamma, that I have no governess?' I asked her at breakfast, not long ago.

Mamma looked at me rather reflectively over her Bath cake. (Her appetite is exceptionally good.) 'Why, Mary Montgomery lets you talk in Italian to her quite often,' she said, 'and we do your letters and sums most days, as we have always done.'

'But Mary Montgomery is your friend,' I persisted. 'I mean, why is there no one in sole charge of my learning?'

'I am always in charge of your learning,' she said. 'Besides, the doctor said that it would be a good idea to halt your education, for a time, and I agreed with him. Your health is poor, Ada, as you know.'

But I don't know that my health is poor; this is simply something that I am told, and while it is true that sometimes things do ail me, when I am feeling well in myself, I forget that there was ever a time when I was *not* well. It's also true that since we came to Hampstead, I have fallen prey to a number of colds, and many headaches, some of which were so pernicious and unpleasant that they caused me to be unable to read my grammar book as fluently as I'd have liked. After the worst such episode, Mamma sent word to my father and told him that I was not well, and although she said nothing to me of his response, I later heard her telling one of her friends that

Lord Byron had professed himself unable to work until he had been informed of my recovery. This made me feel very strange inside – a little proud, and a little mystified also Could my father really love me so much that news of my illness could incapacitate him completely? It didn't seem possible, and yet I saw no reason why anyone concerned should have been lying. In any case, I was doubly relieved when I recovered from that particular period of ill-health.

Puff and I have just reached the landing when we hear a strange, otherworldly wailing from the library on the ground floor. It is like no sound that I have ever heard before. It's a ghostly sort of wail, like the cry of some disembodied spirit drifting over a windswept moor.

'Puff, what in heaven's name is happening?' I whisper.

My Persian cat looks thoughtfully at her paws. A minute passes; the wail continues, rising in volume and pitch, and only then do I realise that we are listening to my mother. There is someone with her, a man, talking in gentle, hesitant, conciliatory tones. It is Grandpapa. Mamma is distraught, and he is doing his best to console her. I want to run down the remaining stairs as fast as my feet can carry me; I want to see her, to see what troubles her, and to find out if I can help.

I am just about to do exactly this, when I hear my own name.

'He spoke only of Ada, I'm told, and left no other message.'

'My dearest Anne,' says my grandfather. (He often calls her Anne, though most other people know her as Annabella.) 'I am sure that he—'

'Oh, I can scarcely put into *words* the feeling – the sudden, vast desolation . . . It was a fever, they say. He couldn't be saved.'

Curiouser, I take a step or two towards the hallway. What is my mother talking about? Who spoke only of me, and why does it matter? Why is her tone so altered? I cannot remember the last time I saw my mother cry; she simply isn't that kind of person. Puff lets out a delicate mew, and the voices, alerted to our presence, change at once. Footsteps resound on a polished floor, and then the oak door of the library opens and Grandpapa emerges. 'Ada, come down. Your mother wishes to speak to you.'

Now my concern for my mother shifts into something closer to alarm. 'Is Mamma cross with me?' I ask Grandpapa, although I cannot think why this would be the case, and know that it surely cannot be.

'Goodness, no; she isn't cross with you. Come, Ada, quickly, and leave the cat.'

Mamma is standing by a bookcase, staring unseeingly at the unlit fire. As we enter, she looks up, and then comes over to me – almost dancing, despite the reddened patch on each cheek that implies recent tears – and takes hold of both my hands. She clasps them so tightly that it is painful.

'Oh, Ada. Oh, my child.'

'What's the matter, Mamma? What has happened?'

'England has lost a very fine poet,' she says. 'But we have lost something far dearer than that – although, of course, you never truly had him at all. When you were a young child, I always thought of you as . . . as *fatherless* . . . and now . . .'

She is babbling, incoherent, as unlike her as I've ever known. I don't know what she is saying, or how to make sense of it. Grandpapa coughs softly, and this is enough to bring her to her senses. Mamma holds herself a little straighter, and breathes with more purpose and control.

'Dearest Ada, your father has died.'

The news is quite shocking, by which I mean that I feel struck by it as though by lightning. For a good two minutes, I am unable to move or speak. I do not feel anything because I do not know how, or what, I am supposed to feel. Certainly, I cannot cry as she seems to have been doing. I would like to, I think, but I cannot. Instead, I say the words in my head, over and over again – *my father is dead* – and wait for something else to happen inside of me.

'You said he spoke of me,' I venture, at last.

Mamma nods. 'He said. "Give her my blessing", or words to that effect.'

Little by little, the high colour is fading from her cheeks. She is regaining control of herself. I try to take in what she has said: that my father, in his last living moments, thought of *me*, and sent me his blessing.

'Where will he be buried?' I ask. 'When will the funeral be?'

But it is clear that the conversation is over, and I have asked too many questions. Mamma only shakes her head, and then leans down to give me a kiss and tells me to run away. And run away I do, going outside to the long narrowish garden that borders the back of the house, whose beds are thick with roses. At the very bottom of the garden lies my Enchanted City, built from wooden blocks of all colours – not just brick-shaped blocks, but cylindrical and triangular ones too – and now I sit down beside it, comforted by its magnificence, and play quietly for quite some time, while everything that I have learned over the past hour circulates in my head, settling in my thoughts. I build a tower here, an archway there, losing myself in the possibilities. I think of my cousin George, who is two years younger than I, and how much I hope to be able to see him soon. Having no brother of my own, I find that I do occasionally want one, and George seems in many ways the likeliest candidate. The thought comes to me abruptly that George's father (also named George) is the new Lord Byron, now that my father, who was once Lord Byron, is dead.

The afternoon wears on; it's a dull, cloudy kind of day, with not much sun to speak of, but I have a sense of it anyway, dipping down towards the horizon. Then, at last, in the act of fashioning a chimneypiece for a red-and-yellow roof, I feel a wave of sadness – a kind of lost, helpless sadness, because I am sad for a father I never knew, rather than one that I knew well – and I lay the blocks down on the grass and start to cry.

Branch Lodge, Hampstead
December 1824

It is my ninth birthday and I am feeling full of *magical* potential. I am early to rise, stealing down the stairs of Branch Lodge, intending to make my way down to the kitchen, where I hope to find Cook and demand some kind of birthday-worthy confection. But at the windows on the upper landing, I pause.

The windows are stained glass, and they have always held for me a real fascination. Mamma's friend Joanna Baillie told me once that the windows were taken from a French convent during the French Revolution – and every time I pass the windows, I look for some hidden detail, something that I haven't seen before. The pictures are of saints, against backgrounds of different colours – blue, green, purple, red – and angels too, and stories from the Bible. I press my nose right up against one of the saints until I can look through the tinted glass and out onto the streets of Frognal – our particular part of Hampstead – and beyond, to the heart of London itself. It's snowing. Little, fluttery puffs of snow are gathering on rooftops, on garden squares. Through the stained glass, the snow looks blue. I start to imagine a world in which snow is always blue. It strikes me as an interesting idea; perhaps something to try to work into a poem.

'Happy birthday, Ada.'

It's Mamma; I spin around, and there she is, in her housecoat. She doesn't usually rise before nine. I run to her and we embrace. 'Do you remember the glass factory?' she says, nodding at the windows.

'A little.'

I *do* remember, although I was quite young, perhaps six. Mamma took me on an expedition to Birmingham. We went to see the glass being made; Mamma is always interested in developments, processes, and wants me to share her interest. I have a recollection of hand-operated machines in which wheels turned, making patterns upon the glass, and being entranced by it. I remember the Malvern hills that we journeyed through afterward too, and how the mist sat like a blanket on the hilltops, making it hard to see.

We stand side by side in silence. Then I say: 'I am imagining a world, Mamma, in which snow is always blue.'

She sighs. 'Oh, Ada. I would like you to notice the world for what it is, in an accurate fashion, and not in the fanciful way that you so often adopt.' But she says it kindly. I have noticed, only in the past couple of years, that Mamma is sometimes a little sad on my birthday. It is as though she is remembering something to do with a time that I myself cannot remember. Sometimes I think that I would like to ask her about it.

*

The Baillie sisters – Joanna and Agnes – come to take breakfast with us, in celebration of my birthday. In their sixties, perhaps – I find it hard to work out people's ages, unless I've been told them – they smile as they come to the breakfast room, light on their feet and full of good wishes.

'What a *treat* it is for us,' says Joanna, who writes plays, 'to see you on this illustrious day.'

'You are looking especially well, Ada,' adds Agnes.

I hope so, for I like to look well. Mamma's friend Louisa Chaloner told me only recently that I am not at all beautiful. I was rather saddened by the comment, and ever since have tried to make sure my hair is nicely brushed and my frock not too dishevelled-looking, even after an exploration of the garden. I thank the Baillie sisters for coming and accept their birthday gift with pleasure. It is an Atlas of Modern Geography – bigger than any other book I own, and heavy to hold. I balance it with care next to my plate, turning each page slowly, examining the worlds contained within it with such absorption that for a while I barely take any notice of the conversation.

'There is so much to see,' I say, more to myself than to anyone else.

Grandpapa smiles at me over his kipper, of which he has not eaten much. He is not as amusing as he used to be, although he is rarely without a smile. Most of the time he dozes, as though there is not as much to incite his interest as there once was. He has also given me a gift – a set of ivory dominoes.

'Anne,' he says. 'What about *your* gift?'

Mamma smiles. She takes a fold of paper from beside her teacup and holds it out to me. I am not sure what to expect. A pamphlet of mathematical puzzles, perhaps – although that would not be anything out of the ordinary, since Mamma might offer me a puzzle any day of the year.

But it is a pair of tickets to Drury Lane. For tonight! I get out of my chair to scamper around the table and give her a hug. 'The theatre! Oh, Mamma!' I have never been to the theatre; Mamma goes fairly often, and afterward writes criticisms of the productions she has seen in her notebook, but she has always left me behind. I am truly beside myself with gratitude. My mother can exasperate me somewhat, especially when I am thinking of a world in which snow is blue, and she is objecting to my free-roaming imagination, but in this moment, I utterly adore her.

After breakfast, the day cannot go by too quickly. I play with Flora Davison in the morning – she is a dear friend of mine, and one whom I seldom see, as she does not live in London. In honour of my new atlas, we play at being World Explorers. We run out into the snow and pretend that we are traversing the vast, icy plains of Norway, with much shrieking and discoveries of bears and wolves and other Wild Things that Dwell in the Fjords, until we are summoned inside by Nanny Briggs. Then Flora goes home, and the hours begin to lengthen in an irritating fashion. In the afternoon, Mamma goes out to pay a few calls. The snow deepens, settling into hillocks and drifts, and I begin to worry that the carriage will not be able to take us to Drury Lane. But then, at about four o'clock, the sun comes out for a late appearance, just enough to melt the snow, and I see the sweepers come out to clear the roads.

In the carriage on the way to the theatre, I look out of the window, delighting in this visit to the centre of a place that I do not as yet know at all. 'What time of day was I born, Mamma?' I say.

'Why do you ask?'

'Because I have never known.'

She half closes her eyes, recollecting. 'At lunchtime. Perhaps a quarter past one. It wasn't snowing that day, but it was bitterly cold. I found it a struggle to leave the house the day before, although I did go out, on an errand of sorts. I remember having to take great care not to slip; the pavements were so icy. By the time I got home, I was quite exhausted and the pains of labour had taken hold completely.'

I can't resist staring at her in the ill-lit carriage, my attention drawn entirely now to the story that she is telling, for it is one that I have never heard. I am rather sorry to have caused her pain.

'What house were you in – Seaham?'

'No,' says Mamma. 'We were in London, at Piccadilly Terrace.'

She looks out of the window, scanning the streets with intent, as though seeing them differently. 'We are not far from there now, in fact, although we shall not necessarily pass it.'

I follow her gaze, seeing London through new eyes. I was *born* here. I never knew.

'And who was there at my birth?'

'Only the *accoucheur*, Dr Le Mann – an unfashionable choice, my friends said, but I liked him – and a nurse.'

'What about my father?' I say. 'Was he at home?'

'He was downstairs,' she says. 'There were others too. Augusta, and a cousin of mine, and perhaps some acquaintances whose names I presently forget.'

I have the most curious sensation, as we are talking. It is as though I am turning the pages of an atlas of sorts, one by one and very slowly, uncovering territory that has, until now, lain undiscovered and totally secret. Augusta, I know, is my aunt – a sister, or half-sister, rather, of my father's, whom I have never met. I consider my next question with delicacy.

'Was my father . . . pleased when I was born?'

'What do you mean?' she says, rather sharply. 'Of course. He was delighted. You were . . . you were very *healthy*. He was quite delighted with you.'

This last repetition is said with weighty finality, and there is a sadness in her voice that is easy for me to hear. We fall back into silence until we reach the theatre. It is snowing again, lightly, as we descend from the carriage. The entrance to Drury Lane is crowded with theatre-goers; I wonder at the fine-feathered headdresses, the elaborate silks and luxuriant cloaks of the women, while the men are also quite elegantly attired. Everyone seems to be enjoying a heightened state of merriment; I hear a snatch of a Christmas carol echoing from the street corner as Mamma whisks me deftly through the crowds and into the theatre. Heads turn as we cross the foyer, and she keeps me close to her side, as though trying to protect me from scrutiny.

'Why, Annabella, my dear!'

Mamma freezes; I can feel the muscles in her hand tensing as she keeps hold of my arm. A woman is bearing down on us – she looks to be of a similar age to Mamma, but in appearance quite different. She is slender, with a face dominated by dark eyes that glitter like charcoal, and fair ringlets cut rather short. She reminds me of a fairy – a dark one.

'Caroline,' says Mamma. 'I am delighted to see you.'

But I know from the tone of her voice that she is not delighted.

'And this must be *Augusta Ada Byron*,' says the fairy-woman, looking at me with interest and adding heavy emphasis to her words.

'I am known simply as Ada,' I say, not afraid at all to speak, although she has unsettled me somewhat. I tend to forget that I am known by people; that my name precedes me in certain circles.

The woman laughs, so loudly that several people look over in our direction. My mother's grip tightens again on my arm.

'Why, of course!' says the fairy-woman. 'Ada . . . the name suits you very well, my dear. Better, perhaps, than—'

'I believe the curtain is due to be raised at any minute now,' says Mamma quickly. 'Come, Ada.'

'Mamma,' I say, as we take our seats in the private box, whose upholstery is extraordinarily rich to the touch, like the top of Puff's head. 'Who was that?'

'A cousin of mine,' she replies. 'Lady Caroline Lamb.'

'What did she mean, about my name suiting me?'

'The woman is quite unbalanced. I would have thought that would have been obvious to you,' says Mamma tersely. 'I hear, besides, that she is not at all well.'

After this, she falls into silence. I begin to fear that I have angered or upset her, although I don't know how or why I have done so. I shouldn't have mentioned my father, I realise; but it doesn't seem fair, when I hear her mention him, unbidden, from time to time. Why should she be allowed to talk of him, but when I do, I am silenced? Surely I should be allowed to ask about my own birth – an event that by definition concerns me quite centrally? Or indeed, why we were not present at his funeral, when so many other people, with connections far weaker than ours to him, were present? I study my programme, abashed and baleful. The play is called *The Road to Ruin*, and no doubt it is sombre, devout and moralistic – just the sort of thing Mamma, who likes nothing more than to reform people, or to study long religious screeds, will enjoy.

I start to wish that I were at home with my new atlas and Mistress Puff.

But as the heavy curtains lurch upwards, Mamma takes my hand and gives it a squeeze, and I remember that this is my special birthday treat, and that I love her very much.

The play turns out to be a comedy, and before the end of the first act we are both laughing fit to burst.

George Gordon Byron, 6th Baron Byron (1788–1824)
by Thomas Phillips (1770–1845)

Bifrons, Kent
June 1826

Now I am ten years old, and we are renting a house on the Dover Road called Bifrons. At the end of a long avenue of trees, and not far from the sea, it's a solid, symmetrical mansion in the classical style. There's a splendid library; finding a book on the history of Kent, Mamma is pleased to learn that the house was once the home to Brook Taylor, a mathematician.

On one of my explorations of the house and its grounds, I discover a picture gallery. At the very end of a long row of framed landscapes, concealed behind a green curtain, is a painting. It's clearly been recently hung, because it seems out of place, somehow, among all the rest. No one should have to resist pulling back a curtain to see what lies beneath; I certainly cannot do so, and so I climb onto a chair, reach for the curtain and manage to drag it back in a single attempt. It is harder than I thought it would be – the curtain sticks a little, and the rings are reluctant to move – and then, all at once, the picture is revealed.

I see a man of perhaps twenty-five depicted from the

waist upwards. His head is turned to the side, as though he is in conversation with an out-of-sight interlocutor. He is wearing a costume of sorts – a headdress, an embroidered jacket – and has a sheathed sword (or that is what I think it must be) clasped against his chest. His eyes are a greyish-blue; he has a cleft in his chin. He manages to look both serious and light-hearted at the same time. There is a painted signature which I cannot read; then I notice the small inscription on the frame itself.

GEORGE GORDON
6th BARON BYRON

A thump of recognition sweeps through me: my *father*! How was it that I have never before seen this picture? It was my understanding that Mamma had no pictures of my father – I asked about it once, and was told that he had hated to have his likeness taken by anyone, and thus there were no portraits, even miniatures, in existence.

Clearly a lie.

Not a day passes, after this, when I don't go to see the portrait, even for a solitary minute. I grow *fascinated* by it, rotating it in my Ada-brain like a spinning top. What was my father thinking, as he sat for the artist? What was he writing at the time? Had he met my mother? To what stage had their courtship progressed? My mind ventures into realms of alternatives and possibilities; every time I go to the gallery, some new thought occurs to me.

But there is one thing that irritates me: no matter how hard I try, I just can't find any resemblance between me and the man in the picture. Even when I press my face close to the looking glass in my room, late at night, and attempt unsuccessfully to mould my features into the same expression that he wears in the picture, I find nothing.

One quiet June afternoon, my new governess and I are working together in the schoolroom. My new governess' name is Miss Charlotte Stamp, and she is a veritable *treasure*. She always knows when my head aches too much to study, and reads aloud to me instead; she willingly follows the will-o'-the-wisps of my inclinations, teaching me about the historical periods that interest me, rather than those that I am meant to be reading about. She notices that I find it hard, sometimes, to grip my pencil, and teaches me to relax my hand when I write. She plays chess with me, and dances with me, and laughs at the things I say. Oh, the things we talk about! Arrowroot and foxgloves and acorns, and the behaviour of water, and how you might construct a boat; and why it is always a good idea to be kind to animals, and what icebergs might contain apart from ice. The days pass with an agreeable quickness under her tutelage.

I am glad that Miss Stamp is here, because I have, I confess, been very lonely. 1825 was a year of change in our little family. My grandfather, Sir Ralph, died and was buried with Grandmama. My mother became known as Lady Noel Byron, and seemed to me to grow slightly in stature with this new name. She inherited a vast fortune. Sometimes I overheard her conducting meetings in the drawing room, in which she discussed her intentions in her usual clear-headed manner.

'I am quite determined,' she would say, 'to do *good*.'

But with power and money seemed to come great fatigue; she spent long periods away at Leamington Spa or Hastings, engaging different physicians and experimenting with cures. At these times, I was left alone with Puff and Nanny Briggs, and largely had to entertain myself. This I did through reading; I had always enjoyed reading, but it was then that I began to subsist on a veritable diet of books. The Baillie sisters were friends of Walter Scott's, and gave me *Ivanhoe*, which I devoured; I borrowed *English Stories* from my friend Flora, and read – with not too much difficulty, for my French was really rather good – some enchanting French fairy tales. I came up with a phrase to describe my burgeoning passion, which was *Gobblebook*, as in 'I am Gobblebook'. And gobble books I did, especially on those long afternoons when there was no one to play with, and no one to talk to; when there was no Grandpapa to crease his ruddy cheeks in an affectionate grin, and there was no Mamma to make sure that I was still doing my sums.

Now I have Miss Stamp with whom to do sums, and I am all the happier for it. We are at present studying the Rule of Three, so important that it is often referred to in books as the Golden Rule. The Rule of Three is essentially a question of proportion; you use your knowledge of two things in order to work out the value of a third, unknown thing. The first question is an easy one, requiring only minimal working-out:

If two loaves of bread cost sixpence, how much will three loaves cost?

'In this instance,' I say, thinking aloud for the benefit of Miss Stamp, 'we will name our quantities as follows: *a*, *b* and *c*, where *a* is two, the number of loaves; *b* is six, the cost of these two loaves; and *c* is three, the number of loaves for which we need to calculate the cost. We will then perform the calculation *c times b divided by a*; that is to say three times six, divided by two, which gives us *nine*. The answer to the question, therefore, is ninepence.'

'Very good,' says Miss Stamp.

We move on to the Double Rule of Three, which I find much harder, because we are dealing now with five known quantities, and one unknown. It can be very confusing. I reread the question in the book which Miss Stamp is obligingly holding open at the right page.

'If six men can mow twenty-four acres in eight days, in how many days can four men mow twelve acres?'

I stare in frustration at the question, scribbling one incorrect equation, and then another. Miss Stamp allows me to notice and address my own errors – this is one of her nicest qualities, I think – and does not tell me the solution. Eventually, gently, she shows me that I need to rearrange the numerator and denominator in one place, and finally the answer becomes clear – six days – and I sigh in relief.

'It's like looking into swirling water,' I tell her. 'Water that's really muddy, but then suddenly grows clean.'

'What a lovely way of putting it,' says Miss Stamp.

'Miss Stamp,' I say suddenly. 'Would you come with me to look at my father's portrait?'

I have not told Mamma about my daily practice of visiting the picture – I prefer to keep it a secret, since I am gradually learning that she reacts to any mention of my father in a strange, unpredictable manner – but Miss Stamp is another matter. She is not the kind of governess I care to keep secrets from, and soon I am leading her through Bifrons to the gallery, safe in the knowledge that Mamma is out. Moments later, we are standing beneath the picture, the curtain drawn back. Usually, I find myself forcefully drawn to my father's face, but today I am more interested in looking at Miss Stamp's. I am keen to know what she really thinks.

'I *do* see a similarity,' she says, frowning a little in her effort to judge our respective physiognomies.

'Do you?' I say gloomily. 'I really don't. I think we are simply not alike at all.'

'Wait here,' says Miss Stamp suddenly, and goes flying off down the corridor. That's another thing I like about her – she is given to impetuous bursts of fancy, not unlike mine. Minutes later, my governess returns with her arms full of fabric – cast-off shawls and fur-lined pelisses and so forth from the dressing-up chest in the playroom. At once, I see what she has in mind; we assemble a costume to rival Lord Byron's: a swatch of tartan, wrapped thrice around my head, becomes a sort of turban, and a black jacket with gold embroidery proves a not-too-distant match for his own.

Miss Stamp, who seems to know more than I do, tells me that the outfit he wears is Albanian. I wonder why; I wonder what connections he had with that particular country.

'Did you know that my father did *not* want me to turn out poetical?' I say, as we fashion a sword out of card, engrossed in our work.

'Oh yes?'

'He wrote and told Mamma so, not long before he died.'

Miss Stamp suppresses a laugh. 'But he did not do so badly by poetry himself,' she points out.

'Perhaps one poet is enough in any family,' I say.

'It might depend upon the nature and quality of the poetry in question,' says my governess, quite gravely. 'Now, Ada, you must stand like . . . like so. Head up a little. *Yes!*'

I am, by now, laughing so much that it's all I can do not to double over. With difficulty, I straighten my spine. I glance behind me, checking once more the specificities of my father's pose. I fold my arms and look meaningfully into the distance. Miss Stamp arranges a fold of material over my arm. 'Wonderful!' she says, clapping her hands – although she does this rather mutedly, lest anyone should hear us.

And suddenly – suddenly – everything vanishes. I can . . . I can *feel* him in the room next to me, his movements, his posture mirroring mine exactly. It fairly freezes the breath in my chest; it is as though (and I will remember this quite clearly for many, many years) there is a ghost in the gallery. Yes. He is here with me. He turns; he catches my eye, and slowly, with approval, he nods and then smiles. It is almost as

47

though he is saying: *there* is *a resemblance, Ada, and don't ever forget it.*

'I won't,' I whisper, hoarse-voiced.

'Ada, are you quite well?' says Miss Stamp.

I look around, collecting myself. The ghost-feeling is gone; all that remains is the gallery, my governess, and some clothes from the dressing-up box.

'You were talking to yourself,' says my governess.

'I forgot what I was about,' I tell her. I do not keep secrets from Miss Stamp, but there are some things, I realise now, that are just too precious to tell.

For a moment, I felt something that I have *never once* felt, in my younger years, for my father – George Gordon, 6th Baron Byron – because I did not have the wherewithal to feel it.

Love.

Bifrons, Kent
June 1826

Not long after the incident of the ghost in the gallery,
Mamma makes an exciting announcement. 'We are to take a
tour of Europe,' she declares over dinner. 'There are a great
many places that I want to go, and it will do you a world of
good, Ada, after your ill-health, to see something of the
Continent.'

The news comes as the most wonderful surprise: she is
speaking of a Grand Tour, in the old tradition, and I can
scarcely believe it. 'Will we go alone, Mamma?' I ask, putting
down my soup spoon with a clatter.

'No, indeed, Ada. My cousin Robert, and a number of my
friends will join us at various times. Miss Montgomery, and
Mrs Siddons and Mrs Chaloner.'

I have always adored Mary Montgomery – there are times
when I think of her as a relation, and not simply a friend
of Mamma's; I believe that Mary is as interested in my
education as my mother is. But while I also like Harriet
Siddons, an actress and passionate educational reformer who
engages in the longest conversations with Mamma on the

subject, I am less enthusiastic about Louisa Chaloner. I have never forgotten that she once told me I was not beautiful.

'What about Miss Stamp?' I say, suddenly worried that my new-ish governess will not be coming with us.

'Of *course* we shall have the pleasure of the company of Miss Stamp,' says Mamma. 'Now that your health is a little better, there is no reason for the pace of your studies to abate.'

Plans develop most enticingly. Clothing and sundry necessities must be bought; letters sent, arrangements made for accommodation and transport; our possessions packed into trunks . . . at times, I am so filled with anticipation that I can barely eat. My dreams, always colourful, grow more vivid and delicious than ever, loaded with lofty castles, rolling hills, elaborately-dressed noblemen; thick, dark forests teeming with wolves, and long golden beaches fringing unfamiliar seas. I pore over the atlas given to me by the Baillie sisters for hours, and Miss Stamp helps me to draw into my commonplace book the route Mamma intends us to take. Mamma says that we will be away for as long as a year, and perhaps longer.

'It will be the furthest geographical distance I have ever been from home,' I tell Miss Stamp, as we sort through the books that we want to take with us. 'The same is true for Mamma too. Why do you suppose she has had such a change of heart? Perhaps the spirit of adventure has come upon her.'

'You must remember, Ada, that England and France are no longer at war; that, to me, seems like the primary reason,' says Miss Stamp, rescuing the books I have piled haphazardly onto a chair from near-collapse. 'There's also the matter of your grandparents,' she adds gently. 'Now they are deceased, your mother is more at liberty to plan this kind of lengthy journey. I believe, moreover, that one of your mother's primary motives for this trip is educational. She wants to visit the famed Hofwyl Institute in Switzerland.'

It is true that Mamma has been talking for some time about her admiration for the founder of the Swiss institute, Dr Fellenberg, and his methods. It is in her nature to need to see how things work, and to show me how they work also; I think of our early visit to the glass factory in the North of England – her pale, serious face as she pointed out various intricacies of the operation. 'Do you see, Ada? Do you see?' she would say, and I would look, and try to understand.

'We must take Walkingame,' says Miss Stamp, selecting a calf-bound textbook from the pile. 'And Pasley's *Practical Geometry Method*. We will have to keep up your arithmetic.'

On my dressing table is a small box, silk-lined, that contains the handful of items that my father sent me in the years before his death. There is a talismanic ring, wonderfully and surprisingly heavy to hold, and a locket that bears the inscription 'Water is thicker than blood'. I wonder if I should take the little box with me – it seems wrong, somehow, to leave it for a year or more, unopened . . . but then I think of the highwaymen that might very well stalk the roads of the Continent, waiting to pounce on wealthy voyagers, and decide that Bifrons is a safer place for my treasures.

'And what's this little book, Ada?' says Miss Stamp.

'Oh, just a notebook,' I say, taking it. 'A book of poems.'

'Your poems?'

'Yes.' I'd almost forgotten about them: a hotchpotch collection of verses, written down in odd moments. Limericks, acrostics – any kind of poem I could think of, really. None particularly good. But Miss Stamp is keen to hear one, and so – rather shyly – I select one that I don't think is too badly-constructed, and begin:

'My name is Ada Byron, and I see the world in numbers.
Once I saw in pairs: eyes, cuffs, slippers;
Then I saw in threes: good, better, best;
Four compass-points: North, South, East, West.
Five upon my fingers, and ten upon my toes.
For the world contains more numbers than anybody knows.'

'Oh, but it's charming, Ada! When did you write that?'

'I'm not sure,' I say, squinting at the date at the bottom of the page. 'I think it was when I had begun arithmetic properly.'

For a while, neither of us speaks. I don't know what Miss Stamp is thinking about, as we continue to sift through the books on the shelves, each choosing what she feels might be most useful for a tour of the Continent, and what might reasonably be left behind. It's a warm day; the windows are shut, and I fall, as I so often do, into a kind of daze. And all the while the books mount up, looking for all the world like the brightly-coloured towers that I once, not so long ago, built out of blocks in our Hampstead garden.

A thought occurs to me, all of a sudden: *worlds* are built out of *books*, just as buildings are built out of blocks . . . The daze deepens; my thoughts spin themselves into an ever-widening web, each filament glinting like a moonbeam shard. I see cities entirely constructed from books, from foundations to firmament - walls of tomes of green and blue and brown, some slim, some sturdy, but each forming an essential, immutable part of the fabric of the architecture . . . It's an entrancing scene. And I realise that this is the feeling of IDEAS – of an *idea coming upon me* – and a wave of such dizzying, blissful excitement that the idea must, perforce, be a good one.

'Miss Stamp,' I say. 'I've just realised something: a decision about my future. I want to become a writer.'

'What an *excellent* idea,' she responds, smiling at me with such approval that I feel like a spring bud, blossoming in the benevolent light of the sun. 'Novels? Plays?'

'I don't know yet,' I say. 'Perhaps I shall not limit myself to any one form of writing.'

'Well, our European expedition will no doubt furnish you with plenty of ideas,' she says. 'Who knows – perhaps you will turn out poetical after all?'

Europe
July 1826

For the duration of the Channel crossing, Mamma and Miss Chaloner huddle together in the small, cramped cabin of the boat, groaning weakly and complaining about the *smell*. I myself am not troubled by seasickness, and am thus free to explore the deck with my governess. It's raining – not a lot; just enough to fleck our faces with moisture – as we admire the hull, and the great funnel.

'The engine of the boat is powered by steam,' I say, remembering what I have read with Miss Stamp about the inventions of Watt and Trevithick. 'The engine turns the paddles of the boat, and this propels it forwards.'

'It's a simple idea,' says Miss Stamp, 'but such a powerful one. It makes you wonder what else could be accomplished with steam.'

'Just you wait,' says Robert Noel, lounging against the rail next to us. I've always liked Robert Noel, who is a kind of cousin of Mamma's; he has a way of making everything sound exciting, even dull things. 'Soon – mark my words – people will be able to travel up and down the country by steam locomotive. Letters delivered in a day! Goods carted from town to town! Imagine it!'

I *can* imagine it. 'There are other things you could do with steam,' I say. 'What about a giant, steam-powered music box, so big that it could be heard across a vast expanse of countryside ... or steam-powered ice skates that could propel the skater incredibly fast along a frozen river?' This is the kind of thing that I would normally say to Miss Stamp alone, but I recognise that Robert Noel is a fellow traveller, and as such may share in our conversation.

He chuckles in an avuncular fashion. 'What an imagination you have, Ada. Be sure it doesn't get you into trouble, now.'

The boat chugs and chatters, cutting a steady-paced pathway through the grey-green waves, until at last the Continent appears: a blurred sweep of distant cliffs, with a ruffle of cloud above it.

I stare at it, awe-stricken. 'I, Ada, have crossed an entire sea,' I whisper, to no one.

'It's amazing to think,' says Miss Stamp, 'of these two countries being at war for so many years.'

'And it's cost this country dearly,' adds Robert Noel.

It is only as we are disembarking that I remember that my father also crossed this same stretch of water. When I do remember, it doubles my sense of adventure and magical promise.

I don't recall much about Calais, or the carriage journey we take thereafter, but the Dutch port of Rotterdam, which we reach within a few days' time, is a revelation to me. I am enchanted by the houses – slimmer, for the most part, than London townhouses, but with an abundance of windows, as though every occupant is a dreamer, perching wistfully on a windowsill and looking out towards the harbour.

'Even the air is different here,' I tell Miss Stamp delightedly, as we watch the boats in the port, the gulls darting and looping overhead. *Everything* is different. The windmills, for example, have a character that is altogether their own; they seem more colourful than English windmills, and bolder. I adore them. There is one particular windmill that catches my imagination: *De Blauwe Molen*. For days, it inhabits my thoughts.

'Use it in a story,' urges Miss Stamp; I think this a very sound idea.

Mamma, meanwhile, eats prodigiously hearty breakfasts every day, all the while poring over literature about the educational institute that we are to visit in Switzerland, and reminding me to exercise diligence with my lessons. I do try, working each morning with Miss Stamp, but I also find time to attempt my first short story, entitled 'The Mystery of the Blue Windmill'.

After Baden and Heidelberg, we travel to Geneva. It's a long, tiring, dusty journey over the mountainside of Jura; Louisa Chaloner has been reading to us from Mariana Starke's guide for travellers, and although I have grown sick of listening to her at times, there's no denying how excited I am that I will shortly see the lake.

'Geneva is a town of some thirty-thousand inhabitants,' Louisa Chaloner intones in her dry, no-nonsense voice, as we begin to descend the mountain.

'I don't know how you can read in these conditions,' says Mamma, whose face is pale with nausea. It is a horribly bumpy road; even Robert Noel and Miss Stamp are quiet and subdued.

Undeterred, Louisa goes on: 'Soon, we shall pass a villa that belonged to the philosopher Voltaire.'

Twisting away from her, I divert my attention to the small carriage window and all that can be seen through it: a thicket of fir trees . . . pretty little cottages sticking like limpets to the mountainside . . . I note these visual treasures, keeping silent count in my head, marking them down to be remembered always. Presently I let out a squeal of joy, so loudly that Louisa stops, annoyed, in the middle of her monologue.

'Oh, Mamma, the lake!'

It has suddenly appeared beneath us – crystalline, tranquil, exquisite – surrounded by glaciers so tall and graceful that they almost defy belief. Robert Noel asks in French for the coachman to stop. We get out, unsteady on our legs, and a moment of silence enshrouds our little group.

'Can it be real?' I say.

'Of course it is *real*,' says Mamma. 'The evidence of your own eyes should suffice to convince you of that. Don't make fanciful remarks, Ada.'

But it is the almost-unrealness that I find so spellbinding, as I stand on the mountainside, with its carpet of tiny flowers, and gaze at the lake. *If only I could paint well,* I think – *or write symphonies, or words of extraordinary beauty; if only I could do something, make something,* achieve *something that could come close to the majesty of this body of water . . .*

I nudge my governess. 'This is why people write poetry, isn't it?' I whisper, so that Mamma will not overhear (for I am not sure that she will share my opinion). 'To try to capture a feeling . . . like this.'

Miss Stamp gives me a beauteous smile.

Louisa Chaloner interrupts my thoughts. 'Geneva itself,' she says, still reading aloud, 'is divided by the river Rhône. On entering the city, we shall cross over two bridges . . .'

Throughout our stay in Geneva, I try, when I can, to work on my story. The Blue Windmill is now situated, naturally, beside a lake of great size and wonder, visited by hundreds of birds, and home to all manner of freshwater fish. But in spite of my ambition, I struggle with the writing. Sometimes the words come easily to me, and I am pleased by the fluency of my ideas; at other times I feel as stale as old Bath cakes, and find myself indulging in frenzies of revising and crossings-out that leave me exhausted at the end of my efforts, and with nothing to show for them but an ache that spreads sharply across my hand, as though I have taxed its bones too greatly.

One Tuesday morning – it's a sultry day with a sticky heat that make my undergarments cling unpleasantly to my legs – Mamma and Miss Stamp and I go to visit Geneva's public library. There's a silver Roman shield on display; we are drawn to it as bees might be to a particularly prominent sunflower, and hover around it in silence.

'How are you finding Ada's *thoughts*, Miss Stamp?' Mamma says, with customary abruptness, as though I am not there.

Miss Stamp seems temporarily at a loss for words. 'Well,' she says, 'I don't know if I can speak for Ada about her own thoughts, but those thoughts of hers to which I am privy seem to me to be of great interest and originality.'

'But what about the *arrangement* of her thoughts?' Mamma persists. 'Witnessing my daughter, it seems to me that she veers from exclamations on the prettiness of the view to a meditation on some question of arithmetic, pausing to sing a scale or draw an outline of a chimney in chalk, and then declaring that she might, perhaps, like to learn a new instrument or two!'

'Indeed,' says Miss Stamp cautiously. It's true, I do behave like this, and she can't really deny it.

Mamma carries on: 'It seems to me, in short, that Ada's mind is most worryingly disorganised.'

At this, she squints furiously at the Roman shield, and then at me, as though comparing us both, and finding me wanting by contrast. There is a pause. Rather morosely, I gaze at the shield. It is a handsome, shiny, heavy-looking thing – exactly what I'd expect the Romans to have made. Someone has beaten away at it for hours, I see, marking it with tiny, identical indentations. In just the same way does Mamma wish my mind to be moulded. It is entirely clear.

What is Miss Stamp going to say to Mamma? I've always

thought of her as an ally; someone who will come to my defence – to shield me, even – if I need it. And, sure enough, Miss Stamp tells Mamma, very prettily, that my mind has no shortcomings insofar as its organisation is concerned.

'Well, Miss Stamp,' says Mamma. 'You do satisfy me with this response, although it remains my strong conviction that my daughter's time would be better employed in mathematical pursuits than, for example, in writing romantic and fanciful stories.'

At no point has she asked me what I think about my own mind, but that doesn't surprise me; she is paying my governess to educate me, and therefore she can regard my intellect as a purchase, a possession, of her own. But if she were to ask me whether I agree – what would *I* say? In a way, I consider her observations of the way my mind flits from place to place to be quite accurate. But what she calls disorganisation, I call something different: the feeling of allowing my thoughts to fly from one passion to another, not allowing themselves to be tied down by doubt, or digression, or ideas about rules – well, that, to me, feels more like freedom.

Mamma has not upset me, and I tell myself that I will not worry about what she thinks about my mind – but, somehow, her comments in the public library work their way a little more deeply under my skin than I would like. I work on my story for another few days, and then – without mentioning it to Miss Stamp – fold the pages in half, tear them twice, and throw them away.

Geneva
September 1826

One day, a week or so before we are due to depart from Geneva, Mamma summons me to her sitting room. 'I think that it is now time for you to engage formally with the principles of geometry,' she says.

I don't know what has prompted this; perhaps she has been thinking further about my mind, and how best to trammel it, or else perhaps she has always meant to give me the book, which she is holding out to me now, at around this point in our journey.

The book is called *The Elements of Euclid*. I open it to its first section, entitled 'Definitions'.

I. *A point is that which hath no parts, or which hath no magnitude.*
II. *A line is length without breadth.*

I look up. Mamma is watching me, almost hungrily; she wants a reaction from me, a declaration of sorts. It feels like a test. Either I will be drawn to Euclid and his writing, or

I won't be; if I am, it will be a victory for her, and if I am not, a failure – on my part as well as hers. But I am thinking so much about what *she* is thinking that I am forgetting to read on.

III. *The extremities of a line are points.*
IV. *A straight line is that which lies evenly between its extreme points.*

The definitions continue, develop, running into pages and pages, deepening in complexity. I turn to another section, mouthing words to myself, absorbing it. This is nothing like fellowship and alligation and the Rule of Three – these are not problems of money and quantity; men mowing acres and boys eating apples. This is . . . pure, somehow. Unassailable. The fundamental truth of shapes.

'When was this written?' I say.

'Oh, hundreds of years ago. *Thousands*,' says Mamma.

The thought of this fills me with an inexplicable feeling – a sense of time passing and triangles and squares and pentagons remaining fixed, immutable, dependable. Inventions change the world and how it works, but the mathematical truths that underlie those changes stay the same.

'What do you think, Ada?' says Mamma.

'It's . . . like poetry,' I say quietly.

Mamma sniffs. 'It is not in the least like poetry. These are *rules*,' she says.

'What I mean is . . . I mean that reading this gives me the

62

same sense of something beautiful and constant, such as I would get from reading a passage of Milton,' I explain.

At this, Mamma nods very slightly. I think she does understand. She herself writes a good deal of poetry, not that I have read much of it. It's not *poetry* that she dislikes; it's more behaviour that she might describe as 'poetical' – having a disorganised mind, for example, or behaving in an unpredictable way. In Mamma's mind, there exists, I think, a certain separation between the notions of poetry and poetical behaviour; this is certainly true in her own case. It may be less true as far as my father is concerned, for I have not yet been allowed to read anything that he wrote.

'But do you like it?' she persists, gesturing to the page.

'Oh yes,' I say. 'I like it very much.'

'That's *good*,' she says.

I have long been an observer of my mother's desire to 'do good'; she is by nature a reformer, one who wishes people and projects to adhere to rigid guidelines. She is unsettled by change, or rather, by change that she has not herself anticipated. On the ferry crossing, for example, she thought that the weather would be fine, and the waves unthreatening; when the opposite turned out to be true, she was very ill indeed, from seasickness of course, but also from the fact that things had not happened quite as she had imagined they would. When a roadside inn that had been recommended to her was full, and we had to find lodgings at another, she found it impossible to be happy there, even for a short time, although our accommodation was perfectly agreeable. If Mamma thinks that my mind is disorganised, I believe that the reverse holds true for her: her mind is *too* organised.

But Euclid provides something on which we can both agree. And now she and I spend our afternoons puzzling over the nature of circles and spheres, circumferences and intersections, and I come to realise that mathematics is a language that we share.

When Mamma organises a sailing trip on Lake Geneva on the last day of our stay there, I imagine that she means it as a reward for my hard work. It's a windy afternoon; the surface of the lake is not as mirror-smooth as it was when we first glimpsed it from the Jura mountainside. Miss Stamp has gone sight-seeing alone, and so it's just the two of us, Mamma and I, and our guide, a tall young man named Franz, who speaks English in a slow, careful, heavily-accented voice.

'How big is the lake?' I ask, as we climb aboard the little boat.

'Nineteen leagues in length, and perhaps three and a half in breadth at the widest part, miss,' he replies.

The lake feels as big as an ocean, hemmed by prim houses on one side and statuesque mountains on the other – and our boat as small as a dust-speck in a soup tureen. I enjoy how strangely unstable it is; the feeling of seesawing.

For a while, Mamma and I don't say much, and I wonder what she is thinking about. The boat circumnavigates the lake, slowly. Then Mamma says: 'As you know, we are to leave Geneva shortly and travel to Hofwyl. Perhaps it would be useful for you to hear some of its history.'

Overhead, the cornflower sky is scuffed with clouds; I tilt my head upwards, counting them, and half close my eyes to listen as she talks. Mamma isn't a natural storyteller, but this is a story that she knows exceptionally well; her voice, often a little stiff and halting, flows smoothly as she tells it.

'It began at the end of the last century,' she says, 'when Switzerland was invaded by the French army. Men and women fought bravely and died, and a good many orphan children were left behind, utterly destitute. In Canton Unterwalden, a philanthropist called Henry Pestalozzi provided shelter for the orphans, and there he set up a little school. His methods were quite unusual: he gave the most intelligent children jobs as his assistants, and enlisted their help in running the school – preparing food, mending garments, and cultivating the plot of land that surrounded them. His endeavours attracted the notice and praise of other philanthropists, and eventually the government offered him the Castle of Burgdorff, in Canton Berne, in which to set up his Educational Institution.

'Now, Pestalozzi had an acquaintance by the name of Philipp Emanuel de Fellenberg, and this young man, who had long paid heed to the phrase: "The rich have always helpers enough, help thou the poor", was an ardent follower of Pestalozzi's ideas. Deeply affected by the principles of the French Revolution, and full of ideas for ways in which the world could change, Dr Fellenberg became Pestalozzi's neighbour when his father purchased the estate of Hofwyl, just a few miles from Burgdorff. Although there were matters on which the pair did not agree, Pestalozzi arranged to hand over the institute to Dr Fellenberg. And so, twenty years ago, a little cottage was built at Hofwyl. The teachers slept on the upper floor, while the ground floor was used as the school room. Lessons took place all morning; the afternoon was spent working in the garden, while in the evening the teachers would prepare the vegetables for the following day.'

'Is it a little cottage still?' I say.

'I believe it has grown somewhat,' says Mamma.

'I like the idea of . . . of changing the way that the world works,' I say.

'So do I,' says Mamma. 'The phrase he clung to – *the rich have always helpers enough, help thou the poor* – is close to my own heart too. When you think, Ada, of the squalor, the cramped living spaces, the lack of opportunity that is the reality for so many in England – why, our lives are charmed by comparison. It's not enough simply to muddle through the daily haze of one's own existence, is it? When there is so much to be *done*.'

She looks at me, eyes bright, and I see someone different, suddenly, on the wooden seat next to me, to the person I used to know. Then, abruptly, she flinches, as though stung by a hidden bee. She looks across the water, scanning the shoreline, frowning as she does so. I follow her gaze. From the edge of the lake, the hills slope up sharply; there, above a plantation of vineyards, upon a ridge, sits a large, square, white villa with a reddish roof.

'There lies the suburb of Cologny,' says Franz. 'And that is the Villa Diodati.'

At this, Mamma catches her breath sharply; watching her hand on the rail, I see how white her knuckles have become. But her voice, when she speaks, is quite level. 'That is the house.'

'What house, Mamma?'

'It's where . . . it's where your father lived, Ada. Ten years ago, now – oh, can it really be *ten*?'

Hearing our conversation, Franz tactfully steers the boat so that our view of the Villa Diodati is unimpaired. I stare at the villa, examining its proportions, trying to imagine my father inside it, ten years ago. A strange transformation is taking place in my head: those early visions that I have cherished of my father – at the edge of the sea, writing at his desk, surrounded by servants – seem to shift somehow and merge with the real-life villa, with its lake view and bed of vines. He feels more *real* to me, now, than perhaps he has ever felt before.

'Your father rented the house in 1816,' says Mamma. 'Another poet, a man named Percy Bysshe Shelley, who tragically drowned some years later, lived nearby. They were very good friends. The night that Mary Shelley thought of *Frankenstein*, there was a storm over the lake. The three writers decided to write stories – ghost stories – to mimic the dramatic weather. Or so it is said. What your father and Percy Bysshe Shelley concocted I do not know, but *Frankenstein* is deservedly a work of some repute.'

She is talking rather glibly, I notice, just as she did a few moments ago, when she recounted her history of Pestalozzi. It strikes me that these speeches have a purpose other than my elucidation: she is trying to fill some kind of empty space – in our conversation, or else in her own head – perhaps for fear of what else might appear unbidden. Miss Stamp has told me, quite recently, about Mary Shelley and her novel, *Frankenstein*, about a man who seeks to traverse the bounds of scientific possibility by bringing another man back to life *by means of electricity*. Clearly, Mary Shelley is a Woman of Ideas. I never knew that my father lived here, so near to the Shelleys.

But there's something else that I never knew, somehow, until this moment.

'Then I was only an infant,' I say slowly, 'when he left. I was not even one year old.'

Silence at this. Then: 'That is quite correct, Ada.'

'Why did he leave so soon, Mamma?' I say.

The wind picks up and the boat surges wildly for a few minutes as Franz adjusts the sail.

'Come,' says Mamma, 'I think we must go back.'

She does not answer my question; I never really thought that she would, but important questions are always worth asking. As we sail back across the lake – it is beginning to rain – Mamma looks back at the house, just once, as though to imprint it upon her memory. She frowns a little, as though such an imprinting causes her a peculiar kind of pain – a pain that is unpleasant, but also, somehow, necessary.

Switzerland
September 1826

Staying up rather later than my usual bedtime, I am sitting at the foot of Mamma's easy-chair in the furnished apartments we have taken in Canton Berne, listening to the conversation between three learned and lively-minded women. Mary Montgomery and Harriet Siddons have come to join us in our travels; Robert Noel, meanwhile, has left us to attend to other matters. In a couple of days, we are to visit Dr Fellenberg's institution.

Mamma is in a visible state of anticipation – she is usually too self-possessed to be demonstrably excited – about visiting the famed academy. I can tell from her manner of speaking – faster than usual, and a little breathless. 'Of course, dear Harriet, it is on *your* recommendation that I thought of arranging this visit,' she is saying. She is drinking a cup of chocolate with her usual gusto – we have it at home, sometimes, but at home it is nothing like as rich and sweet as it is in Switzerland.

Harriet Siddons is an actress – she once played Juliet at Drury Lane – and always speaks with clarity and emphasis.

'Why, everyone knows that education in our country is quite *shockingly* in need of reform,' she says, her voice resonating in the room. 'Impractical, ill-considered and, more than anything else, *unfair*. Think of how many people are simply denied the right to an education.'

'What people?' I say.

Harriet Siddons looks at me sternly (she is not, in fact, a stern person – just a rather emphatic one, as previously stated). 'Poor people, for a start,' she says, as though I am very foolish for not understanding this.

I sit up a little straighter, listening now with real interest. For so long I have allowed myself to stop listening as soon as Mamma brings up the subject of Dr Fellenberg. Now I am intrigued; I have never thought about this before. 'Do poor people not . . . do they not receive an education at all, then?'

'Why, no, Ada,' says Mary Montgomery, from her corner. She is bolstered by cushions, to make her position more comfortable, for she is troubled by continual back pain. Her lovely face is a little tired-looking in the firelight. 'How could they, when they must work for a living, often from childhood?'

Mamma says: 'What is needed is useful, practical training: the provision of a set of skills that children might be able to use for the rest of their lives. That is what they aim to do at Hofwyl.'

'No messing about with things like *Latin*,' says Mrs Siddons, making a wry, disgusted face. 'Not like—'

'Indeed,' says Mamma tightly. She goes on: 'I am looking forward to seeing the place for myself. More than I can possibly say.'

'Annabella,' says Mrs Siddons, who is always outspoken, 'you can't deny that your husband's Harrovian education is the very *opposite* of the model you seek to know more about; now, can you?'

My mother rises from her chair. 'Let us not talk about him now; not here, not in front of Ada.'

Thinking about this later, I'm puzzled. Mamma showed me my father's house on the lake not two days previously, but she cannot allow her friends to mention his education. Why? It doesn't make any sense. I think about it, treating it as a riddle, for hours – then, I realise the difference. Harriet Siddons was *criticising* Byron, finding fault with the way that he was brought up, and that is something that Mamma cannot permit. Our little sailing-trip earlier in the week was something very different.

If anything, I decide, it was a pilgrimage.

I have other questions besides this one, and decide to ask Mrs Siddons, since she was the one to mention my father in conversation. I choose my moment carefully, waiting until Mamma is resting, and Mrs Siddons is sitting alone on the balcony with a small pile of correspondence.

'Mrs Siddons,' I say. 'May I ask you a question about my father?'

'Why, Ada, certainly you may,' she says in her usual

forthright way, though it strikes me that she *looks* a little hesitant.

'I've been thinking about my father's departure to the Continent, and I know now – though I hadn't realised this before – that it was in 1816. That is right, isn't it?'

Mrs Siddons replies: 'I remember his departure, as a matter of fact, quite clearly – it was in the newspapers, you see.' She smiles wryly. 'Let me think. The war was over, of course . . . yes, it was 1816, Ada.'

'And he . . . he never came back?'

'No indeed.'

She picks up her pen, balancing it between her heavily-ringed fingers, but doesn't write anything.

'Why was it in the newspapers?' I say.

'Well,' says Mrs Siddons. 'He was famous – still is, of course, even after death. What he did was always of interest.'

'And why did he never come back, not even once?'

'Ah, Ada, I don't know if I can answer that. Perhaps he preferred the ways of foreigners. Many do, you know.'

This doesn't entirely convince me. Now she scans a piece of correspondence, and then starts a letter on a fresh piece of paper, and I don't feel that I can disturb her further. But I can't dismiss this new knowledge: Byron left England when I was the smallest of infants, and never returned . . . I hadn't realised that he left so soon after my birth. For some reason I can't quite express, I feel saddened by this. My existence was not enough to tempt him to stay.

*

72

Mamma is at her most voluble in the carriage on the way to the institute the following morning, telling Miss Stamp the history of Pestalozzi.

'Pestalozzi championed something that he called *Anschauung* – "the perception of the senses",' she is saying, as the carriage slows to a halt outside a tall gate. 'Dr Fellenberg then expanded the principle, adding the concept of action, as well as perception. Education by action! Just think, Miss Stamp. It was – and still is – a revolutionary approach.'

I listen with interest to this as we disembark, and the gates are unlatched to allow us to walk through. Education by action sounds very much like the sort of thing I would enjoy. I do not consider long hours at a table – education by *in*action – to be particularly exciting, and this is how my own time is largely spent. Perhaps, as a result of our Grand Tour, Mamma will revise her ideas about how I, her own daughter, am meant to be educated? It's an exciting thought.

On the other side of the gate is a group of lofty, generously-sized buildings, in the Swiss style, with pointed roofs; they are surrounded by a pleasantly-sized courtyard, in which is a tall climbing-frame and a number of trees. Regimented gardens lie beyond on three sides. The courtyard is *full* of boys – some of about my age, and many much older – running, playing, exercising . . . there are even a few on horseback, and I watch them curiously; I have always wanted to be able to ride, and have never been thought to be strong enough.

A wise-looking man with very little hair and a quiet, precise manner approaches us. This must be Dr Fellenberg himself. 'Milady,' he says, taking my mother's hand.

'It is a *great* pleasure to meet you,' Mamma replies.

'What an atmosphere of quiet industry,' says Mary Montgomery, walking with the aid of her cane. Dr Fellenberg is taking us on a comprehensive tour of the institution. We speak to teachers and pupils alike, looking at what is taught, and how, and all express admiration for this peaceful, purposeful school.

'This is a place of equals, as you know,' says Dr Fellenberg. 'We have rich pupils and poor ones; old pupils and young ones. They are friends, truly, each feeling sympathy and understanding towards the other, no matter what their circumstances are. This is a school for everyone.'

'Dr Fellenberg,' I ask, 'why are there no girls?'

'But there are indeed girls here,' says Dr Fellenberg, smiling, with a gesture towards the garden, around the back of the largest building, and there we see at least a dozen young women going about the business of weeding a vegetable patch. 'My wife is in charge of the girls,' he adds. 'They too are in need of the skills we aim to provide, especially if they are to earn a living.'

The girls are now walking in pairs across the garden. I admire their practical-looking dresses with big pockets for carrying things in, and the way each girl has a basket piled high with implements or produce. One girl, red-haired and long-legged, has a smear of dirt on her cheek. I envy it. She looks at me suddenly, and we smile at each other.

At the end of our visit, Mamma seems exhausted, but elated. Harriet Siddons and Mary Montgomery are talking excitedly as the carriage takes us back to our apartments, but Mamma sits back, hands folded. In her eyes is an expression that I know very well, for I recognise it as one of mine: that glittering, magical-potential look that speaks of *ideas*.

'Mamma,' I say, 'is . . . is an idea coming upon you?'

I assume that she won't answer me, or say she doesn't understand, but she does. 'I have so much money, Ada,' she says simply. 'As you know, I am determined – utterly determined – to do good with it. Well, I am quite resolved. I shall set up a school, following in the footsteps of Dr Fellenberg and Pestalozzi. I shall get the best advice, and find the best teachers. I've no doubt that I can do it.'

And I have no doubt, either. Mamma is a very determined person.

Bifrons, Kent
June 1828

I am sitting in one of my preferred hiding places – the little box room next to the maids' bedrooms, high up on the very top floor of Bifrons. Slant-ceilinged and filled to capacity with boxes of papers, trunks, and odds-and-ends, it is an excellent spot for Gobblebook, but also for thinking, uninterrupted.

It is nine months since we returned from our continental travels, and in many ways, I feel extraordinarily changed. I am different. Older (twelve and a half, which seems almost impossibly grown-up) and taller (a relief, for the doctor did not think, before we left, that I was growing quite as well as I might) and *wiser.* I am wiser in many ways. I can speak better in French; I have read thirty-seven books (Miss Stamp and I kept a faithful record); I can now complete Euclidian problems with speed and accuracy. Sometimes the beauty of geometry permeates my dreams: a galaxy of vertices and planes, glinting like palaces of ice.

And I have acquired not only the wisdom of *books,* but also of people. I know that, for all her protestations about the educational purposes of our tour, Mamma was, in many ways, giving space and time to her feelings for my dead father. It really was a pilgrimage of sorts. Yes: we visited Hofwyl, not once but twice, and I've no doubt that Mamma truly needed to see it. But our stay in Geneva, where we saw the house in which he had lived, was no less important to her. I'm sure of that.

There was more to come. After a time in Turin, on the Po River, where you could see the Alps in all their magnificence no matter where in the city you were, we went to Genoa. Here, Mamma rented a *palazzo*. It was simply the most exquisite place I had ever seen. Huge, square, grey – a veritable castle – it overlooked the bustling port town from a high-up resting place amongst the hills.

'I am never happier than when I can see the sea,' I said to Miss Stamp, as I waltzed from room to room.

One afternoon, a visitor appeared: a plump man of middle age with a kindly face and luxuriant moustaches. It transpired that Signor Isola had been engaged to teach me music and drawing.

'Do you like music, Miss Byron?' he asked me.

'I love to sing, though perhaps I could be better at it,' I told him. 'While here on the Continent I have heard, on many occasions, the most beautiful organ music in churches.'

'What made you like it so much?'

Thinking carefully, I replied: 'Because of the *patterns*. The notes in each register complement each other. It seems a simple thing, but actually it must be very complicated. It must take a composer of great genius to create such music.'

Mamma said to Signor Isola: 'Ada's father wanted her to be musical. It was his wish.'

'Lord Byron himself had a fine singing voice,' said Signor Isola, nodding wisely.

'Oh!' I said. 'You . . . you knew my father?'

'Why, yes. He lived here, in Genoa, for a time – five years ago, it must be – before he went to Greece.'

And so, once again, it seemed that we had come to a place that my father had intimately known. Signor Isola came every day, ostensibly to teach me, but I found that he stayed long after the lesson was over, talking to Mamma about my father. I would have liked to have been part of their conversations, but was not invited. Leaning over the banisters of the *piano nobile*, I would do my best to overhear what they were saying.

'He stayed in the Casa Saluzzo, if memory serves me well,' Signor Isola was saying one evening. 'A lovely place, with the most wonderful views. Ah, but I don't know if he was happy here in Genoa. Many's the time that I would see him, head lowered, at the water's edge, and frowning as though all the cares of the world were visited upon him . . .'

Such tantalising snippets as this one would occasionally reach me. I heard only one other snippet, and it was Mamma this time who was speaking, but she was not speaking in English. I fretted over it all night, for it seemed to me important. I wanted to know.

At my singing lesson the following day, I plucked up the courage to ask Signor Isola himself.

'Tell me, please, some of things that you have been speaking about with Mamma,' I said. 'They concern my father, and so they also concern me.'

Signor Isola took out a large, splendidly-embroidered silk handkerchief and wiped his brow, with exaggerated slowness, before replying: 'Your mother wishes to know my impressions of Lord Byron, and I have been telling her what I remember.'

'And what did she say to you last night?'

'What do you mean?'

'It wasn't in Genoese,' I said. 'I thought it might have been Latin. A phrase of some kind. A quotation?'

'Ah, yes. *De mortuis nihil nisi bonum.* "Speak nothing but good of the dead",' said Signor Isola.

'I don't understand.'

He shrugged. 'Your mother, she is a proud woman. She will not tarnish the name of a great poet with public slander; and even in private, to you, his child, she will say little.'

'But . . . but what is there to say?'

'Lord Byron was, many say, a genius. Those people do not often exercise the same *moral restraint* that others, less blessed with exceptional talent, are wont to do.'

'What does that mean, if you please?'

'Ah, Miss Byron, it is really not for me to say. He was a man about whom there was often . . . What is the word?' He made a searching motion with his hand, as though rummaging through some drawer in his mind. '*Gossip,*' he said at last. 'Oh, yes, there were plenty of stories! Next time, perhaps, I could tell you a little more . . . But then again, you are only a child. Let us practise now a rising arpeggio, if you please, commencing on Middle C.'

That was the last time that I saw Signor Isola. But for the rest of our tour, the tantalising questions raised by our stay in Genoa remained with me, and now that we are returned to England, they remain with me still. I must – I *must* know what happened! Why did my mother and father separate when they did? Did they argue? Was there a misunderstanding of some kind? A tragedy?

Was it something to do with me?

It is, I decide, not unlike a Euclidian puzzle. Human Geometry. I imagine now my parents as shapes – my obstinately rational mother I cast as a square; my father, less symmetrical, a triangle. The angles of the triangle add up to 180 degrees; the angles of the square to 360. The floor of the box room is dusty enough to allow me to draw the shapes with a finger. Inscribed within a circle, it is possible for their respective points to meet in only two or three places. In short, they do not match. There are sharp, uncovered edges; differences in behaviour.

I wonder, did my parents love each other at all?

'I know *she* loved *him*,' I say aloud, staring hard at my diagram as though it contains the answer. 'I know she did. Why else did we travel to all those places that he had visited? But why does she never talk about him – or rather, when she does, it seems that there is so much that she cannot, or is unwilling to, say? And . . . did *he* love *her*? If he didn't, why . . . Why am I here?'

The problem seems worryingly insoluble. My grandparents, who might have been able to shed some light on my questions, are dead; Miss Stamp did not know my father, nor my mother until she was engaged as my governess. I resolve to talk to some of my mother's friends at the next suitable juncture – although I am doubtful that they will give me any meaningful information.

The window, I notice, is as grimy as the floor. Wiping away a thick film of cobwebs and dirt with my skirt – Nanny Briggs won't be pleased about it, but never mind – I peer through the film glass and down to the gravelled pathway at the back of Bifrons. Sudden movement startles me – a blur of silky fur, shimmering out from beneath a bush – before I realise that it's only Puff. She is circling something on the edge of the flowerbed, prowling like a tigress, occasionally darting forth to take little vindictive nips at what looks, at first glance, like a heap of funeral garments.

Taking care to first brush away my Human Geometry from the floorboards, I hurry down to investigate.

The heap of funeral clothes turns out to be a poor dead crow. Puff is dancing elatedly about, looking for all the world as though she killed it herself, which she may well have done.

'Come away,' I tell her, kneeling down. 'Naughty Puff! Then again, I suppose you are only following your instincts.'

The bird is only recently dead, I think. I try to dissuade Puff from eating it; she has of late become incredibly fond of feasting on the corpses of birds. I feel sorry for the crow, and also curious. I would like to examine it. After a moment's thought, I scramble over to the greenhouse, locate a pair of gardening gloves and return, emboldened, to scrutinise the bird. Tenderly, I take one wing and stretch it out so that I can see it well. I must make a sketch of it, I think; and when the flesh has decomposed, I will be able to study the skeleton properly, and make a sketch of that as well.

I feel it then, that web-like funnel-feeling: the world expanding and contracting around my ears, the daze swallowing me whole for a short while . . . undoubtedly, *an idea*. I sit for a moment longer, the wing resting between gloved fingers, and then dash pell-mell into the library, and this is where Miss Stamp finds me a couple of hours later, surrounded by notebooks and loose sheets of paper.

'My goodness, Ada! What are you doing?'

'Oh, Miss Stamp,' I say. 'It's absurd – why has nobody thought of this before? Man *should* be able to fly! I feel *intoxicated* with the thought of it. Look!'

She leans over the pages, trying to decipher my writing, which always descends into lamentable squiggles when I am excited. 'This,' I explain, 'is a design for a pair of fully-functioning wings, for a man – or woman, of course – to put on and fly with. I shall try to make them myself to see what can be achieved.'

'As long as you take greater care than Icarus did,' ventures Miss Stamp, with a smile.

'I will write a book to go with my inventions,' I tell her, 'called *Flyology*. With illustrations.'

'Oh, Ada,' says Miss Stamp. 'I am glad that you have not entirely abandoned your dream of being a writer.'

She smiles broadly, and I smile back, feeling – for some reason – relieved. 'I never wanted to abandon that dream,' I say slowly. 'But I do worry that Mamma will say that Flyology is too fanciful. I shall make sure my designs are sound; then, perhaps, she will approve of them.'

'That seems an excellent plan,' says Miss Stamp.

'I can't help my imagination, sometimes,' I say, thinking about it. 'It just *wants* to do things, and I can't stop it, you know.'

'Ada,' says Miss Stamp, 'if I had your imagination, I would be very proud indeed.'

It is perhaps one of the nicest things that anyone has ever said to me, and I make up my mind to remember it always. For perhaps half an hour, my governess and I discuss my newly-christened Flyology. Miss Stamp suggests that we consider Da Vinci's sketches for inspiration, but I point out to her that he did not actually succeed in designing fully-functioning wings, as I mean to do. We talk also of the Montgolfier brothers, who were, we think, the first to come up with the concept of human flight, by means of hydrogen-fuelled balloons. Miss Stamp raises the question of safety, and we talk about this for quite some time.

'All good inventions must involve *some* risk,' I say. 'Just look at Mr Harris, the balloonist. He invented a special valve to allow gas from the balloon to be discharged slowly. A most important discovery.'

'He died while flying his balloon, did he not?' says Miss Stamp.

'Yes, he did,' I say. 'But he died for the cause of scientific discovery. A most noble reason.'

'Would *you* be prepared to die for your own inventions?' asks my governess.

Thinking about the matter in all seriousness, I am not sure how to answer. No one, surely, can consider their own death lightly. But I think of my father, and also of my mother: each, in their own way, a person of remarkably strong convictions. My father believed absolutely in his work. (I am sure of this.) My mother believes absolutely in her duty to do good. I, Ada, must believe equally absolutely in my own causes.

I say: 'If my invention – whether it is a flying machine or something else entirely – proves to be of indisputable use to society, then, yes, I think I would be prepared to die for it.'

'That is a brave intention indeed,' says Miss Stamp. 'As long as there is to be no dying while I am here.' She goes on: 'Oh, Ada, I shall miss you.'

The words arrest my pencil mid-motion, and it slips from my fingers, landing with an apologetic clatter on the floor.

'Miss me? But . . . where are you going?'

'I am going to be married. I have just spoken to Lady Noel Byron. I shall leave before Christmas.'

'You will come back,' I say, wanting it to sound like a question. Instead, it has the querulous, tremulous tone of a vain command.

Bifrons, Kent
November 1828

I sometimes think that I give up on things rather quickly, but Flyology is different. Perhaps it is because I know that Miss Stamp is leaving. The design of our flying machine is to be our last collaboration, and as such I wish to invest all my energy in it. I continue with my lessons, working diligently enough at my French compositions and algebraic equations, and filling my commonplace book with essays on the Napoleonic wars and maps of Europe, but in the afternoons – or whenever there's time – I work on Flyology, and Miss Stamp helps me.

To begin with, we concentrate solely on the wings, making small models in different materials – mainly wood or paper – and writing detailed notes on how they are to be made to work. The days shorten; winter draws near, sweeping chill-frost winds from the sea along the Dover Road. I have begun, over the years, to notice how the lack of daylight affects my mood – and, to some extent, Mamma's too.

'I feel odd,' I say to Miss Stamp, one afternoon. We are

walking about the grounds of Bifrons while it is still light –
Miss Stamp is a great believer in the benefits of exercise.

'In what way, odd?' says my governess.

'I shall try to explain. The more work we do on Flyology,
the more I feel like a wing myself. Sometimes I feel that I
am at the highest point of a lifted wing – do you know what
I mean?'

Miss Stamp nods quietly, avoiding a puddle of dead leaves
that the gardeners have yet to clear.

'At that highest point, I feel as though I can do anything
and be anything and that everything is beautiful,' I say. 'And
then . . . and then at other times I feel like the same wing at
its lowest point, sort of *flapped* downwards.'

'How often do you feel like this?'

'I don't know,' I say, not sure whether I ought to have
embarked upon this topic at all. 'Perhaps once a day I feel an
up-stroke, and once a day a down-stroke. And then . . . at
different times of the *month* I might feel worse. Or better. Or
simply more up and more down in a day.'

Again, my governess nods. I can talk to her about things
such as bleeding in a way that I cannot talk to Mamma. It
was Miss Stamp who found me in the nursery, a few months
ago, in a state of silent shock, and showed me where the
sanitary napkins were stored, and how to tie them correctly.
I often feel very disconnected to my body; Miss Stamp
reminds me (in clever, gentle ways) to observe the changes
that take place in it, and to try and understand those changes.
She is so easy to talk to about everything. She told me that

there are ancient links between monthly bleeding and the cycles of the moon – this fascinated me deeply, to the extent that I have entered into regular correspondence with Mamma's old tutor, William Frend – now an elderly, white-haired gentleman – about astronomy.

'And how does that make you feel?' says Miss Stamp.

'Truthfully,' I say, 'it makes me feel very tired.'

My governess says: 'I wonder, Ada, if perhaps we ought to pause our work on Flyology for now.'

'Oh, but we can't!' I stammer. 'Not now, not when we have so much more work to do. Miss Stamp, only think: if one were only able to fly . . . why, one would be able to see a rainbow *in its entirety*. I have always wanted to know why a rainbow is curved, as it appears to the eye. Perhaps, if one could fly high enough . . .'

We have by now reached the stables. The strong, musty odour of straw and manure greets us as we push open the swing-door. My governess picks up her feet carefully as we make our way down the narrow corridor towards the tack room. The four Bifrons horses whinny and snort, hoping for carrots.

'Not today,' I tell them. 'I'm sorry. We are making a *flying visit*.'

I glance gleefully at Miss Stamp, to see if she appreciates the joke, but she still has a rather fixed, anxious expression.

The small, disused tack room is a fairly new discovery – recent terrible weather led me to investigate the Bifrons outbuildings for sources of possible amusement, and in the tack room I have found a world of delight: a laboratory, essentially, in which I can experiment with my Flyology plans. From the various hooks that hang on the walls I have hung ropes and saddles and scuffed girths. Now, as Miss Stamp watches – she is part-assistant and part-safeguard in these Flyology sessions – I hoist myself halfway up a rope and begin to swing, an Ada-pendulum, from side to side.

'Do be careful,' says Miss Stamp.

'I am always careful,' I tell her, swinging more vigorously. The rope creaks on the hook, sounding like an animal in pain. I can hear one of the grooms shouting something to a stable-boy, an instruction of some kind.

'I do very good thinking when I'm swinging,' I say. My heartbeat is quick, the blood rustling agreeably in my ears. There's such a delicious rhythm to it: this way, that way, the slither of rope against wooden wall . . .

An idea comes upon me.

'Oh, Miss Stamp!' I say. 'Remember the steam boats on the lake at Lucerne? Well, if we can use steam to power boats, then why not machines that can fly? What if . . . what if we were to design a flying machine in the shape of a horse – larger, of course – with a steam-powered engine?'

My governess gives a little shriek as I let go of the rope at the top of an upswing and propel myself in an arc across the room. I land in a heap of straw, laughing uproariously. Miss Stamp hurries towards me. 'Oh, Ada, are you all right?'

'Better than all right,' I say. 'We must go back to the library now, and draw some more diagrams.'

Bifrons, Kent
February 1829

Miss Stamp has gone, and there will never be another governess to match her. I am quite sure of it.

She left, as she said she would, just before Christmas. I cried on the morning of her departure, refusing at first to go downstairs to say goodbye. It was Nanny Briggs, who always thinks about the well-being of everyone in the household, who persuaded me that Miss Stamp would be sad if she and I were unable to say our farewells in person.

'I have a gift for you,' Miss Stamp said, as the last of her trunks was hoisted onto the roof of the carriage.

Red-eyed, I accepted the pages, which were tied together with pale pink ribbon. 'What is it?'

'It's something of yours, actually.'

I looked down. It was my story – the one that I had worked on with such care in Geneva – 'The Mystery of the Blue Windmill'.

'I . . . I didn't think it was very good,' I said.

Angered by what I perceived as its imperfections, I had thrown it away; Miss Stamp had quietly retrieved it from the waste-paper basket and brought it back to England. There she had copied the story out in her beautifully neat writing, and kept it until it was time to bid me goodbye.

'I did,' she said, as she kissed me. 'I thought it was very good. You'll achieve great things, Ada. I know you will. But you must believe in yourself.'

Mamma was watching this exchange. She said nothing, but she was wearing one of her many Mamma-expressions, all of which I am adept at reading. This particular one – a pinched, tight, nostril-flared look – suggested to me that she, personally, was not sure that I would achieve anything of note, and certainly not by means of writing stories.

I think about Miss Stamp often – she is married now, of course, but I will always think of her as Miss Stamp. I hope that she is happy, and wonder if she misses me at all. The days, so full of excitement and colour and interest when we were abroad, feel dull and flat now, like a landscape of scattered rocks and dried-up rivers and dust. Even Puff gives me less pleasure than she usually does – really, she has turned quite feral now, and spends all her time tracking down mice in darkened corners. I feel listless, achy, uninterested in things. Where I used to feel ups and downs – those winged emotional states that I tried, once, to explain to Miss Stamp – now I feel a sort of level lowness. It is as though there is a heavy coverlet on top of me – one made of lead, or woven rope – a coverlet that I cannot lift.

One rainy February morning, I find that I cannot get out of bed.

'I don't . . . I don't feel right,' I say, slowly, to the chambermaid. 'My head . . .'

The chambermaid goes to fetch Nanny Briggs. She is gone a long time; I try again to get out of bed, and fail. It is as though the various parts of my body have ceased communication. At last, my nurse appears. It is difficult to explain to her how I am feeling. She presses a hand to my forehead.

'You're running a fever, Miss Ada,' she mutters. She peels back the cuff of my nightgown, and exposes a ruddy, raised rash that extends all along my arm. 'It may be that you've caught the measles,' she says.

I don't want measles. I've had chickenpox before, long ago, and remember only too well the sweltering, soporific itchiness of it; the muddle-headedness. 'I don't have *time* to be ill, I fret, as Nanny Briggs changes my nightgown. 'I'm working on Flyology. If I don't invent the machines, then then someone else will!'

'Hush now, and don't babble,' she soothes. 'You'll be right as rain in no time.'

She holds a cool, damp flannel to my forehead. It feels wonderfully comforting. Perhaps she is right: I will just rest for a day or two, until the worst of the illness passes, and then I can return to my study: to Flyology, and my books, and everything else that I enjoy.

But it is a long, long, long time – three years, all told – before I am well enough to get out of bed again.

Part Two: 1832–1833
Age sixteen to seventeen

I had a dream, which was not all a dream.
The bright sun was extinguish'd, and the stars
Did wander darkling in the eternal space,
Rayless, and pathless, and the icy earth
Swung blind and blackening in the
*   moonless air . . .*

From 'Darkness',
by Lord Byron
July 1816

Brighton
June 1832

My mare's name is Locket, and she is a slender, dappled creature – as beautiful a steed as I could ever have wished for. For so many years, I wanted to ride, and now, finally, I can. Locket (she isn't actually mine, rather borrowed from my instructor, but still I like to pretend that I am a genuine horse-owner) trots in her elegant, sure-hoofed way along the crescent. We are in Brighton for the summer, to take the sea air. I pass our hotel, where Mamma is resting, and head towards the enticing stretch of the seafront. The morning is brilliant and clear-skied; seagulls dive and caw above the ocean spray, while holidaymakers, in companionable twos and threes, stroll in leisurely fashion along the pier.

Down at the water's edge, I slither down from the saddle and undo the straps of my *tricot* drawers, which are secured tightly over each riding boot. Removing the boots, I hurl them away from the shoreline. They land with a crush in the pebbles. Then, rather furtively, I peel off my drawers and roll them into a careless bundle under one arm. Yes, Mamma would be horrified; but Mamma isn't here, and neither, for once, is my instructor. I am alone, a rarity, and something of which to take advantage. Barefoot, and delighted to be so, I wander along the edge of the water, holding Locket's reins in one hand and hitching up the skirts of my riding habit with the other.

I, Ada, am stronger every day.

Oh, the delight of being *in* my body again, able to *move* again, after so long! I take a couple of little shuffling dance-steps into the sea for good measure, enjoying the icy thrill of the water between my toes. A high-pitched peal of glee whistles from my throat, unbidden, as I look out across the Channel, relishing the extent of it, its possibilities, its freedoms. A young man passes me, a Dalmatian at his heels, and for a brief moment I catch his eye, before returning to my watery dance of independence.

Those days of illness were dark ones – literally dark, because I was, at times, half-blind. It started with measles, but turned into something that the doctors did not understand. I was almost completely bedridden, and only sometimes able to scribble a short, shaky letter in pencil to Cousin George or Flora Davison, or be carried downstairs to sit in the garden. Mamma wondered if I had some kind of spinal weakness – something akin to Mary Montgomery's condition, perhaps. But nobody really knew anything at all. My illness took on a timeless quality: the hours melted like rancid butter, and I stewed in a lonely, aimless haze, punctuated only by the visits of doctors and their clockwork rotation of prescribed treatments.

Dark days indeed.

But two good things came out of those suffocating, nocturnal times. I can see that now. The first was that I was given the freedom to read as I chose. Although I wasn't always clear-eyed enough to enjoy it, and I certainly couldn't call it Gobblebook (I wasn't fast enough to gobble a thing), I read widely, not limiting myself to any particular avenue. Books on astronomy proved especially valuable; perhaps, in my introverted state, I relished something that would make me think of the stars. My own body was letting me down: why not turn to celestial bodies instead? German fables, French verses, my old atlas . . . I picked up each book as I chose, when I wanted to, without worrying too much about what I hoped to achieve by doing so.

The second thing was also to do with reading. One evening, Mamma came and sat by my bedside. We were living now in Fordhook Manor, in the village of Ealing, just west of London. The house had belonged to a writer named Henry Fielding; Mamma had chosen it because Ealing was where she wished to set up her school. It would follow the principles set out by Dr Fellenberg, with whom she had established a fast-paced and copious correspondence. The enterprise seemed to exhaust and revive her in equal measure; I had never seen her so absorbed, so devoted to any one cause, and Mary Montgomery had told me that Mamma was making excellent progress.

But on the night that she came to see me – it was just past my fourteenth birthday – she seemed neither enlivened nor exhausted; just rather intense, and with a sense of something she very much wanted to say.

'Ada,' she said, 'I think it's about time that I gave you this.'

I confess, I was expecting the Collected Works of Pythagoras (or some other Ancient Greek purveyor of theorems), and not what she now held out in front of me: a red, leather-bound book that said only, in embossed letters of gold, BYRON.

'I have— I've wanted to read his work for a long time now,' I said.

'I know you have. And I think, now, you are old enough.'

She left me then, which was nice of her – there are some things, like going to see the villa my father rented by Lake Geneva, that we could do together, but other things that we might each prefer to do alone. Oddly enough, I did not read the book at all that night; I slid it under my pillow for safe-keeping, and waited until I had something better than an oil-lamp to read by. Then, over the course of perhaps a week or two, I began to read my father's poems. The experience was an extraordinary one; I had the sensation of tugging back a green-velvet curtain, once again; but this time I was unveiling entire continents of thought and feeling, not just a painted portrait . . . I met each poem as though I were being introduced to a succession of dinner guests, and evaluated, wondered at, and delighted in each in turn. I hadn't expected the poems to be so funny – I'd imagined romance, of course, and tragedy, but not the kind of direct, easy-to-understand narratives that seemed to dance off the page, loud as fanfare.

I laughed at some, and cried at others, and was puzzled by many. Sometimes, I would take from the silk-lined box that sat silently on my dressing table the talismanic ring that my father had given me when I was an infant, and hold it in my hand as I read until it grew hot against my skin. One poem in particular, 'Darkness', spoke to me in my own darkness, reaching out across the margin between life and death, between the time of his writing it and the time of my reading it, and I read it over and over, and it comforted me.

And now that I am well, and strong, and able to live my life again, I feel that I know my father far better. My puzzle has additional pieces, although many still are missing. My childish dreams of the poet beside the sea are gone, replaced by my memories of Geneva, and Genoa, and the soft lines and shapes of the portrait by Thomas Phillips, and now, too, my father's verses. And I have learned something from his poetry that I had always known anyway, simply by instinct: Byron really did love the sea.

Voices, carried on the salt-sprayed breeze, pull me out of my reverie.

'Just *look* at that young woman walking along without her shoes!'

'My dear, don't you know who that is?'

'Why, of course – but I barely recognised her! Goodness, Ada Byron is grown so *plump* and pale!'

I look up at the promenade, guiltily startled, and see a trio of sharp-nosed, elderly women in extravagantly-trimmed silk bonnets peering down at me. Before I can stop myself,

I raise a hand in a kind of military salute and give them a cheerful grin, although inside I am furious. Now it is their turn to be guiltily startled – clearly, they had not expected me to hear them, and they scurry away like the three blind mice. My triumph is blighted by gloom; I put on my stockings and walk Locket back to retrieve my boots – only slightly scuffed – and we return to the hotel.

'Why is it that I must persistently be stared at and commented on, everywhere I go?' I say to Mamma over lunch. She is doing justice to a plate of mutton – it looks like far too much food for one person, but this is unlikely to deter her, and I have always admired the robustness of her appetite. She lays down the letter that she is reading and gives me her full attention.

'What has happened now, Ada?'

Omitting the detail of the drawers and boots, I tell her of the conversation I overheard, and she is pleasingly outraged on my behalf. 'A person who has been as ill as you were might reasonably be both plump and pale, but there was no need for them to make personal remarks,' she says. 'Your father had a tendency to put on fat too. He would attempt the most outrageous diets – nothing but soda water and biscuits, or a plate of crushed potatoes with vinegar – but really, he couldn't maintain any kind of regime. And besides, it would make him terribly morose.'

I look thoughtfully at my plate. Lack of food makes me morose too; is this a way in which I resemble my father?

'As long as your dresses still fit you in a seemly fashion, Ada, I see no reason for you to mind what they say,' says Mamma cheerfully, as I pick up my fork and knife.

'It's not just the personal remarks,' I tell her, eating my breast of partridge (quite delicious it is too). 'It's being known at all, when I am not famous in my own right, just famous for being someone's daughter.'

Mamma says: 'That's why we used to come to Hastings and not Brighton; it was quieter there, and more private. I did my best to protect you from scrutiny when you were young. People would point, and stare, and it was quite hideous.'

'You used to say that we were proud lionesses,' I say, remembering. 'Queens of the Jungle, nobler beasts than they were, and *not to take any notice*.'

We say the last phrase together, and laugh out loud.

Mamma picks up the letter again. 'I've secured a new tutor for you, Ada – a James Hopkins. He comes highly recommended and is very intelligent, they say. His family lives close to us in Ealing. He is engaged elsewhere until Christmas, so we may expect him thereafter.'

'What will he teach me?'

'Shorthand – so that you can attend lectures, you know. It will be of great use to you, I'm sure, in addition to your other subjects.'

This news is only mildly welcome. My tutors and governesses have, over the years, waxed and waned like scholarly moons. Sometimes Mamma might pay over two hundred pounds a year to some magnificently-referenced instructor, only to tire of them within weeks. (I think sadly of Miss Lamont.) During the dark days of illness, I was not tutored much at all, and certainly not with the intensity of previous years. I corresponded with three people. The first was William Frend, that kindly old man who would write to me about astronomy, advising me to sketch the moons of Jupiter, or keep a look-out for an eclipse. Then there was Dr King, Mamma's physician, who had brought the cooperative movement to Brighton. And there was also a lady named Arabella Lawrence, an acquaintance of Mamma's, who is very interested in education. To all three I wrote letters, when I was well enough to do so, and they would write back, suggesting things that I might want to read.

Now that I am better, Mamma's interest in my education has, of course, properly resumed. I had hoped that she might have extended some of her newfound philosophical principles (education by action and perception and so forth) to me, her child, but alas, she reserved such pedagogic developments for the pupils at the planned academy. Nevertheless, I am glad to hear that the new tutor is male.

'At least your letter does not bring news of a Fourth Fury,' I say, half under my breath; at this, Mamma looks up sharply.

'What's that, Ada? Oh, come now; you must stop calling them that.'

'But they *are* Furies.'

'They are simply good friends of mine who seek to oversee your moral development,' says Mamma, in a tone of great reasonableness, although what she has said is in no way reasonable. She lays her fork and knife together so that they bisect her plate neatly at its diameter. My partridge finished, I do likewise.

'There is nothing wrong with my morals,' I say to Mamma.

'There is nothing wrong with exercising caution nonetheless,' she counters in her annoyingly unflappable way. 'Especially when you are – as you have yourself pointed out – "talked about". No matter what you do, Ada . . . you must always be sure to keep *straight*.'

My own fork and knife are askew. Leaning over, she adjusts them, so that they are exactly parallel.

Fordhook, Ealing
August 1832

Mamma and all three Furies are taking tea in the garden, under the sycamore tree. Mamma might not think of them as Furies, but I personally cannot think of them as anything else, and truly I cannot stand them. They hang around the house like horse-flies, creeping down corridors, waiting to pounce on any perceived wrongdoing.

When the Furies first arrived at Fordhook, about three months ago, I thought they were house guests. I did not imagine myself to be under their watch; this realisation came upon me gradually. I was out in the garden, not long after their arrival, conversing with a boy who had come to attend to the yew hedges, when Fury the First – Frances Carr – happened upon us like a witch descending from a storm cloud on a broomstick and hauled me away, squawking all the while about propriety.

'Why shouldn't I talk to him?' I demanded.

Rendered inarticulate by her haste, the Fury merely squawked again, dragging me along as though I were a puppy in need of training.

On another occasion, I was in the library, writing in my commonplace book. I moved away to fetch a German dictionary, wanting to translate a line of Goethe's; I looked back towards the table to see Fury the Second – Selina Doyle – leaning over my notebook, attempting to decipher my writing. From then on, I adopted a kind of code to mitigate against such attempts: a feverish scramble of swapped letters and dog-eared Latin, as hard for me to understand as it would be – hopefully – to anyone else.

And *then* there was the incident with the Spanish Count, who so kindly gave me lessons on the guitar during our stay in Brighton. Alfonso Galiano had a rich collection of family histories that he recounted to me in thrilling detail – his brother was a renowned cartographer and explorer – and in me he recognised both an ardent listener and a willing pupil. I strove to match the tricks of his flickering fingers as they danced over the fretboard, and practised each scale and chord he gave me with brow-bent diligence. I thought it deeply unfair when the Furies pooled their investigative sensibilities and told Mamma that the Count and I were exchanging 'looks of a perceptibly loving nature'. Only one Fury was even in Brighton at the time! I protested to Mamma that they were making up lies and nonsense, but the lessons were abruptly stopped.

(As for the loving looks: I, Ada Byron, have *not yet* experienced love. If I had, I'd have put up more of a protest at the termination of my guitar lessons. But there was something interesting in the way the Count would lay his long, elegant fingers on my wrist as he repositioned my hand, and he did like to look into my eyes for longer, perhaps, than was necessary, as he explained the constituent notes in the chord of D minor. I would find myself gazing into his eyes too, and thinking that it was something not unlike the gravitational pull between planets – two moons locked into mutual orbit, neither quite able to pull itself away.)

Now, as the Furies crowd around the wrought-iron tea-table, I, who have managed to my delight to climb up into the heart of the sycamore (I am getting stronger and stronger and stronger), peer down through the green-loaded branches and eavesdrop without remorse on their conversation. Since they are putting me under surveillance, I see no reason why I should not do the same to them. Intent as they are on their victuals, none of them has noticed me. Only Betty, the parlourmaid, glances up fleetingly in my direction from her position behind Mamma's chair; but I don't think that Betty looks especially kindly on the Furies, who are exacting and petulant, and I doubt that she will give me away.

'It is my sincerest wish,' Mamma is saying, 'that Ada should not become . . . like her father.'

The Furies make clucking-sounds of agreement. 'Why, yes, dear,' they chorus, as unoriginal as braying donkeys. 'Of *course* you must wish that.'

'That is why I am so grateful for your vigilance,' Mamma says. 'Especially when my own health is not good,' she adds forlornly, helping herself to some cake.

At this, I snort. I have come to the conclusion that there

isn't really very much wrong with Mamma's health. She eats like an ox; her digestion is sound; she is a solid sleeper. She could walk a marathon if she wanted to with that fierce, fine energy that she can summon at a moment's notice. She simply likes the attention of doctors, such as her physician, Dr King. Their attention warms her, as a lizard might be heated up in the sunlight. She also enjoys retreating to spa towns in order to take the waters there, and focus on the rituals of healing. For these reasons, she persists that her health is not good.

Fury the Third, Sophia Frend, looks up sharply. 'What's that?'

I freeze, solidifying the breath in my lungs, hugging the trunk of the tree.

'Oh, a squirrel, perhaps. The woods around here are full of them,' says Mamma, who has not looked up. 'The fact is that we must all be on the look-out for any signs of moral deviance on Ada's part,' she goes on. 'She is at that age, now, when one might reasonably expect such strains to emerge in her temperament.'

The Furies make wise noises, and it is all that I can do not to fall out of the tree with indignation. How *dare* she accuse me of . . . of moral deviance – or of having the potential to show such a thing? What have I ever done to make her think this might even be possible?

Later on, in my bedroom, I turn to my father's verses for the answer. Is there moral deviance contained within these pages? Perhaps, yes, you could say so. I scan the pages almost at random, looking for particular details that I remember from previous readings of behaviour that my mother would find questionable. In *Don Juan* – an epic collection of sixteen cantos – I find more than enough examples of things that would send my mother's eyebrows skywards, not least the proclivities of the hero. And then there is Manfred, a tortured soul who has committed some unspeakable wrongdoing by indulging in an illicit affair with Astarte. The more I read, the more I find. But why should my father be judged on the basis of the character of his creations? (For that, I am convinced, is what Mamma has done.) She ought to realise that the poet and his work are not the same. And furthermore, she does not realise that by alerting the Furies – and me, as well – to my potential moral deviance, she is only encouraging me, I think, to experiment with those boundaries. Yes: Mamma might view the prospect of my turning out like my father with horror and anxiety, but I, for my part, feel no such trepidation.

For would it not be a matter of considerable pride to follow in the footsteps of one of England's greatest poets?

Fordhook, Ealing
October 1832

Ever since we first visited Dr Fellenberg at the institute at Hofwyl, the idea of setting up a school of her own has remained fixed in my mother's mind.

'I am more resolute than ever, Ada,' she says, as the carriage sets out to the Church of St Mary, about fifteen or twenty minutes away from Fordhook. It's a chill-winded, drizzly autumn morning and Mamma's eyes are marble-bright with purpose. 'As you know, my first attempt at a school was unsuccessful,' she is saying. 'I had not at the time the requisite deep understanding of Dr Fellenberg's methods. The children fought like wild beasts and did not seem to thrive under my programme of baking, arithmetic and music. Now I know better.'

I nod, listening. I was so unwell during the time to which she is referring that I had no knowledge of it until recently. I missed so many episodes – domestic incidents, and chapters in Mamma's life, such as this first attempt at a school – that I feel sometimes as though I am a student of history, poring over a primer of the years I lost to my illness. King George died two years ago, and his brother William is now on the throne. The electoral system has been transformed by the Reform Bill; Mamma told me of the rioting that broke out all over England when the bill was rejected by the House of Lords. Before I fell ill, I wasn't much interested in politics; now, though, I am starting to see how politics is the loom on which the fabric of the lives of ordinary people is woven. It is machinery, and it must be challenged to work well, and altered if it does not work well.

'Why Ealing, Mamma?' I say. I've always wondered at her insistence on this particular location. I like it – it's romantic and verdant and overlooks the metropolis of London from its westerly viewpoint just as Hampstead does, from the north – but I've never known why Mamma so much wanted to come here.

'Because this place is a natural garden – almost a Garden of Eden, if you like. I know it may not seem so, on a cold day, but here – long ago – the hungry people of London were fed by its gardeners. Its natural position overlooking the city and its expanse of fertile land made it an ideal site. But after the Napoleonic blockade was lifted – just around the time of your birth – the place became rife with unemployment. Ealing was suddenly full of wild young men – wayward vagrants with no meaningful occupation. They need training, Ada, and a clear sense of purpose.'

The carriage deposits us at the church hall. Mamma is nervous; she is pretending not to be, but I recognise the way that she licks her bottom lip from time to time, and the short, shallow breaths that she takes as she trots up the steps. Still, she is grace and assurance personified as we enter the hall, to find a sizeable council of parishioners seated at a round table. In their inky top hats, the men are dignified and distant, the women, in their gloves and bonnets, the epitome of formality likewise. I don't know any of them, though it is likely that these people are the richest and most influential dignitaries of Ealing. Then there are the clergymen, just as severely dressed, and not a smile to be seen on a single countenance.

'Lady Byron,' says a pewter-haired man with a corpulent frame.

'This is my daughter, Ada,' Mamma says, to no one in particular.

I think I can guess at the outcome of this meeting already. But if Mamma too is made uneasy by the atmosphere, which rivals the weather outside in frostiness, then she hides it well. 'I can hardly conceal my excitement,' she says, 'in putting forth this proposal. At last, we will be able to address the prevalent problems among the young people of Ealing – vagrancy, unemployment, delinquency and disenchantment. With a school that prizes purpose and practicality above all else, we will offer training in agricultural methods, ways in which they can earn their living . . . skills that they can put to use, *for the rest of their lives* – drawn closely from the methods of Pestalozzi and Dr Fellenberg. If we can simply—'

Somebody – an elderly man with a face as lined as sheet-music – interrupts her. 'But these are foreigners. Pestalozzi, Fellenstein . . .'

'Fellenberg,' Mamma says.

'Why should their principles be of any interest to young Englishmen? It seems an absurd idea.'

'That is not our only reservation,' says another man. 'You make no mention of corporal punishment in your outline of the school's methods.'

'I have visited the institute at Hofwyl twice,' says Mamma. 'The children manage their own behaviour; there is no need for corporal punishment.'

'I don't see how you could possibly keep order without corporal punishment,' says a dry-voiced woman in an opulent cloak.

'But at Hofwyl—'

Now a clergyman, lip quivering, and scarcely able to speak due to his palpable indignation, pipes up. 'Lady Byron,' he says. 'In addition to the objections raised by others, what seems to me, on reading your plans, quite shocking, is that you do not intend the school to follow any kind of religious teaching.'

Mamma says: 'I wish the school to be open to children of all belief, or to children of no belief at all.'

There is, at this, an audible gasp of horror. It is news to me; Mamma is a religious woman – the school of Christianity that she follows is called Socinianism – but I can see, I think, why she has said what she has said. She does not wish to close the door to anyone of any belief. This is admirable; I wonder why these people cannot see it, even though they are church people.

'Lady Byron,' says the first of the elderly men. 'Although

we commend the good intentions that clearly underlie your propositions, we are not able to countenance any funding for such an undertaking as you propose.'

Mamma gets to her feet. I do the same. We are being dismissed. Then Mamma turns, taking in the whole of the room, and I hear in her voice a passion and emotion that I seldom hear, that lend a richness to her tone, like a fire lit in a cold grate.

'People are starving,' she says. 'The degree of separation between the richest of the upper classes and those who exist in a state of poverty is one that cannot be borne. Industries are changing; agriculture is changing; education must change too, or else it will not be able to support the people who need it most.'

Mamma is quiet on the journey home, and I summon the courage, after a little while, to ask her whether she had any real expectation of a favourable response to her scheme. She sighs. 'You are right, Ada,' she says. 'Given my commitment to allowing children of any belief to attend the institution, I could not have expected the clergy to welcome my proposals. Perhaps, too, the principles on which my scheme is based are simply too *different* in nature to what those people understand by the concept of "education". And yet . . . I am seeking a solution to the problem of delinquency in Ealing, and as such I hoped that they would offer *some* form of support – it is a shared problem, after all. But it does not matter. My resolve is not lessened in the slightest. I shall use my own money – I have plenty of it.'

*

Unsurprisingly, Mamma proves as good as her word, and immediately sets about directing – with all her customary zeal – some of her considerable fortune into the school that she eventually names Ealing Grove. The first headmaster she chooses is not suitable – he does not enjoy taking orders from a woman. As is her wont, she treats this as only a minor setback, and before long has secured another man, a Mr Atlee, far better-suited to the post. There are not many pupils at first, but those that do attend seem happy and purposeful and intent on their learning. This much is clear to me on my first visit. Ealing Grove reminds me, in so many ways, of Hofwyl. Mamma has even arranged for the development of some allotments – long, narrow strips of land which can be cultivated – where the children are instructed in various agricultural skills.

'Why can't I be a pupil here?' I say to her, half-jokingly, as we wander through the allotments together, watching the children at work.

'You aren't what I would define as *in need*,' says Mamma, stepping delicately over a rake.

'A teacher, then. I'm sure I know enough about some things, like French, for example, and—'

'Ada,' says Mamma. 'You will never be a teacher.'

'Why not?'

'You haven't the temperament, for a start.'

'I have been educated to such an extent,' I point out, 'that it seems a shame for me not to use it in some way. Do you not think so?'

'My parents gave me the best education possible too,' replies Mamma. 'But not so that I should have to enter a profession. No: the point is that you should be acquainted deeply with a range of subjects, from languages to mathematics, without, of course, neglecting art and music and current affairs. It is important to know as much as possible about the world in which you live. And for you, moreover, the intellectual discipline is highly beneficial. You do not need to *use* it, as you say; it will be useful regardless. And one day, Ada, the benefits of your academic instruction will be quite clear. You will have the clarity of mind to know what you are doing is *right*; to try to make a difference to the community around you, as I myself endeavour to do.'

'But what am I meant to *be*?' I persist, although I know what she is going to say.

'You'll be a wife and mother, Ada. And a very good job you'll do of it too.'

This she says so simply, so matter-of-factly, that at first, I accept it as some kind of universally acknowledged truth. But it sparks something in me – a little wisp of silvery flame – and as we continue our walk, I begin to think: *Why must I be a wife and a mother? Why must I do only this, and nothing more?*

We don't discuss it further, but once I have started upon this thought, I find that I can't let it go, and return to it in the way that Puff might worry at a ball of wool. There must be something else, I think, that I can do with my life.

Surely, surely, there must be.

Fordhook, Ealing
February 1833

The occasion of someone new arriving to teach me is a familiar one. It has happened so many times, and I am used to the pattern of it: the breathless, eager governess, armed with her ambitions; the tall, grey-haired man of letters, primed by my mother for wise tutelage. Oh, I have grown very accustomed to it indeed. But when my shorthand tutor finally arrives on a Tuesday morning, I find myself totally unprepared for my reaction to him. A breathless, eager governess he is not, nor grey-haired man of letters; he turns out to be someone far, far more interesting.

I am waiting at an upstairs window when he arrives, and the first glimpse I have of him is a bird's one – just as if I were still hiding in the sycamore tree. There he is: a young man – not tall, slightly built, though it's hard to tell from where I'm standing – walking briskly up the steps to the front door. He moves with confidence: rare for one who has never been here before. He wears a fawn-coloured top hat; the tail of his frock coat flies behind him. Now the bell peals with a great, theatrical clang and Fury the First appears at my elbow.

'Come, Ada. Mr Hopkins is here.'

Mamma is in the process of subjecting the newcomer to a short interview in the entrance hall. I come down the stairs, mulishly slow, holding up the progress of the Fury who is coming down behind me, and hoping she'll trip. I also feel shy suddenly, and unsure of myself. I've never been tutored by a young man before. The tutor seems unaware of our arrival; he is talking to Mamma, gesticulating as he speaks. He laughs: it's a rich chuckle that echoes on the marble floor. He has a very straight nose that turns up just at the end, as though drawn by a pencil that was suddenly lifted from the page. Mamma is smiling; she seems pleased by him.

'Do you have far to travel, Mr Hopkins?' she asks.

'No, no. A pleasant walk across the fields, in Hanger Hill. Our house is the Old Rectory – perhaps a mile or so from here.'

Mamma says: 'And here is Ada.'

At once, Mr Hopkins spins round like a wind-up figurine. The smile broadens; his eyes – they are brown – narrow almost into parallelograms as he does so. He comes towards me, holding out his hand, which I take. 'What a great privilege it is for me, Miss Byron, to have this opportunity.'

I look at him, absorbing it all: the tilted nose, the rum-dark eyes, the longish hair, which is the colour of burnt butter beneath his hat. His is a pleasant, intelligent, open face – he is not handsome, precisely, but then I myself am not beautiful. I sense a hovering Fury, realise I haven't spoken, and mumble indistinctly, 'I am most pleased to make your acquaintance, Mr Hopkins.'

In my head, though, I do not think of him as Mr Hopkins. He is *James*.

Over our first lesson, I find out more. James Hopkins is twenty-two. He is a graduate of the University of London, a secular institution, only recently set up, of which Mamma approves. He has taught shorthand to many young ladies, and enjoys it. He *smells* nice; this is an unusual thing for me to observe, but he does – it's not a scent that I can find words to describe, but I like it nonetheless. I find myself quite unable to concentrate on anything he says that pertains to shorthand.

'The Art of Writing,' he says (he is soft-spoken, and quick in his delivery), 'is, quite simply, one of the most important things that a young person like you, Miss Byron, can study today.'

'Why is that?' I say. We are sitting in the library; the door is ajar, and from time to time footsteps are heard marching past, doors swinging shut in other parts of the house. I wish – as I so often wish – that this lesson could take place outside. The trees are wintry spindles and the wind is high, and I would naturally prefer not to be spied on.

James Hopkins shifts in his chair – he is sitting at the head of the mahogany library table, and I to his left – so that he is almost facing me. 'Let me ask you another question. What is writing *for*?'

'It's for . . .' I consider. It's a good question. I think about all the different kinds of writing that I have, in my shortish life, enjoyed; and the different kinds of writing that I've aspired to try myself. I've thought a lot about the fact that I love to write, but not necessarily about *why*. But I'm never silent for long. I think of my father in the Villa Diodati, contemplating the silvery pattern of moonlight on water as he composed his verses. 'It's for telling stories,' I say.

'Always?'

I hesitate, feeling stupid, and correct myself. 'Not always, no,' I say. 'It's . . . it's for the communication of ideas.'

There's that shy-wide smile again; his teeth are wondrously even, although one, on the upper left, is missing. 'Yes, Miss Byron. That is quite right. Without the communication of ideas, how would we be able to make any progress in society? It all comes down to writing.'

'But is it really an Art?' I say, wanting to prolong the discussion now.

'*That* is a good question. Yes, writing is, absolutely, an Art. Let us think about the matter carefully. Imagine that you are at a lecture. Someone is speaking of a new development in . . .' He pauses, struggling to think of something.

'The mechanics of . . . of flying,' I supply. He looks a little taken aback. I supply an alternative: 'Or the movement of the planets.'

'The planets! Yes! Very good,' says James Hopkins. His hands fly apart as he speaks, moving almost in time to his words. He has long-boned hands, expressive ones. For a moment I think about moving my own hand to touch his – but, of course, I don't do anything of the kind. Behind us, the door creaks, and Fury the Third drifts in, making a pretence of searching for a particular book in the shelves. I know when I am being watched. James Hopkins, meanwhile, does not even notice the intrusion, so focused is he on his discourse. 'There you are, in the front row, at the lecture. You have been invited to make notes for the speaker. Those notes are to appear in a prestigious publication. You are delighted – immensely proud to have been given such a task. You have a pen and some paper. You are quite ready (or so you think). The lights are dimmed as the speaker takes his place on the podium and the lecture begins. He starts to talk. He speaks fast – much faster than you had anticipated.'

James Hopkins speaks very fast himself; I cling to each word, absorbing it all as though it were poetry. 'Alas! You have dropped your pen. A gallant young man to your right picks it up.' The smile again. 'You've missed a bit, but it doesn't matter. You will remember it later, you think. The lecture continues. You are writing, writing . . . faithfully, you copy down what the speaker is saying. But you can't catch it all; in your efforts to keep up, whole words, and then whole phrases are missed. Soon, the entire transcript becomes devoid of meaning. You leave the lecture hall disheartened, wishing that there could have been some way to capture those words for posterity. For what good is a half-communicated notion? Why, none at all.'

He pauses. The dramatic effect is profound. I am gazing

at him, mouth half-open, waiting for what comes next. The Fury indulges in a fit of coughing as she carries a pile of books out of the room.

'That,' says James Hopkins, 'is why we learn shorthand. Now, Miss Byron, will you take up your own pen, if you please, and write something for me.'

'What should I write?'

'Oh, anything at all; it doesn't matter what it is.'

My fingers are not precisely steady as I dip the nib of my pen into the inkwell. I want to think of something clever to write, something that will impress him. A line from a poem of my father's comes to me, then, and I inscribe it in my best copperplate.

I had a dream, which was not all a dream.

'How interesting,' says Mr Hopkins, who has watched me closely. 'Most people, you know, if invited to write something of their own choosing, simply write their names. You must have an original mind.'

I can feel my cheeks colouring and wish that I could be more in control of myself than this – as in control as he seems to be. Does he know what it is that I have written? It depends, I suppose, on whether he is acquainted with Byron's verses. I say: 'Those are not original words.'

'No, indeed. They are the opening line of "Darkness", are they not?'

'I . . . yes, you're quite right.' He *does* know my father's work. Perhaps everyone does.

'Now, Miss Byron, I have made some observations of the

way in which you write,' says Mr Hopkins. 'Do not be offended when I say that your posture, when you write, is a little stiff, with too much tension in the shoulders.'

'Oh,' I say.

'Furthermore: you place too much pressure on the page. The letters are clear and legible, but only because you took great pains to make them so. What would happen, I wonder, if you were to write them *fast*?'

Dipping my pen afresh, I rewrite the line. I think about what he has said – my posture is too stiff, the pressure exerted on the page too great – but I don't know what to change. I feel mildly insulted, although this is ridiculous, since it is his job to help me to improve; more than this, though, I am desperate to impress him. In an attempt to write at speed, I lose my grip on my pen on a down-stroke and score a jagged diagonal line down the page. I stop, rueful and dissatisfied.

'Don't give up,' says Mr Hopkins. 'Try again.'

'It's impossible. I can't write any faster and make it appear in any way legible.'

Ah, but there's the smile again, just when I am feeling almost tearful with frustration.

Mr Hopkins opens a leather-bound box and takes out a curious-looking object – it almost looks like an ornament of some kind, made from wire and – I think – ivory.

'What is that?' I say.

'An "aidergraph", or Hand Guide, as it's generally known. It will help to hold your hand in place, while preventing unwanted flexion in your fingers.'

'No,' I say firmly.

'It won't hurt.'

'Oh, very well,' I say. He secures the aidergraph – it is like a sequence of interlocking ivory rings – and asks me to move my wrist, to extend each finger.

'How does it feel?' says Mr Hopkins.

'I hate it,' I say. 'I don't like to be bound by things.'

'At least try the line again, before you take it off.'

He must be mad, I think, to imagine that this oddity will make a positive difference to my writing. But I want the lesson to continue, undisrupted by any refusal on my part to go along with his plans. And so, I dip once more, and roll my pen ever so slightly between my fingers before I lay the nib to the page, experimenting with my new range of motion. The aidergraph no longer presses quite so unpleasantly – perhaps the unpleasantness of it was inferred, rather than truly felt – and as I write the line for the third time, I find that the letters that form themselves are smoother, somehow, than they were before.

'Good,' says Mr Hopkins. 'That's very good.'

My hand is trembling – not from the exertion, but from the heavy-hot self-awareness that suffuses me. Can he tell? I wonder. Even when I was very young – five, six – and had to lie perfectly still upon the board in the nursery, feeling like dough beneath an angry rolling pin, the afternoon weighing down my bones ... I never felt as awkward and uncomfortable as this. I must say something; I've been silent too long, and he will think that I am being rude. I look at him and say: 'Will I make progress, Mr Hopkins?'

'Oh, yes,' says my tutor. His eyes are not brown, I realise now: they are greenish-brown, a cross between rain-soaked moss and tree bark. For good measure, he smiles a final time. 'Certainly, Miss Byron, you will.'

Fordhook, Ealing
February 1833

It is our third lesson. I have made far more of an effort than I usually would to make sure that I am nicely dressed, hair brushed, face scrubbed. I sit in a kind of agony of anticipation, making mistakes on purpose in the hope that Mr Hopkins will lay his hand over mine in order to correct them. So far, he has not done so.

I am learning, he tells me, the Lewisian model of shorthand, pioneered by a Mr Lewis. 'An interesting character,' says Mr Hopkins. 'He has a strong Cockney accent and a fondness for doggerel verses, but I am personally quite convinced that he is something of a genius. When I was studying for my final exams at university, I injured my hand quite gravely by writing too much in the wrong style. My brother had seen Mr Lewis give a lecture, and recommended that I seek his advice. Within weeks, he had corrected my posture, shown me how to wear the aidergraph, and had altered my handwriting so much that my own mother suspected my letters had been written by another. Really, Miss Byron, he saved me. That's why I am so very passionate about teaching his method to as many young people as I can.'

For ten minutes or so, he tests me on my knowledge of the Stenographic Alphabet. I have been committed in my private study of these simple shapes and lines – so like a code, or secret language, that I find it quite enchanting – and he applauds me for my efforts. 'Excellent, Miss Byron,' he says. 'I believe we are ready to begin the next chapter: The Beginnings of Long Words.'

'I like long words,' I say, with far more enthusiasm than I generally afford to my teachers.

'As do I,' says Mr Hopkins.

James Hopkins comes twice a week, on Tuesdays and Thursdays. It is lesson five, and my penmanship is now much improved; I no longer require the support of the aidergraph. Mr Hopkins, as usual, is all smiles; he tells me endless anecdotes involving his university days, and the things he learned; he asks me how I am with an expression of genuine interest and concern. But nothing else has happened and I am growing positively faint with frustration.

Invited to 'write anything I like' by my painstaking tutor, I think for a while and then decide on a line of Catullus'; I have been reading a good deal of poetry recently with my Latin tutor, who comes on Mondays: a lean, bespectacled man with streaks of grey in his hair, who clears his throat with compulsive regularity. The line is, I realise, a risky choice. I hope – I really do hope – that it will get some kind of reaction from Mr Hopkins, for I do not think that he will fail to infer its meaning.

Da mi basia mille, dein mille altera.

There: that is as big a hint as I can possibly give. What will he make of it? His eyes are downcast, focused; he is still scrutinising – or pretending to scrutinise – my writing.

'Would you like me to translate the line?' I say.

'I know the translation. *Give me a thousand kisses, then a thousand more.* Isn't that right?'

'Just so,' I say, still watching him.

'Hmm,' he says. 'The formation of some of these consonants is very good.'

'Thank you,' I say.

'I don't know if you have taken due care over this double "L".'

'Where?' I say, knowing where – I felt it myself, that slight slip of the fingers as I wrote the conjoined letters; a double 'L' is written almost as a C-shape, and I did not do it justice. 'Here?' I point, disingenuously, to the wrong place in the line.

'No, Ada.' He laughs, moving his hand to mine. '*Here.*'

I laugh too, then stop. 'Oh!' I say. 'You called me "Ada".'

'I apologise, Miss Byron. I should not have done that.'

'But I liked it,' I say.

We stare at each other. 'I think . . . I believe that I did too,' says James Hopkins.

He does not withdraw his hand. He is not quite close enough to kiss me, in his usual position just around the corner of the table, but he could move so easily, just by shifting his chair a couple of inches, and I lean my body towards him, imperceptibly, to make the prospect of so doing a simpler one. Yes: he could kiss me now, if he wanted to. Or: *I* could kiss him, abandoning convention altogether, embracing the kind of rare, rash action of which, perhaps, Lord Byron might have approved. A spatter of sparks from the fire brings me to my senses; of course Mr Hopkins will not kiss me now; he would not, could not do such a thing, not here, in the library, with a Fury on Duty somewhere not too far away. But even so, I can see that he is thinking about it; his lips part, perhaps without his even realising it, and his left hand drums a pattern on the table in what I am quite sure is an unconscious rhythm of desire. The room is so silent that the tick of the clock over the mantelpiece is suddenly heartbeat-loud.

And then the peace is shattered by Fury the Third, who comes bustling in to tell us that the lesson is almost over. James Hopkins moves his hand in an arrow-quick second, and by the time Fury the Third is upon us I am meekly reading aloud a marked passage from *The Ready Writer*.

It is a mercy, I think later, that the Furies know nothing of shorthand. If she had been able to read the line that I had written, the Fury would have been instantly alerted to my desires. As it is, she seems to have suspected nothing.

Mamma likes to visit the children at Ealing Grove as often as she can – two or three times a week, at the very least – and she is pleased, albeit mildly surprised, that I, almost as often, offer to go with her. I am particularly interested in the allotments. 'I like your principle: education taking place outdoors, as well as in. Learning by doing,' I tell her.

'Quite so,' says Mamma.

'Besides, I might want to become a farmer one day,' I add. Mamma ignores this.

Two young boys of perhaps twelve or thirteen are helping their teacher, a Mr Cross, to dig a drainage ditch. It's hard work, and I wish that I could help them – it would be good for me to ask something more of my body than walking and reading, and besides, the young boys look as though they could do with assistance. Mamma ushers me on, to where a greenhouse is being constructed. She issues a volley of crisp questions at one of the gardeners; while they are engaged in conversation, I drift away to where some new fencing is being installed. In one corner, alongside the fence, sits a wooden shed. That too looks new. It seems that my mother has truly spared no expense.

A cry of pain startles me; I turn back to see that one of the boys has taken a tumble over his spade. I fly over to him in seconds, reaching him before Mr Cross does. Mamma is not far behind. I kneel down and help the boy up. 'What is your name?'

'Stephen, miss.' I'm glad to see that he is warmly dressed; it's bitterly cold at the moment, especially on these allotments, where there's not much to block the wind.

'Does it hurt when you move your foot, Stephen? Try to turn the ankle – gently, though.'

I support the boy's weight as best I can while he moves his foot from side to side. 'Does it hurt?' I ask again.

'No, miss. Not too badly.'

'He'd better go indoors at once, and have it seen to,' says Mamma. 'I'll go with him myself.' She casts a dark look at the earth, as though disappointed in its failure to offer her students adequate support. 'Ada, you stay here with Jack, and keep him company until Mr Cross and I return.'

They disappear, one on each side of the hapless Stephen (I suspect that he was in greater pain than he admitted), leaving me with the other boy, Jack. He seems unwilling to go on with his digging for the time being, and so I ask him instead about his studies, and whether he enjoys his life at the Academy. Jack, knowing perfectly well who I am, is politely enthusiastic.

'How about the gardening work?' I say, looking around. 'It seems hard. Not to say dangerous.'

'Oh, no,' says Jack. 'We enjoy the time outdoors, and whatever we produce is ours to sell. And it'll be spring before long. Once the land is better prepared, we'll be able to grow things, miss. Potatoes and parsnips. Mangel-wurzel.'

He is about to enter into a long disquisition on vegetables. Keen to avoid this if possible, I say: 'And what of these new buildings?'

'Well, miss, that, over there, is the greenhouse. And that's the storage shed. Brand-new it is. Took a week of work for the carpenters and the pupils alike. It's awfully nice inside, you know, with chairs and a table, and even a rug.'

'I'd like to see it,' I say, which is true: anything to get out of this cold wind. But I have other reasons, besides the cold and idle curiosity. Burning in my Ada-brain, which is always busy, like a needleworker's hands, is the smallest seed of an *idea*.

Fordhook, Ealing
March 1833

Mary Montgomery is staying with us at present, and I am greatly relieved to have her companionship. Not a Fury, never a Fury, she has offered to take me out for the morning. We have come to the Strand to visit the National Gallery of Practical Science, more commonly known as the Adelaide, named after the Queen. The street is crowded: a man is selling bread from a cart, while a crowd of gawkers outside a shop window holds up our progress.

As we reach the gallery, I see a handwritten sign proclaiming: COOKING WITH GAS: A NOVEL METHOD BY MR HICKS. A tow-headed urchin with scabbed knees glowers at us from a doorway, and I remember what Mamma said about the separation between rich and poor. It jolts me – I suppose that I see the evidence of her words only when I am in the heart of London. When I am removed to the green pastures of Ealing, it's easier to forget.

I've always been impressed by the fearless way that Mary forges through crowd-filled spaces, in spite of the fact that she finds it difficult to walk. With the aid of a slim walking stick, she is a determined figure in her voluminous walking-out dress; people stand back when she passes, making room for her.

The gallery comprises a central room, long and high-ceilinged, with a domed roof and an upper walkway, and smaller rooms sprouting from this middle atrium on both sides. The walls are a pretty pale colour, a cross between the sky and the sea – a fitting choice, I think, for a place devoted to curiosities of the imagination. A model canal – filled to the brim with water – divides the main room lengthways; little mechanical boats float upon it, serene as swans, and there are several people watching their progress intently. From the upper level come the thudding footfalls of visitors looking at the paintings.

We have a little time before the cooking demonstration begins, and so we wander about, not looking for anything in particular. A pocket thermometer in a glass case, a lithographic press, a number of curious fossils . . . then my eye is caught by a handsome, weighty-looking instrument, the likes of which I've never seen before, at the other end of the gallery. There is a man standing in front of it, in workmen's overalls. In his hands he shuffles a deck of rectangular cards – they are rather larger than playing cards. He is, perhaps, making sure that they are in the correct order.

'That is a Jacquard loom,' says Mary, who has followed me. 'It was designed by a Frenchman, Joseph Marie Jacquard, at the beginning of the century. Truly a unique invention, this.'

'What does it do?' I say. 'Weaving?'

'Silk-weaving, yes. Do you know how weaving is commonly done?'

'The weft is woven over and under the warp,' I say, 'so that you have an interlacing pattern.'

'That is quite correct. Now, this loom is able to do something rather more complicated. You've heard of the term "figured fabrics"?' says Mary.

'Those silks with pictures on them,' I say.

'Yes – very, very expensive fabrics they are too. They might feature sumptuous landscapes or fruit or flowers. There's one hanging in the drawing room at Fordhook. It would take two weavers a day to weave perhaps an inch of silk, and no more. Slow work.'

'Indeed,' I say, enjoying the story. 'So why is this loom different?'

'See those cards there? With the holes in them? Those cards are punched in particular configurations that correspond to whatever pattern or picture is desired. They were Jacquard's invention.'

We watch as the weaver feeds the cards into a mechanism at the top of the loom.

'How do you get from the pattern to the punched holes?' I ask him.

'It's done by the card maker,' he says, 'so I'm not rightly sure. As far as I'm aware, the pattern's painted onto a grid. If a square on the grid is painted in, then he'd punch a hole in the card. If the square isn't painted in, then there'd be no hole.'

I think about this for a while, and realise that I *understand*. The small round holes remind me, somehow, of musical notation – another system in which a pattern is represented by a series of identical circles, differentiated by their placement. It is beautiful – both simple and complicated at the same time. Now the mechanism draws down the series of cards – they are laced together – with a rattling sound. I am just wondering what will happen next when the weaver says: 'Wherever there's a hole, a pin will pass through it, and a hook will raise a warp thread, if you understand my meaning.'

A kind of feverish excitement tingles at the back of my neck as I watch the shuttle travel up and down, industrious, precise, and the pattern – it is a fairly simple one, of different-coloured triangles – begins to appear.

Mary says: 'How long, would you say, it takes you to weave a foot of fabric? On your own?'

Without looking up, the weaver says: 'I could weave double that in a day, ma'am, with no trouble.'

Mary turns to me. 'An incredible difference. Just think, Ada, of the possibilities! Any picture you could dream of, all reduced to a series of punched cards.'

I gaze at the loom with new admiration, my Ada-brain ticking over with this delicious information. *Just think of the possibilities*, said Mary. Yes: the possibilities. Any picture at all, produced not from a drawing, but from a series of holes in a particular configuration . . .

'Come, Ada. The cooking demonstration is about to begin,' Mary says.

I bid a wistful goodbye to the loom and follow her. We enter a small, circular exhibition space with a high ceiling, lamp-lit and absolutely packed with people. Most are women, but I can see a handful of men too, glossy in their black coats, laughing, looking around impatiently, waiting to be amused and enlightened.

'Look,' says Mary. 'That's Michael Faraday.'

'Where? I can't see—'

She ushers me in front of her, pointing subtly to a man in the centre of his group, and there he is: short – perhaps shorter than I am, with a mass of curly hair and coal-dark eyes. He looks to be about forty. Unlike the jostling, jocular crowd, he is silent, standing patiently in front of the exhibition stand. Michael Faraday is renowned for his work on electromagnetic induction. Mamma has always been especially fascinated by him; she'll be delighted to hear that Mary and I have actually seen him in the flesh.

'He gives lectures,' says Mary. 'Wonderful lectures. We'll go, Ada.'

'I would like that.'

'How is your shorthand progressing? Is it as dull as you anticipated?'

At this, I suppress laughter: that I could ever have been unenthused by the prospect of learning shorthand. How ignorant I was! 'No,' I say. 'It's not dull in the slightest. A most useful skill, and one that I find increasingly worthwhile. All my life, Mary, I have found writing quite hard – not the ideas bit, or even the spelling and grammar – but the writing, the physical writing. I never knew why; I just thought it was something to be endured. But Ja— Mr Hopkins says that I have too much laxity in my fingers, and now he has shown me how to exert far better control over my hand.'

'Ada, that's wonderful,' says Mary, though she looks slightly taken aback by the level of detail I have just offered her in my response. 'The better your shorthand is, the more you'll get out of the lectures. Ah! Mr Hicks has arrived.'

We watch, fascinated, as a tall man with luxuriant moustaches introduces himself and his novel method of cooking. Mr Faraday is watching too, leaning forward to better see the cooking apparatus, the flame that leaps up, yellowy-orange, when Mr Hicks holds a match to the gas. An assistant brings a plump, plucked pigeon on a metal skewer, and soon the air of the exhibition space is filled with the tang of roasting meat.

'This pigeon, ladies and gentlemen, will be fully cooked – roasted to perfection – in precisely twelve minutes' time,' says Mr Hicks, in a matter-of-fact, rather nasal voice. Oohs and ahhs of excitement from the crowd. One woman turns to another and says: 'Why, Emily, but this will change everything.'

At home, over lunch, I tell Mamma about our morning. 'Mr Hicks roasted mutton, as well as pigeons,' I say, summing up. 'And Mr Faraday was there.'

'Goodness,' says Mamma, who is very keen on mutton. 'I am glad to hear that your mind was suitably exercised by the excursion.'

'Oh, it was,' I say. 'A lady commented to her friend that it would *change everything*. So much is changing now, isn't it?'

Mamma agrees, and then makes an interesting point. 'You must remember that – in the short term, at least – the Jacquard loom did not change everyone's lives for the better.'

'What do you— Oh,' I say. 'I see. The weavers.'

'There were riots, I believe, in the city of Lyon. Looms smashed in protest. Replace too many men with machines, without considering any viable alternatives, and there will always be consequences.'

Mamma thinks very seriously, and very often, about the welfare of everyone. She was being quite truthful when she uttered that phrase of Dr Fellenberg's: 'The rich have helpers enough; help thou the poor'. When the Reform Bill was passed last year and the rotten boroughs (those with one or even two parliamentary representatives, but no constituents, thus creating a deeply unfair imbalance of representation) were abolished, Mamma tells me that she thinks her cheers might have been heard all the way across the farmland of Ealing and in the Palace of Westminster itself. Yes: her civic-minded sense of doing good is probably one of her best points. I will admit that.

Another thing happened today, however, and I will not be telling Mamma about it; Mary has counselled me not to, and I trust Mary to advise me correctly.

As she and I were coming out of the Adelaide, we saw a woman standing across the street, unmistakably watching us – or rather, watching me. Used to being stared at, if not comfortable with it, I made to follow Mary into the carriage that was awaiting us. But the woman, seeing that we were about to leave, began to wave earnestly and to mouth my name. Then came a flurry of carriages and barrows, rattling at speed along the road, and I lost sight of her.

I was about to climb up into the carriage when I looked around, and there she was at my side. She was a little taller than me, rather buxom, with untidy, darkish-fair hair and a sweet, rather foolish expression. 'Ada,' she said. 'Is it really you? I sent a prayer-book to you for your birthday – oh, two or three years ago now. Did you never get it?'

From the carriage, Mary called: 'Come, Ada; we must be on our way.' But I was momentarily transfixed, searching my memories for a face that matched the one that was now before me. Familiar? A little, yes, perhaps . . .

And then I said: 'You are my Aunt Augusta.'

She smiled, revealing small uneven teeth. 'That's right. Your father's sister. Well, half-sister, really. Oh, to finally look at you, grown so tall! Your face . . . it is so like his – yes, yes, I can see it!' Reaching out with a hot, dry hand, she touched a finger to my chin. 'They say you have your mother's intelligence too.'

'I—' But I didn't know what to say to her, to this Aunt Augusta whom I had never before met.

Another cry from Mary, this time shrill with impatience, which was rather unlike her. 'Ada! Do hurry up; the carriage can't wait here indefinitely.'

'I'm sorry,' I mumbled to this newly-discovered aunt, in

whose face I was just able to detect glimpses of my father. 'I can't . . . I have to . . .'

She smiled and made a funny, tangled gesture with her head – a cross between a nod and a shake – and before long the carriage was rattling away. I looked back, just once, and saw her, standing alone on the pavement, still wearing that sweet, wistful expression.

'It would be best if you didn't tell your mother that we saw Mrs Leigh,' said Mary on our way home.

'Why not?'

'They have a difficult relationship. Without going into too much detail, I believe she continually asks your mother for money. Being a kind-hearted soul, and having promised your father to look after Augusta, Annabella generally capitulates.'

I sat back, not quite satisfied with this.

Now, watching my mother finish everything on her plate, I wonder again if there might be another reason. Perhaps there was an argument of some kind between Augusta Leigh and my mother, something bitterly divisive, irreparable . . . Augusta seemed like a gentle-natured woman; could she, perhaps, have taken my father's side over my mother's cold-natured treatment of him?

Did my mother do something that Augusta simply couldn't forgive?

Fordhook, Ealing
March 1833

Lesson six. James Hopkins is sitting waiting for me in the library. When I enter, he gets up, with a formal bow and I think: *He regrets what happened last time, when we held hands.* Yes: he seems nervous, chattering more than usual about Mr Lewis and his work, telling me in detail about a new pen that he wishes to buy, and the particular brand of ink (Stephens' indelible blue-black) that he holds so dear. The lesson begins. Nothing happens out of the ordinary, much to my annoyance, and after a while it strikes me that perhaps he thinks that I regret the hand-holding, and is waiting for a signal on my part. Some kind of assurance that I myself do not regret anything.

I wait for the Fury on Duty to perform her usual check – a brief circuit of the room, skirts sweeping the floor, sometimes a proffered excuse, sometimes no excuse at all – and then I say: 'It is rather dull always sitting in these upright chairs, don't you think?'

'Well,' murmurs Mr Hopkins. 'Good posture is quite crucial for good penmanship.'

'Certainly,' I agree, feeling suddenly bold, 'but I wonder if we might be more comfortable in those chairs by the fire.'

And that is how we end up side by side, knees very nearly touching, on the richly-upholstered chairs. No more polite right-angles. I look at the clock; we have almost a full hour left, and I don't think we shall be disturbed. We look at each other. A bead of sweat lies on Mr Hopkins' temple. It is rather warm in the library.

'What shall we talk of now?' I say. 'Letter formation? Speed of script?'

Startled, he falters for words. 'I—'

'Or else, perhaps,' I say, edging a little closer, 'we ought not to talk at all?'

There's a blink-brief moment in which I watch him trying to grasp the intimation; I can almost see the realisation flicker across his face, causing those rum-dark eyes to widen most attractively. He closes his mouth, perhaps to form the M of Miss Byron, but he gets no further. Pre-emptively, I move, leaning into him with such fluency that I suddenly cannot believe that I have never done it before; my right hand reaches for his left wrist, encircling it, while my left hand travels audaciously round his right shoulder, drawing him towards me. With alacrity, he mirrors my actions, as though he has simply been waiting for permission. Our eyes meet: in his I perceive a question – *May I? Shall we?* – and I smile quickly: yes. Only the width of a sheet of paper separates our faces.

I have one last impression of his features before they dissolve entirely, and I am enveloped in new information: the pulse I can feel that is not my own; the smell of someone else's clothes, someone else's skin; the heat of another body. His lips: firmer than they look, but soft too, fitting somehow with mine as though we are pieces of the same puzzle. He tastes of the sea: salt and myth and the tiniest hint of danger.

It is exquisite.

For the first time in a long time, my body is *alive*; I lost so much feeling in it, for so many years, that for a while I felt like nothing more than a brain in a glass box. Now I am in possession of all five senses – and the thrilling thing is that I am connected to his possession of his senses too; I can feel his, and he can feel mine, and we are each enriched by our perceptions of the other . . .

'Oh, Miss Byron,' says James Hopkins, as we pause in order to breathe properly.

'Ada,' I say reproachfully.

'Ada,' he says. 'You are . . . quite . . .'

Amusingly, for one as naturally verbose as James Hopkins, it seems that words fail him entirely within the context of romantic entanglement. Such an intriguing expression crosses my tutor's face; it almost makes me laugh. I tell him: 'You look as though you are trying to find the square root of a large prime number.'

'Something like that,' he says. He stands up, abruptly, and I realise that the telltale clatter of Fury footsteps is signalling the end of this delicious – and utterly illicit – moment. We hurry back to our usual position at the table, but this time – perhaps our movements are dulled by sensory intoxication – we are not quite quick enough. As Fury the First enters the room, we are just in the process of taking our seats, and James Hopkins is adjusting his collar, which has become rather dishevelled. Even so, Fury the First might not have noticed anything amiss – we are entitled, after all, to get up from our chairs from time to time – were it not for our expressions. Mine, I know without glancing in a mirror, is guilty. James, meanwhile, has that same look of a man who is trying to find the square root of a large prime number, and failing to achieve his mathematical goals.

'Ada,' says the Fury, her voice as dry and crackly as the library fire. 'I don't know what you have been doing, precisely, but I don't like the look of it.'

'Shorthand, Miss Carr,' I say, keeping my voice even and serene. 'What else would we be doing?'

'Why were you not sitting down?'

'It's nice, from time to time, to take a turn about the room,' I reply. 'Especially when one's hand is tired from writing.'

The Fury advances, the lines around her mouth pronounced in distaste. 'Your tone is one of intolerable impertinence,' she says. At no point does she address my tutor; if there is fault here, then the fault is clearly mine. 'I believe that you have been behaving improperly.'

James Hopkins gets to his feet. 'That is . . . quite untrue,' he stammers. I notice that he sounds far less sure of himself than he usually does – the velvety patter is quite gone from his delivery.

'You have offended Mr Hopkins,' I say. 'You should apologise.'

'I? Apologise? I never heard such insolence. Ada, you are to leave the room at once.'

I never before realised how closely aligned are the states of romantic excitement and righteous anger. I do now, as I run from the room, not looking back at either of them (and how embarrassing it will be for them both). My love for James is matched in intensity by my loathing for the wretched Furies – especially this one, Miss Carr, who has dared to order me about in my own house! The only reason why I obeyed her is because I saw no point in inciting any further sanctions on her part; already, this episode will no doubt be poison-dripped into Mamma's ear; I will be cast in the worst possible light, and perhaps – just perhaps – Mamma will be prevailed upon to relieve my tutor of his post. That would be unbearable. My heart is still pounding unplayable rhythms as I reach my bedroom, slam-shut the door with far more force than is necessary, and throw myself down on the carpet.

Oh, James, *James* . . . I work my fingers into the carpet, just as I wrapped them into his hair not fifteen minutes ago, as my body bordered his absolutely and his lips and mine made a pattern of their own. What can I do now? If he is allowed to continue to teach me – and after all, there is no proof that anything untoward has taken place between us – I can only assume that we will be subjected to even greater vigilance than we have previously endured. I am bound by expectations, by routines, by arrangements . . . I am a hand in the grip of an aidergraph, but instead of a benign wire-and-ivory device that seeks to help its wearer, and not hinder her, I am trapped, trapped, and will always be so.

Oh, how I hate them all: the Furies, with their watchful, vengeful natures . . . this house, that imprisons me . . . and my mother, who orchestrates my every move. I am close to tears, and think how much I will enjoy them – the ocean-burst of despair will engulf me, and quieten me, eventually – when it comes to me. An *idea*. The faintest glimmer of a plan, a star only just perceptible to the eye of the diligent astronomer. Yes: I think I can see what to do. And for my plan to work there must be no tears. Not now.

I get up, dust down my dress, and go in search of some paper.

When I return to the library, Mr Hopkins is still putting away his books and papers. Fury the First is watching my tutor closely, as though she suspects that he may be planning to steal some silverware. I stand meekly in the doorway, the picture of wronged innocence.

'Ah,' says Fury the First, seeing me. 'What is it, Ada? Have you come to apologise?'

She is not a witch, I decide, but a toad. She is neither powerful nor skilful enough to be a witch; I hereby demote her to a witch's accessory. She is also irredeemably stupid, to think that she can predict my actions so easily.

'I am very, very sorry, Miss Carr,' I say. 'I was impertinent, I know. I should not have spoken to you in the way I did.'

Slightly mollified, she says: 'Indeed, Ada, you should not.'

I edge into the room, one foot-shuffle at a time. Subtlety is crucial.

'I just . . . I resented . . . I was saddened that you should have thought ill of my behaviour,' I say, approaching the mahogany table with measured steps.

Fury the Toad holds up a hand, warning me to come no further. 'Your lesson is over for today,' she says.

'I only wish to borrow *The Ready Writer* from Mr Hopkins,' I say. 'Since our lesson has been cut short, I would like to be able to continue with the chapter that we had abandoned.'

She cogitates; clearly, she has been persuaded by the idea of my continued progress – and thus my mother's approval – for she nods slightly, and gestures to me to take the book. Mr Hopkins is holding it – I go to him, demure; he offers me the book, and I thank him.

'Farewell, Mr Hopkins,' I say. 'I'll see you on Tuesday, for our next lesson.'

Fury the Toad does not seem to take issue with this; either she is fully convinced of my repentance, or else she believes that she was unjust in her accusations. Not, of course, that she is likely to apologise to me if the latter is the case. But no matter: I, Ada, am more than a match for a toad-like Fury. She, and Mamma and anyone else, may think that Mr Hopkins and I will meet again on Tuesday, but the reality is that we shall see each other far, far sooner than that.

For as I took *The Ready Writer* from his long-boned fingers, I was able to fold – stealth personified – a twist of paper into his hand.

Fordhook, Ealing
March 1833

The chapter which follows (one that exceeds the riches of even that worthy tome, *The Ready Writer*, in every imaginable way) takes place, appropriately, by moonlight. I have set the stage as best I could, and provided – in Lewisian shorthand, of course – the clearest directions possible.

> *The allotment shed.*
> *Midnight tonight.*

Will James be there, though? That is the question: when I gave him the slip of paper, there wasn't the slightest chance of his being able to read it in front of me; I imagine that he waited until he had reached the end of the driveway, and was perfectly out of sight of the house and all its incumbent Furies. Then, only then, would he have read the note. Will he have understood it? The symbols themselves, yes. The meaning? Presumably. If he does not know where the allotments are, he has only to enquire casually as to the exact location of Lady Byron's educational establishment. James Hopkins is not stupid. He will, I am sure, be able to find me.

The next question is: how I am to get there myself, undetected? Keeping myself awake in a fever of dry-throated anticipation, I burn a candle down to a waxy nub and wait for the rest of the house to go to sleep. For the first time, Fordhook takes on the aspect of something more than bricks and mortar: it is as though I am crouching in the grasp of some giant beast, and must wait until it finally succumbs to slumber before I can slither from its curved claws. I am patient. Midnight is a long way away. The sounds of a wakeful household dwindle – the occasional cough; water being poured away; a muffled bidding of goodnight from someone to someone else. Mamma is a solid sleeper, and her chamber is some way from mine. I'm more worried about the Furies. Will they, perhaps, be keeping watch?

But I peer onto the darkened landing just after eleven o'clock and find no cause for alarm. The house is asleep: Furies and servants and all. I am unsure what I should wear. It seems overly familiar to wear my nightgown – as though we are married! – but I have *every intention* of being familiar, or at least every hope, and it would be highly suspicious to be caught wandering around the house fully-dressed.

I think about climbing out of the window – this would be romantic – but think better of it. The servants' staircase will do perfectly well. Just as I'm leaving the room, I catch sight of myself in the looking glass: a girl in a long, white, high-collared nightgown, her hair in a loose cloud around her head, rather than rigidly parted and secured. For once, I look just the way I feel – I can't quite explain why this is the case, but I know it to be true. I am the girl in the mirror far more than I am other Adas.

I never fully appreciated my mother's decision to set up an academy within walking distance of Fordhook Manor until I had to walk there in the middle of the night. In my thick hooded cloak and boots, I feel different again as I steal down the driveway and along the lane, keeping towards the hedgerow and holding a gaslight in front of me. I am Ada the Adventuress, exploring the unknown terrain of nocturnal Ealing. I am not afraid of the secret sounds of the undergrowth, the rat-like chirrups, the hoots of night birds. I am going to meet my lover – for surely that is a word that I can use when I describe him – and I am quite fearless. Only when I hear the sounds of drunken revelry, and spot a party of young men – they have the look of officers – staggering towards me on the other side of the road, do I panic, shrinking behind a tree and waiting until they are gone.

Once I reach the allotments, I feel emboldened again. I mustn't be late; what if I am, and he has arrived already, but doesn't wait for me? I can't bear the thought of some *Romeo and Juliet*-style tragedy; James Hopkins and I are not under any circumstances to be parted. I run down the central pathway, passing the shapes that I have known quite well by daylight, that are rendered ghostly and strange by moonlight.

(For there *is* moonlight, a great gleaming belt of it, and I am glad of its presence.)

The shed looks deserted; no light gleams from its single window. I unlatch the door cautiously, my lamp aloft. Darkness, and the smell of damp and cut grass, and then a form, human-like, looms out of the shadows and I cannot stop myself from making a small noise of alarm: a whistling gasp, like air let out of a balloon.

'Oh, James,' I whisper. 'You startled me!'

'But you *were* expecting me,' says my shorthand tutor. 'Weren't you?'

'I hadn't any doubt.'

I sound confident, but I don't feel it; I am suddenly shy, not sure what to do next. He moves closer towards me, presses his body against mine, takes hold of my hands.

'This is definitely not Good Behaviour,' I mutter.

'I'm, er, afraid not,' says James.

'Oh, well,' I say. 'I never cared much for it.'

He kisses me, and it's a different kiss: less the tentative flicker of two butterflies whose wings fleetingly touch, and more the magnetic meeting of entities: water and stone; paper and flame. Extraordinary words go through my head, as his hands steal inside my cloak, finding my waist. *James*, I think. *Ada. Kindling. Darkness. Home.* It is most curious: my Ada-brain seems somehow separate from my body; it is as though I am floating above myself, dissociated, observing, and yet I am more closely aware of everything going on inside me than I have ever been before. It is though my body has its own kind of brain – hard to explain, I know, but true.

It is like a silent dance, this Ada–James pairing in the shadow-dark shed. There is no music but the tides of our breathing, the scuffle of feet on floorboards, the distant calls of owls; there are no set patterns to follow, and yet we seem to know how to move, as though some long-ago teaching, deeply ingrained, resonates in our bones. A nudge, a curve, a dip, a slope, an invitation, an acceptance . . . Yes. It is like a dance, and I want never to forget it. I don't know how we advance (or decline?) from vertical to horizontal, but we do; now I am lying on the floor of the shed, on a woollen rug with scratchy filaments that I would find, in any other circumstances, quite aggravating . . . I am still clad in my cloak, but James is without his greatcoat, and we neither of us is wearing boots, though I do not remember removing mine. I have never felt the weight of another person before, so close to me. Now I rejoice in it: the warmth of him, his breath on my neck, the feel of his shoulders.

'Miss Byron – oh, Ada. I—'

'What's that?' I say, sitting up, patting the cotton folds of my nightgown, exposed where my cloak has fallen open. There's a sudden wetness spreading over my leg; something like water, or . . .

'My ink bottle. It was in my pocket,' says my tutor.

For some reason, both of us find this incredibly funny. Perhaps it is because he has told me – on many occasions – how fond he is of the particular brand that he uses. In any other circumstances, this tragic loss of ink might be viewed as a real calamity.

It's not until the next morning, when I wake up – feeling like a different person – that I wonder how I am going to explain the fact that my nightgown is covered in ink. In the end, I decide that the best thing to do is to hide the offending garment behind my washstand. I have plenty of other nightgowns; I am sure that no one will notice. When Nanny Briggs – not the most perceptive of people, but one who is deeply attuned to all matters domestic in a way that I, Ada, never shall be – does ask me where it is, I feign ignorance. 'Why, Nurse, I don't remember the last time I wore it,' I say. 'Didn't you take it away for darning?'

Gullible as she is, my poor nurse goes away, shaking her head, and no doubt chastising herself for her poor memory.

For a while, at least, the shed, built so beautifully for purpose, finds another purpose altogether, and offers shelter to two people whose interests lie somewhat outside of the usual allotment pursuits. These dull strips of land become an unlikely location for Paradise: a veritable Eden, indeed. And Eden is an appropriate comparison, because there is bliss – more than I ever could have imagined – but there is also transgression. Each time we meet, my awareness of the fact that it is *wrong* becomes slightly more acute – rather to my annoyance. Catullus, I realise, was not quite right: one can give a thousand kisses, and then perhaps a thousand more, but ultimately the kisses must be replaced with a question, and the question is one that I put to my shorthand tutor, on the night of our third encounter.

'James,' I say.

'Yes, Ada, my dear?'

'I want to know what happens next.'

I know his face so intimately that I can imagine, rather than see (it's terribly dark, and our lamps are low) his face – eyebrows raised, a half-smile, an earnest blink. 'We agreed,' he says delicately, 'that we ought not to . . . go any further.'

A blush of heat smoulders beneath my eyes. 'I know,' I say quickly. (We did agree this – in a strange, breathless conversation where each unfinished phrase carried a kind of wordless urgency – and I am glad we did. I may be prepared to transgress – midnight assignations with my tutor are precisely the kind of moral deviance that Mamma has sought to prevent – but there are boundaries to those transgressions; boundaries that I only realised I had in the moment of our discussion, and I am glad that we *did* discuss it. Certain garments, in other words, have gone unremoved.)

'What I mean is,' I say carefully, 'is . . . well, I am wondering if you love me?'

At this, he laughs – surprise and affection, and a touch of exasperation, as though I have asked an awkward question. 'Ada, you funny little thing. Yes – yes! Of course; of *course* I do.'

'And I love you,' I reply in a whisper. The words hold such sudden import that I am almost afraid of them. It means more to me than I had thought it would, somehow, to hear that he loves me; I feel something open up inside me at the words – a kind of yawning hunger. Now that I have heard those words, I want to hear them again and again. I did not realise how much I wanted to be loved. For the first time, I feel honestly *known* to another human being – not as Ada Byron, a figure to point out in the street, but as a girl in a nightgown who is somewhere she shouldn't be but is all the happier for it. And as I say those same words – those heavy-soft syllables – I know that they are true: I *do* love him. I am the trail of light that follows a comet; what he teaches, I will learn; and where he goes, I will follow.

'Do you think I would make you a good wife?' I say.

'You would make an exceptionally interesting one. I should never be bored.'

'Is that all I am – interesting?'

'Oh, no indeed. You are all kinds of things: amusing, intelligent, determined. You . . . you do what you say you will do. Not many people are like that, Ada.'

I am rather enchanted by this, although I feel bound by honesty to inform him that I do not always succeed in my endeavours. 'Once,' I tell him, 'I thought I could invent a flying machine – powered by steam, you know, and in the shape of a horse.'

'What an extraordinary idea!'

'I was so delighted by it,' I say, remembering those feverish experiments in the tack room at Bifrons; the pages I covered in sketches and hypotheses. 'But I fell ill in the midst of

154

it all, and by the time I was better again, I realised that I couldn't do it. Not really.'

I couldn't do it . . . It is a secret hithertofore never revealed to another living soul, and I think I love James all the more, for being the one to whom I have told it. I nestle into the hollow of his neck, silent for a moment, content to listen to the sound of his heartbeat. This is our usual position, on the rug (which we have moved in order to hide the ink-stain on the floorboards), and beneath the moonlit square of window. A swatch of moonlight glows on my tutor's wrist, and I outline the shape – a polygon of sorts – with my finger.

'We'd have to run away, though,' says James.

'To . . . to get married?'

'Yes. We'd have to go to Gretna Green.'

I try to imagine my mother's face, were she to receive a letter from me explaining that I had eloped. I am not convinced that she would be best pleased.

'Would your mother be surprised?' my tutor asks.

'I don't know. Perhaps. Then again, she does tend to *expect* the worst of me. She asked the Furies to watch over me, after all,' I say.

James Hopkins points out that Mamma might want to employ other friends to do the same office in future, since the Furies have quite notably failed in their charges.

'She quite specifically said that she didn't want me to turn out like my father,' I continue, remembering now the conversation I overheard from the tree.

'Do you know what she meant by the remark?' James asks.

'Hush! I can hear something,' I say, half rising to look out of the window. 'No . . . no. It's only a fox, I think. What she meant, I suppose, was that my father's morals were those of a genius, an artist, and as such perhaps were unconventional.'

I realise, as I'm speaking, that I don't really understand; I am simply paraphrasing Signor Isola, with whom I discussed my father in Genoa – and I was fairly sure that Signor Isola had not known Lord Byron nearly as well as he claimed to. 'What do *you* know about my father?' I say.

'He was one of the most famous poets of our time.'

'Everyone knows that. What about his personality? His character?'

'Why, Ada, I don't know that I feel qualified to comment on his character. I didn't know him.'

'That doesn't seem to stop people from commenting.'

'Indeed: the newspapers make commentators of us all. I suppose everyone thought they knew him, in a way – through his work, if not his reputation.'

'*Was* he morally deviant?' I say, getting the impression that James knows more than he is saying; that he is selecting what to say, as a dandy might muse over his choice of cravat.

'I . . . well, Ada, did you never – did you never hear any of the rumours, the stories? I suppose you wouldn't have. I was quite young myself; you were even younger, and shielded besides, presumably. Lord Byron certainly lived an eccentric, extravagant lifestyle. He had a caged squirrel, I believe, and a number of other exotic pets. I believe he even had a pet bear when he was at university.'

I am quite thrilled by this: not everyone, surely, has a father who would have thought of such an unusual pet.

James goes on: 'He was – by all accounts – a man of extreme habits: dieting one day, gorging himself the next. He spent a lot of money.'

'He was rich,' I say, not sure whether I am asking a question or making a statement, and realising as I say the words that I don't actually know how rich my father was. My mother is rich, certainly; but was my father?

'I believe he *was* rich, initially. But I think that when he left England he was in considerable debt.'

'Oh!' I say, digesting this. But how little, how little I know; I can see that now. The childish visions of desks and servants, castles by the sea, float in a kind of bitter cloud around my head, and then slowly dissolve. 'I . . . I had always thought that he . . . just wanted to live abroad.'

'I think that he was fleeing his creditors,' says James softly.

In the dusty gloom of the shed, I can only see James' face in indistinct profile, but his voice tells me that he is not comfortable telling me things that I had not previously known about my father. Echoing my own thoughts, he says: 'Ada, I don't know . . . it doesn't seem appropriate for me to tell you all this.'

'But who else is there to tell me?' I say, slightly shrill, forgetting to whisper, rising up onto one elbow and putting my hand on his wrist. 'Mamma won't say anything. I don't have an older sister, or an aunt . . . well, I suppose I do have Aunt Augusta, but I can hardly—'

At this, James begins to cough uncontrollably. He sits up. 'We should go.'

'But there's so much more I want to ask,' I say. I am torn suddenly – I have made the person to whom I feel closest grow distant, and that is something that I never want to do again. But James has revealed to me things that I've never known about my father, and – in spite of the nature of his disclosures, for clearly my father *was* a character of somewhat loose morals – I feel closer to my father because of this, and want so much to enquire further.

It is a curious dilemma.

Fordhook, Ealing
April 1833

Disaster strikes like an unforecasted storm on the morning of our eleventh lesson.

James is reading aloud from a pamphlet that he has brought, penned no doubt by the indefatigable Mr Lewis: *'The brilliant accomplishment of good writing is as sterling gold, whose intrinsic value will remain unalterable through all the vicissitudes of life,'* he is saying, as the library door creaks open. Fury the Second is on duty today; we are so used to her heavy-footed tread as she circles us that neither of us looks up. Then I become aware of a changed energy in the room – I am peculiarly sensitive to the moods of my mother, and I know before seeing her that it is she who is standing there. Her entire body is rigid with fury; here is Fury personified, and far more frightening and dreadful, for all that she is rather short.

James gets to his feet at once.

'Mr Hopkins,' says Mamma. 'That sounded like an interesting piece that you were reading.'

He bows. 'Yes, milady.'

'You hold the accomplishment of writing in high regard.'

'I do indeed.'

'Which is, of course, why I hired you to tutor my daughter. Is it, or is it not the case, that you use a particular kind of ink, Mr Hopkins?'

'Of . . . of ink, milady?'

'I believe that you have claimed as much. Indelible blue-black writing ink, from a company called Stephens.'

James nods, defeated. Mamma continues, each word placed for maximum dramatic effect (she takes particular care over the word *indelible*). 'Not many people use this ink, I believe. It is expensive, and has only relatively recently been made available.'

'That is so.'

'Then perhaps you will explain to me, Mr Hopkins, why it is that not only has an extensive spillage of this particular blue-black ink been discovered staining the wooden floorboards of one of the allotment buildings, but also a nightgown belonging to my daughter, that she ingeniously, but not ingeniously enough, hid behind her washstand?'

She is just too clever, my mother. Nothing escapes her; I realise now that my greatest sin – greater by far than whatever carnalities I have indulged in – has been presumption. I assumed that because Mamma wasn't often actually here, because she tasked an array of Furies with watching over me while she herself alternated between rest cures and continued plans for social reform that, somehow, she wasn't aware of what I was doing. I was wrong. I am guilty of presumption, and laziness besides; I should have visited the shed by daylight and washed away the ink, instead of moving the rug into a different place, hiding the stain, and hoping no one would notice.

My mother, gifted mathematician that she is, has put two and two together, and made four.

'I have made enquiries,' Mamma goes on. 'The housemaid says that on at least two occasions she has noticed that Ada's outdoor things were damp in the early morning. One of the teachers at the Academy recalls looking out of his window, late at night, and seeing what he thought was a candle somewhere in the grounds. 'You should consider yourselves fortunate that you weren't discovered on the spot by Mr Atlee.' At this, she half closes her eyes and bites her lip, as though uttering a silent prayer.

'N-n-nothing happened, milady, I assure you,' stammers my tutor. I don't look at him; I don't look at either of them. In spite of the evidence, which is considerable, I wouldn't have done what he has just done – admit guilt. I'd have come up with a story, something to explain the ink on my nightgown; I'd have denied all knowledge of the shed. But it's too late now, and Mamma seems not at all pacified by James' promise.

'You are to leave this house immediately,' she says.

He gathers his books with the speed of a wounded soldier, horseless and fleeing from the site of a battle that has been lost. Mamma escorts him out, one hand flared like a claw at the small of his back, as though she wishes she could push him over and send him sprawling down the front steps. I melt into the library shadows as they pass, neither of them casting a glance in my direction.

'James,' I whisper.

But it's too late; he's gone.

All the feeling in my body has turned to liquid; it bubbles up in my blood, riddling me with rage and frustration and a kind of flat, dull sense that, once again, Mamma has *won* . . .

Distantly, the front door slams; footsteps crunch; my banished tutor leaves Fordhook for the last time. My hands shrink into balls, my nails cutting into my palms, tears misting the corners of my vision.

'Why must she always win?' I say bitterly to the empty room. 'It is as though she is my enemy, and not my mother.'

I wait for her to come back, but she doesn't. It is beginning to rain; slow, lardy drops are gliding sluggishly down the pane, making a mockery of my tears. Why hasn't she come back? Rather aimlessly, I leave the library, ears alert. Passing the drawing room, I hear the Furies, murmuring in shocked whispers.

'All this time, my dear – all this time, why, under our *very noses*!'

'Come, Selina. He seemed such a nice young man—'

'It was Ada who led him astray.'

'Now, now, we cannot be sure of that . . .'

'But do we *know* what actually happened?'

'He says . . . the young man claims that nothing improper took place . . .'

162

'Oh, I find that very hard to believe!'

'Dearest Annabella is quite beside herself. She has gone to lie down, and we shan't disturb her until morning.'

It is so like Mamma, I think, as I beat a retreat towards the kitchens, to be rendered prostrate by her own victory. I can just imagine her, lying flat on the coverlet, demanding a tincture of something, a cold compress. What about *my* feelings? Who is going to minister to me, in my moment of defeat? I am light-headed with self-pity. And rage. Without even really noticing the direction of my steps, I make for the boot room, where I put on my outer garments, my walking boots, and suddenly I am outside, in the rain, pulling my hood up over my head. I stride down the driveway, wanting to plant my footsteps in the exact spaces where James stepped not so very long ago, but the ground is slithery with mud. Where I am going? I think I decided the moment she sent my tutor away, although I didn't know it at the time.

Didn't I promise myself that where he went, I would follow? I meant it. I will follow him unto the ends of time, or failing that, to his house. The only slight problem being that I am not entirely sure where he lives. A walk across the fields, he said, but in which direction? Scanning my memory for snatches of half-forgotten conversations, I walk on. At the end of the lane is a forked path; where I would turn left for the parish church and Ealing Grove, I turn right, find a gate – I am sure that this is the way; I am sure he described it so – and climb over it, and find myself in a barren field. There *is* a path – well, more of a nettle-strewn track; I keep slipping on the ground, and realise that I am wearing someone else's boots. A hollow marble-roll of thunder; the rain doubles. I can feel seams of droplets along my eyelashes. I start to wonder if I should turn back; but I don't want to, for what is there to go home to? Furies, and lessons and disappointment? No: better to drown in this joyless field, on my own terms, than be subjected to a life that I no longer want to lead.

I cast myself as the heroine of my own tragic romance. As I trudge along the path, I can almost see the words unfolding on the page before me.

Ada, who had suffered most unjustly at the hands of the Furies – and, of course, her own mother too – was finally unable to bear the life that they had so painstakingly laid out for her. The storm was bitter; the rain sliced through the heavens like butter knives, and yet she felt nothing but freedom as she forged a path towards the humble house where her lover lived . . .

Carried away by my own composition, I walk smack into a gatepost, and let out a squeal of surprise. Looking about, I see houses: a small cluster of them, painted pale colours, with thatched roofs. There's no one about, but by now it is raining so much that I wouldn't expect to see anyone outside.

The Old Rectory. That's it: that's James' house; I'm sure of it. Rain-drenched, riddled with so many emotions that they have all, by now, dissolved into one, I stand rather confusedly outside the door. An iron bell dangles from the lintel. I look up at it, hesitate, and then, instead, take hold of the door-knocker. But just as I'm about to knock on the door – a single tentative tap of brass – the door swings open and a woman looks out.

'Can I help you?' she says.

I open my mouth, incapable of speech, furious with myself for not utilising my slippery cross-field tramp to fashion for myself something to say at the end of it.

'But . . . you are Ada Byron,' says the woman, and I realise that she is James' mother.

'Your hands are the same,' I say, through chattering teeth. 'You . . . you have the same hands.'

'Come inside,' says the woman, perhaps not understanding this. 'Come into the warmth.'

She draws me into a small room with a lit fire; the walls are crowded with oil paintings; a small harpsichord sits, loved-looking, in the corner. All at once I feel the pull of a *home* – not a rented mansion with a hundred uninhabited rooms – but a real, family home, where siblings share secrets at the end of a long day. Perhaps, I think, I can come and live here – at least until we are married. This woman looks as though she would make an excellent mother-in-law, and I shall be an exemplary daughter. They might not have very much money, but I shall be able to contribute plenty, I'm sure. If Mamma agrees to the marriage, that is. But at the thought of Mamma, the glass sphere of my daydream begins to acquire long fractures. She would never agree to the marriage. James Hopkins does not have a title; he has no land; he is not of my class . . . It will not matter that we love each other absolutely. She will not care.

'Wait there, if you please,' says the woman, motioning for me to make myself at ease, and disappears with a rustle of fabric. Not wanting to sit down, I stare into the fire, and then take in the colours of the walls, the furnishings, so that at least I will always be able to remember the house where James Hopkins lived.

When the woman returns, she is accompanied by a tall man with dark hair, broad shoulders and James' upturned nose. Behind them, with the abashed tread of a child caught stealing, is James himself. For a moment, he looks at me, and then he looks away, as though it is too painful to meet my gaze. And I realise that short of running away, eloping, there is really nothing that we can do, James and I.

This entire affair has been a misadventure.

'Miss Byron,' says the tall man, who must be James' father. 'We must take you home.'

Fordhook, Ealing
April 1833

Freedom. It's something I think a good deal about. What makes a person free? What gives one person the right to exert any kind of direction over another? Why should a parent seek to control their own child with such overwhelming, unilateral dominance that the child's every action is more or less predetermined? If they are acting out of love, out of genuine concern, does it make this control more justifiable?

This is the question that I ask myself, as Mr Hopkins takes me back to Fordhook in a borrowed carriage. The rain thrums aggressively on the roof; as we sit in embarrassed silence, I can practically hear the man's thoughts, as uncomfortable as too-tight boots. *What happened between this young lady and my son? Who was the instigator? What, oh what, will Lady Byron have to say?* Several times, he clears his throat, reaching for words that never come. Rounding a bend, we roll onto the flat plain of the hilltop; if it wasn't raining so heavily, we'd be able to see the metropolis below the trees, busy with its machineries, its engines, quite disinterested in whatever small, inconsequential drama might be taking place above it.

'We are good people, you know,' says Mr Hopkins, breaking the silence. His voice is very different to his son's – coarser, lower. 'We don't want any scandal.'

At this, I look at him, levelling my gaze to his. 'Are you thinking about my father?' I say.

The question seems to jolt him; he opens his mouth, dumbly, like a herring. 'I'm thinking about everyone,' he says.

Part of me is angry. Two lovers have been forcibly separated, and all this man can think about is family reputation. Does he have no regard for the happiness of his own son? Could he and his wife not have supported our being together – rejoiced in it, even – rather than dispatching me back to Fordhook like a parcel that must post-haste be returned to its sender? Do they care nothing for the romance of our situation?

'I would have gladly married him,' I say.

'That's as may be, Miss Byron,' he replies.

A vision swims into my imagination: we stand, James and I, in the Fordhook drawing room, before some designated officiant. We are demure; we are elated; our hands are, perhaps, just touching as we prepare to murmur our vows. Then the vision darkens and changes: the Fordhook drawing room vanishes, and in its place some unknown chapel appears. James is there – a little older, his hair a little darker, but otherwise no different – but now it is someone else by his side. She is un-Ada – tall and fair, perhaps, with an expression on her face of soft satisfaction. She has never visited a shed at midnight, and never will.

At the thought of James marrying someone else, a single tear wobbles down the side of my nose; I turn my face to the window, so that Hopkins Senior will not see it.

I am not present at whatever conversation takes place between James' father and Mamma upon my return to Fordhook. I can only imagine that it is brief and perfunctory. Perhaps the Furies hover at the fringes, lending support to Mamma; or perhaps they don't. I am expecting to be summoned to my mother, but it is Mamma who comes to find me, later, in the garden. The rain has stopped, although droplets are still pattering irregularly from the trees, the only sound in an otherwise still space.

'I blame myself, Ada, more than I can say,' she begins.

This startles me; whatever I was expecting (remonstrations, accusations, dire warnings of as-yet-unheeded consequences), it wasn't this.

'I have not been present enough,' Mamma goes on. 'I know that now. Even when you were a baby, you know . . . my own mother would tell me that I was going away too often, spending too much time in spa towns. She would tell me to come home, and I *wanted* to, Ada, but at the same time I just didn't have much confidence in myself as a mother. Your grandmother and your nurses would do a better job than I would.'

It isn't like Mamma to admit fault. She indicates to me that she wishes to walk around the rose garden, and I – rather grudgingly – fall into step beside her. She goes on: 'Perhaps, in my efforts to ensure that you received the same thorough education that I myself received, I placed too many restrictions on you. Too many governesses, too many lessons.'

Thinking of the board that she made me lie on, unmoving, as a correction for inattention or poor work, I make a little sound at the back of my throat.

'I should not have been surprised that you threw yourself into the arms of the first young man who took notice of you,' says my mother. 'I was your age once; I remember how it feels.'

I doubt this.

'In coming home willingly, I do believe that you have understood the error of your ways. Ada, I want you to know that I . . . I do forgive you.'

The rose beds are rocky-looking and drenched; the rose bushes spike out like brittle webs at all sorts of angles. Briefly, I picture myself as a rose, thorns razored smooth, expertly pruned into submission. Then I cast the image aside; it is a dull one.

'I believe that, if we all exercise *great caution*, no word will ever escape of this matter,' says Mamma. She looks at me sideways. 'You do understand, don't you? No reference must ever be made to what has taken place with your tutor. I want no mention of him in your letters (certainly you will not be writing *to* him), and I shall make no mention of him in mine. If we can endeavour to forget his name entirely, so much the better.'

We have walked around the entire perimeter of the rose garden, and are back where we started. 'Well, Ada? And what do you have to say?'

I wonder if she wants an apology; she sounds as though she does. And, in a way, I *am* sorry. What James and I did was wrong; there is no escaping the fact. If we *had* run away together, the outcry we'd have caused would have been barely imaginable. Especially given the fact that I am Byron's daughter, and famous for it, whether I like it or not. But I am angry too, and the emotions serve to cancel one another out, as neat as a balanced equation. Mamma's speech was a pretty one. But in making it she proved, once again, that what she really wants to do is to control me, and any stories that concern me, and any situations that involve me. For all that she claims to regret the amount of control she has exerted over me, the reasons underlying her actions are proof of the reverse.

'I understand,' I say at last, not very loudly.

She pouts, as though she expected something better, something more. Then she walks back towards the house, stepping quickly, holding her skirts a few inches above the wet ground. I watch, loving her and hating her at the same time and almost equally. Above the house, the clouds have the swirly look of chilled milk, and I stare at them furiously, willing them to drift apart into cottony puffs. If I stare for long enough, pouring into my gaze every morsel of intensity that I possess, could I summon a rainbow? I wait a minute, and a minute more, but no rainbow appears. Mamma is now a tidy dark-clad figure in the distance.

Another picture is growing in my mind: my father on his way to cross the Channel for the final time, the horses galloping so madly that it is all he can do to hold himself upright in the carriage. His creditors are at his heels. He leans back, eyes closed, exhausted by it all. He is not only escaping from those to whom he owes money. For a moment, he has a vision of my mother's face: cold, drawn, effortlessly calculating . . . and he thinks to himself that he will soon be free of her and her infinite need for control. He laughs bitterly; his valet looks over, solicitous, but Byron doesn't care to explain. Perhaps he thinks of me, his daughter – longingly, forlornly – before turning his thoughts once more to the journey ahead.

Staring at my mother's retreating form, I say under my breath: 'I understand why my father left you.'

Surrey Zoological Gardens,
May 1833

On another of her regular visits to Fordhook, Mary Montgomery sees that I am ill at heart and proposes an excursion to the newly-established Surrey Zoological Gardens.

'It will take you out of yourself, Ada,' she promises, as we begin the carriage journey, which will take the best part of an hour.

I am interested to see the Zoological Gardens, a place I've never been, and know little about. I am also glad of Mary's company. I *do* need to be taken out of myself; it is six weeks since James Hopkins was banished from my life, and I feel that I have retreated inside the bubble of my own thoughts, simmering with resentment and confusion. On the surface, I have shown a good deal of contrition, offering my heartfelt apologies to all involved – the Furies, and Nanny Briggs, and, of course, Mamma. I deceived them, and deceitful behaviour is shameful.

I even allowed, last week, a physician friend of Mamma's – Dr Combe – to examine my head. Dr Combe is a phrenologist, which is to say that he is devoted to the study of the appearance of the human skull. I sat perfectly still as he laid his hands on my head, allowing him to press the bumps and the bones, the plains and hollows, feeling all the while – rather irrationally – that he was trying to get at my secrets with his probing fingers.

The diagnosis the doctor gave Mamma was nothing I couldn't have told her myself. 'Ada is a young woman of unusual intelligence,' he apparently said. 'But she is very wilful.'

I can't imagine this came as a surprise.

But in spite of my show of regret, I am still quite bereft, adrift with longing, unable to concentrate on any of my lessons. Every night I summon a memory of James' face – the tilted nose, the burnt-butter hair – and each night I am saddened that the memory is growing fainter. After a few weeks, I am beginning to worry that my much-improved shorthand is the only thing that survives from the time I spent with James Hopkins.

Heartbreak is not my only concern. Two days ago, Mamma announced in her rather abrupt manner that I am to be presented at Court. It was framed not as a request, but as a command. When I was younger, I used to confide in my cat, but there is only so much that cats can offer in return, and I do feel as though I could do with some advice. I resolve to ask Mary what she thinks, at some appropriate moment. The carriage travels over Vauxhall Bridge, and I watch the water of the Thames, entranced by it, green-grey, both busy and tranquil in the May morning light.

'Just think how useful this place would be for the student of botany or zoology,' says Mary, as we disembark at the entrance to the Zoological Gardens.

I wasn't, I confess, expecting such expanses of water – they cover an extraordinary portion of the gardens. I think at once of Lake Lucerne and Lake Geneva, mapping the memories of those places over the sight that is presently before me. There are more birds than I've ever seen before in one place – swans that glide across the glass surface of the water, stately as porcelain sugar-bowls; flamingos that stand one-legged in the shallows. We visit the elephant house – not, at present, home to any elephants, to my disappointment, but to a collection of wapiti deer – and the aviaries, where large birds of prey loom darkly in corners, ruffling feathers, while a flock of curassows (hailing, apparently, from South America), steals our attention for several minutes. There are trees from almost every part of the globe and each is labelled, to show where it originally came from. Mary tells me that a good many rare shrubs have recently been donated by the Duke of Devonshire; indeed, there is almost no square of land that is unadorned with some kind of plant.

'Truly,' says Mary, 'it's a treasure trove of knowledge. Don't you think, Ada?'

I am about to agree that these gardens are indeed rich in learning opportunities, when something catches my attention. A young man and a young woman are leaning over the wall of the bear pits. While they are clearly supposed to be inspecting the bears – who have retreated, rather shyly, from view –

I can see that they have only really got eyes for each other. How well are they acquainted? I wonder. They are being chaperoned discreetly by a kind-faced middle-aged woman (not unlike Mary in appearance), who stands at a little distance, her gloved hands folded. Have they ever stolen away to an allotment shed in the middle of the night? Probably not. They don't look as though they possess enough imagination for that kind of gesture. But I envy them all the same, for Mamma would never have allowed me to come here with James for a decorous stroll under watchful supervision. At the thought of Mamma, I sigh rather loudly, and Mary asks me what the matter is.

'Mamma says I am to be presented at Court,' I tell her.

'Well?' says Mary. 'You are seventeen now. Do you not wish to be?'

'Not especially,' I say.

'Why not?'

But I can't quite explain why not. It is something to do with convention. Being presented at Court is the correct thing to do; somehow, this makes me not want to do it. 'Why should I be like everyone else?' I say, as much to myself as to Mary. 'It seems such an obvious thing to do. A dull thing to do.'

'It will make it far easier for you to find a husband,' says Mary practically.

I open my mouth, and close it again. I *did* find a husband, I think, remembering that dear, fire-warmed room where James Hopkins' family must still sit, every evening, singing songs and telling stories and uttering kind words. He just wasn't the right husband. And so, given the fact that Mamma and I obviously disagree about what might make a suitable husband, why should her method meet with my approval?

'Does it really matter so much whether I find a husband or not? You don't have one.'

'You are right, Ada. I am an old maid,' says Mary. 'Dependent on my own wits, and the kindness of others, and an invalid besides. Is that the sort of life that you want?'

I tell her truthfully that if I end up half as wise and perspicacious as she is then I will have been very lucky indeed. The lovers have moved on, and in their place are a mother and daughter, both rather overdressed for a walk in the gardens on a fine morning. They don't seem to be much interested in bears, and instead are looking around at all and sundry, pointing out anything that catches their eye.

'I hear that the Governor of Barbados has donated a pair of panthers to the zoo,' says the mother. She has a strident voice, easily heard.

'Oh, let us go and find them, Mamma!' giggles the girl, who is, I think, a little older than me.

'As you like, Clara,' says her mother. They walk right past us, and for a moment the mother's gaze travels over us – first me, then Mary, and then back to me again. I've seen that kind of look – half-lazy and half-alert – before. It means, sure as anything, that I've been recognised. Really, I don't know why I am recognised so often. It's not as though my portrait appears in the *Morning Post* every week, and I don't bear much of a resemblance at all to my father, though I still, quite often, go to look at his portrait to check. And yet there is something about me that makes people take notice. They stop and stare, and nudge each other. People have been doing this for as long as I can remember.

'Ada, what's wrong?' says Mary, when I hang back, turning on one heel.

I hold a hand up, as though to say: *wait, please.* Sure enough, a moment later the mother's voice competes with the birdcalls of the gardens – impossible for us not to hear, and probably for many other bystanders too.

'Clara, did you see that young woman? Very pale, with brown hair, just there by the bear pits? Why, that was Ada Byron. Oh, the things I've read about her lately – it would curl the hair on your head, it really would! It is said that she is the *most vulgar woman in all England* – some rumour, you know, about an affair . . . It's been hushed up very nicely by Lady Byron. But frankly, I shall be amazed if anyone marries her now.'

Mary and I stare at each other. I say: 'Is this . . . was that true, what she said?'

Mary Montgomery, who is always pale, has coloured like a boiled lobster. 'Oh, that wretched, prurient woman! Idle gossip – really, it is the worst thing. Ada, don't give it a thought.'

'But . . . she mentioned a rumour. Something she'd read.'

'I believe there *was* something in one of the papers,' says Mary. 'Your mother tried her best. But someone, somewhere, heard of the affair, and the newspapers got wind of it. That's what happens in this country. They'll print anything, and mostly lies ... and people do believe what they read, unfortunately. Oh, Ada, don't look so stricken.'

She clicks ahead, hoping that briskness will stir me. She is also, I think, implying that I really ought not to have stolen away to a shed at midnight and run off to the home of my tutor if I really minded what people would say about me. And, of course, she's right. I didn't realise how it would feel: the shame dark unpleasantness of being read about by those who don't know me. Which newspaper was it? Perhaps she doesn't know; perhaps it doesn't matter. But I can imagine that newspaper, spread open to the pages reserved for gossip and speculation, wedged beneath a saucer, sluiced by tea ... a paragraph to be read out at breakfast, laughed over, shared ...

Ada Byron is the most vulgar woman in all England.

I've always liked a superlative, but not that one, not for myself.

Mary has got some way ahead; I run to catch her up, my feet marking the pebbled pathway with urgent dimples.

'Mary,' I say carelessly. 'I wonder if perhaps I should be presented to the King, after all.'

Mary Montgomery smiles. 'Why not, Ada? I think it a very good idea indeed. And your mother will be delighted.'

Brighton
May 1833

And so we are returned to Brighton, to the hotel on Preston Street that Mamma favours. It is the eve of my presentation to King William, and I cannot quite believe all that has happened in a year. I sit on the windowsill, wishing that I could see the sea – it makes its presence felt, tantalisingly close, with its water-whispers and gull chorus, but is not quite within view. I remember the Ada who rode her horse alongside the water, who danced at the edge of the sea, so relieved to be released from the clutches of illness. That Ada was newly free, and rejoicing in the sensation of it; to her I made a promise, which was to wriggle out of the bounds and strictures in any way that I could, and *live*. Did I keep my promise? Well . . . I tried.

I did what I could, and I thought I was free, but I wasn't really.

Watching the evening merrymakers jostle and wander along the road towards the seafront, I reflect that my attempts to live and be free came at a certain cost – to my reputation, and to Mamma's happiness and sense of pride. And as much as I might pretend not to care about how my mother feels, I *do* care. I feel that same sense that I've always felt of wanting two things: to please her, and to please myself. Those two irreconcilable things. Tomorrow, then, I will try to make amends – to rebalance our relationship, which is never an easy one.

A knock on my door. 'Come in,' I say.

It's Mamma. She has my white dress over one arm; Nanny Briggs has been letting it out at the hips. It's my best dress, rich satin overlaid with embroidered tulle. With it, I shall wear a headdress of feathers with blond lappets, as well as Mamma's diamonds. Fleetingly, I wish that my shorthand tutor could have seen me in such an outfit.

'There,' says Mamma, hanging it with care in the wardrobe. 'Nanny Briggs has done a very nice job. You'll look beautiful, Ada.'

'What will you wear?' I say.

'Dark crimson, I think, and my white-feather hat.'

'That will look very fetching,' I say, meaning it.

Mamma sits down delicately on the chaise longue. 'I don't want to be an embarrassment to you,' she says. 'My own mother was never dressed quite right, somehow, when she accompanied me during my London Seasons. She used to talk too much, and too loudly – I could see people laughing at her, discreetly, and it made me feel terribly self-conscious.'

If this is supposed to make me feel sorry for her, it doesn't; I feel sorrier for Grandmama, whose heart was far bigger than Mamma's ever will be. But I do recognise what she is doing, by coming to my room this evening; a bridge, delicate as one fashioned from matchsticks and crepe paper, is being built. We haven't spoken, she and I, not properly, for weeks, apart from an emotional, twisting conversation in which she tried to exact from me a promise that I would behave myself at the ceremony.

'I am grateful, Ada, that you've agreed to do this,' Mamma says.

Gratitude isn't her strong suit; more likely, she is glad, and relieved. Does she know that I know about the story in the paper? I wonder if Mary has told her that I knew; I think perhaps that Mary has not. But I imagine she will never forget it, and neither will I. *Ada Byron is the most vulgar woman in all England.* If presentation at Court can go some way to addressing the coarseness of this comment, then I will be glad to make such an appearance.

'I . . . I thought it as well,' I say.

Not everyone reads the papers, after all; and not everyone believes what they read. In time, Mamma must be thinking, that harsh, vindictive little paragraph will be forgotten, buried under the weight of other harsh, vindictive little paragraphs with other people as their targets.

'And one day – not soon, perhaps, but one day – you will make the right kind of match, I'm sure of it. A man with money, and a title. An old title, preferably – a hundred years or more. Yes: that is what we must hope for.'

She bids me goodnight, and goes out. I stay at my spot by

the window, watching the lights of Brighton as they grow dim, and the moon that shows whitely in the clouds like a chipped china saucer. I picture a wedding: Mamma dabbing a genteel tear from her cheek as I make my eternal vows and an *old title* is bestowed upon me. Me, stout and finely gowned, at the head of a long, polished table, raising a glass by candlelight to a shadow-faced man who sits at the other end, so far away that I'm sure he will barely be able to hear me if I tell him a secret. A brood of titled children, pursuing me fatly, like ducklings, as I stride across some ancestral lawn in search of solitude.

And now another picture: scenes of tomorrow. A hushed, ceremonial chamber, bedecked in finery. Rows of dutiful debutantes, as nicely-trussed as Christmas geese, hair braided and bright. Me on Mamma's arm, making slow-steady progress – shuffle, shuffle – towards the throne. Will there be music? Singing? An announcement, I think: '*Miss Ada Byron, presented by her mother, Lady Noel Byron.*' Yes. Will King William – genial, grey-haired – and Queen Adelaide – namesake of one of my favourite places, some thirty years younger than the King – raise their royal hands for me to kiss? Or shall I simply curtsey, and then look up at them through lowered lashes? What will they say? Will I be thrilled, cast for once as the princess in the fairy tale, rather than the changeling? Will I be relieved to have appeased, if only temporarily, my feather-hatted mother? (And what bittersweet relief it will be, when I scarcely know from minute to minute whether I want to kiss, comfort or condemn her.)

Or will I, perhaps, feel nothing at all?

I blink, and the picture fades, as quickly as it assembled, and now there's only the moon, watching me over the water. I think about hope; of all of the things to hope for, to dream about, to long for . . . is this really the only thing? A man with money and an old title?

I wonder.

Part Three: 1833–1835
Age seventeen to nineteen

Fordhook, Ealing
June 1833

My favourite letter has always been the letter *I*. The simplest of strokes, middle vowel in a family of five, it stands upright as a soldier, boasting its lines of symmetry. It's a near-relation of the number 1, another marker of primacy. *I* is a pronoun: not the foghorn-blast of *me, me* – just a simple proclamation. *I* am the centre of my own universe. *I* am the most important person in my own world. It echoes in my head, a lyrical bending of tongue to palate.

I, Ada.

I think it so often – *I, Ada, have ridden a horse; I, Ada, have kissed my tutor* – and I love the way it sounds. Perhaps it is because I'm an only child; I grew up thinking only (or else mostly) of myself, because I had no sibling.

And now I, Ada, have been presented at Court, it seems that a husband must be found for me. One of the first events that I attended was a state ball at the Palace at St James' – no small affair; someone told me afterward that over seven hundred guests had been present. Proceedings began at ten o'clock. For once, I was glad of Mamma's company; there was such an air of ornate splendour about the occasion that I was in danger of being entirely overwhelmed. I gazed in wonder at the gentlemen in full court-dress, the knights laden with insignia, the ladies in their dresses of impossible finery, as they entered the state rooms. All along the staircase stood the Yeomen of the Guard, motionless as bronze casts as we passed.

'There is the Prince Royal of France,' whispered Mamma. 'That gentlemen there – no, don't stare, Ada – is the Russian Ambassador. And there is the Duchess of Kent.'

The throne room had been prepared for dancing; the throne and platform had been temporarily removed, and in the corner was stationed the quadrille band. In the ballroom there was another band (a special piece of music had apparently been composed for the Duke of Orléans), and a raised platform on which had been placed seats of gold and red damask for their majesties. Between the two ballrooms was a drawing room, and I noticed a smaller room set out for cards, and another with tables stocked with ices and other refreshments.

When the King and Queen entered, the band played *God Save the King*, and then the dancing began. First a gallopade, and then a quadrille . . . I participated in neither of these, preferring to watch as the Duke of Brunswick made his way into the centre of the room with his dancing partner. Then a young man approached with a low bow, introducing himself as Mr Edward Cowley, and I accepted his invitation to dance, for I knew the steps to the mazurka quite well, and was keen to demonstrate them. I don't remember what we spoke about as we danced – the usual formulaic pleasantries, no doubt. Mr Cowley danced quite well, with both elegance and confidence. Midway through the mazurka, I felt a sudden, sharp jolt of unhappiness – it struck me with all the haste of a fever – that I was dancing with someone who was not James.

'Are you quite well, Miss Byron?'

'Oh, yes,' I said. But I could see Mamma watching me now, from the edge of the dancing.

'Who was that young man?' she asked, when the dance was over and my partner had excused himself.

'A Mr Cowley,' I said.

'A man with no title,' she said at once, as I had known she would.

'Mamma,' I protested. 'It does not to me seem fair that your thoughts should advance to matrimony so quickly. It was only a mazurka.'

But after that, my enjoyment of the evening faded, and by the time supper was served at one o'clock, I was longing to go home. Mamma had reminded me of the purpose of my attendance at such things as state balls – not to eat, and dance, and wear fur-trimmed dresses and pearls – but to be seen by the right people and, in time, to *meet the right person*.

Now, some weeks later, I still find myself unsure about how I truly feel about it all. I am supposed to look attractive, rather than merely presentable – something I've never thought too much about. There are so many formalities to be observed that I feel positively baffled at times and long to do what Mamma always does when she's had enough of something, and lie down for an hour or so in a darkened room. Sometimes, indeed, I do slip away early, pleading a headache that is no lie; but at other times I enter into the spirit of the proceedings as best I can, because that is what I promised that I would do.

Wherever I go, whomever I meet, Mamma is never more than six feet away, watching me discreetly as she converses with one of her acquaintances. Ever since the James Hopkins Affair, she has dispensed with the Furies and now prefers to chaperone me herself – although there are occasional excursions with Mary Montgomery to look forward to still.

But my Ada-brain longs for something else; something *more*. There's only so much enthusiasm I can summon for dresses and slippers, refreshments and dance steps, over and over again, a pattern that becomes a parody of repetition.

And then there are the things that I actively dislike, such as the women who sit clustered in a corner, bosoms heaving in low-cut dresses, flapping their fans in front of their faces. Sometimes – I am sure of it – one of them leans in to the others, cheeks salmon-pink with pleasure, and hisses:

That's Ada Byron, my dear!

And the eyes watch me then, tracking my progress as I circle in a quadrille, or talk with other young ladies of mundane matters. The fans flap faster; another woman leans in, with another tempting morsel to offer.

Oh, but I heard the most scandalous rumour – you'll never guess . . .

And so it goes, from one drawing room to the next.

Why, that's Ada Byron, you know . . .

Goodness! What do you suppose is the truth behind that extraordinary tale about young Ada Byron?

Do I imagine them, these whispers? I have too much imagination, I think, sometimes, and I can't control it. Once I start imagining something, it's hard to stop . . . my butterfly brain skitters with what-ifs, and to me those whispers are as loud and clear as racecourse announcements by the time I have finished imagining, I wonder, therefore, what the fresh-faced young men to whom I am introduced know, and what they are thinking, and whether they could possibly countenance an affiliation with the *most vulgar woman in all England*. I would like to share my anxieties with my mother, but it just doesn't seem to be the kind of conversation that we could have together. I long for a friend, like Flora Davison, but she is not doing the Season.

I have no one in whom to confide, and for all that I am busier than I've ever been, I have never felt lonelier.

There is one kind of person, incidentally, who appears undeterred by malicious whispers, and that is a breed of gentleman known as The Fortune Hunter. Mamma holds forth on the subject one morning over breakfast, cautioning me to steer well clear of these objectionable types.

'I don't see how I am to avoid such people,' I say. 'You presented me at Court; you *wanted* me to have suitors.'

'Yes, yes,' says Mamma, tearing impatiently at a bread roll

with her small teeth. She chews, swallows and goes on: 'Suitors, yes. Fortune hunters, no.'

'How on earth is anyone to tell the difference?'

At this, Mamma looks vague, and mutters something about 'a particular gleam in the eye'. 'My point is really this,' she continues, liberally buttering another roll. 'If you are a young woman of means, you need to marry a man of wealth so that you can be sure you are not being married for the sake of your money.'

'What if he *has* money, but wants more?'

'Ada, you are being extremely tiresome,' says my mother. 'You simply have to make the correct judgment; that is all.'

'Is this how *you* felt when you were doing your London Seasons?' I venture. 'Was this a concern of your parents too?'

'We are not talking of me,' says my mother, in a conversation-closing tone of voice.

Rather rashly, I decide to press the point. 'How did my father appear, when first you met him?'

There is no more butter to spread. Mamma lays the butter knife down so that it bisects the dish. I wait for her to change the subject, or else to return to hectoring me about fortune hunters and the like. Her hand slips, and the knife clatters to side of the dish. She retrieves it and holds it for a moment, tilting it so that it reflects shards of light. Then she says: 'Hmm. I don't know that I recall the precise moment of our meeting . . .' The knife tilts again, and for some reason – one that I cannot fathom now, and perhaps never will – she appears to change her mind. 'No, I do remember,' she says.

'It was at Lady Melbourne's, at her house in Whitehall. Byron fairly turned the room inside out when he entered; he had a way of doing that, you know, even though he was lame in one leg and had a habit of holding onto the backs of bits of furniture, moving a little like a crab from place to place. Not a proud, bold stride into the centre of a room, as you might have expected. But he dressed quite exquisitely, and besides, he was famous. Really, extraordinarily famous. Musicians would lay down their bows. People would fall silent, just waiting to see what he would do or say.'

'Were you in awe of him?'

'I don't know that "awe" would be the right word. I was . . . *intrigued*. Yes, that describes it well. We fell into conversation, although I don't remember what we talked about. We met several times afterward, and then entered into a correspondence – a long one, of several years.'

This is more than she has ever told me. Far more. I risk one last question. 'Did you ever fear that *he* was a fortune hunter?'

Mamma coughs; a bit of bread has slipped down the wrong way. At once, three solicitous waiters spring to her assistance and it is some time before she is recovered enough to speak. 'Lord Byron,' she hisses, wedging her napkin into a starched ball, 'was never interested in my money.'

Later on, I find myself dwelling on this exchange, pressing at the edges of it, scanning for cracks. James Hopkins told me that my father was hugely in debt when he left for the

Continent. Was he in debt *before* he married Mamma? And in which case, why did he remain so – since Mamma, I know, was then a woman of considerable means? Did money lie at the root of their troubles, or was there some other reason?

I have puzzled and puzzled for so long that every time I come up with a hypothesis, I struggle to reconcile what I know to be true with what I imagine to be possible. But my theory is that my mother's behaviour while they were married was somehow so abhorrent to my father that he was forced to leave – first the marriage, and then the country. The debts must have figured too in the situation. But that is the best that I can come up with. (For all her flaws, I do not consider my mother capable of actually *incurring* debts.)

Yes, I think she tried to do all those things that she tries to do to me: to 'trammel' his mind; to curb his natural tendencies; to subject him to constant scrutiny, mindful of moral deviance. And if I, a young woman, find it almost too much to bear, then what must Lord Byron have thought? As a poet – a man for whom the flow of words must have been as crucial as lifeblood – he must surely have felt stifled by her indefatigable desire for control. How many times have I heard the word 'reform' upon my mother's lips? My poor father: I can just picture her attempts to reform his nature – perhaps, each time he lifted a glass of wine to his lips, she urged him to set it down untasted . . . perhaps she proposed that he peruse one of her long religious tracts, in the hope that he would better himself . . . And, of course, the great tragedy would have been that there was nothing really so wrong about him or his character; it was simply that my mother likes so much to try and make people better.

Vainly, I try to imagine myself there: a mouse scuttling along the skirting-boards, witnessing that first conversation. What is Mamma like? I picture her serious face with its rosebud mouth and prim brows. Does she smile, laugh at his jokes? No: I think she asks him a question, a searching one. She is perfectly sombre, while he is all gaiety and light-hearted wit. Perhaps he is interested by that, by the fact that she, Anne Isabella Milbanke, is different. But what a distance from that point to a point of an actual proposal of marriage: honestly, it's as absorbing as the trickiest of algebraic conundrums.

Sometimes, therefore, when I'm attending a party, it is not of myself that I am thinking at all. Nor am I thinking of whatever the bright-eyed, rouge-cheeked women might be muttering behind fanned fingers.

I think instead about my parents, and what they might have said to each other at those dances, nearly twenty years ago.

London
June 1833

There are moments, aren't there, when *everything changes* . . .

Those moments are often most clearly definable with hindsight. At the time, we don't realise what is happening; it's only later that we look back and appreciate that we have witnessed something of importance. Sometimes, however, we *do* realise. Take, for example, the first time I saw my father's portrait. I was only young, but even then, I knew that it marked a stepping stone along the path to finding out more about him – since, at the time, I knew so little. There are other examples: my first glimpse of Lake Geneva; the moment I saw the poor, dead crow and knew that one day someone would surely find a way to design a flying machine . . . and, perhaps, the moment I looked down from an upstairs window and saw the tailcoated figure of my shorthand tutor, and knew that he was a person I would want to know better.

Yes: life is full of such moments, if you keep watch for them.

At a party that is otherwise indistinguishable from so many similar parties – a mixture of the usual dukes and dignitaries – I meet, for the first time, Mr Charles Babbage. I believe that I hear his voice first of all – gruff, a little lion-like – occupying a register all of its own. He is talking, as far as I can make out, about the benefits of silence – an odd conversational choice for a crowded gathering. Looking for the speaker, I see him, in the middle of an attendant cluster: broad-chested, thick-necked – yes, really rather like a lion.

'That is Mr Babbage,' says Mamma. 'I have lately been reading his book, *Reflections on the Decline of Science in England*. He proposes a more formal attitude towards research, and laments the lack of funding for science from the government and the Royal Society. It was most interesting.'

It doesn't take her long to arrange an introduction. We move a little way away from the rest of the party, where the noise is rather less intense, and for some time I say little, preferring to observe the exchanges between Mamma and Mr Babbage – two people of repute making what they will of each other. Typical formulaic phrases and pleasantries are exchanged, but in Mr Babbage I get the impression almost at once of a man who cares little for formulae. There is a fascinating energy about him; I watch the way his eyes dart this way and that, following whatever flickers of light or movement might momentarily entice him; he rolls sometimes onto his heels, and rocks a little back and forth before settling himself once more upon the ground; his hands play patterns against his sides, as though an invisible piano is concealed somewhere about his person. He has an interesting way of speaking: he is brusque and excitable, like a child in anticipation of presents, and sometimes interrupts himself mid-sentence.

'The Difference Engine, my dear lady,' he is saying. 'It is rather a preoccupation of mine, and has been – yes, it has been for some time. Tell me, Lady Byron – what do you understand by the term "counting machine"?'

Mamma pauses for thought; I know that she will not want to sound ignorant. 'A mechanical device for calculation,' she replies carefully. 'Pascal created one, did he not?'

'Yes, indeed,' says Mr Babbage. 'The "Pascaline", as it was known – Pascal invented it in order to assist his father with tax calculations. It was a small machine. Used a wheel mechanism. Then there was Leibniz – all this was a hundred and fifty years ago, perhaps more, mind you – *his* machine could add, subtract, multiply and divide – more than Pascal's could do. Couldn't advance from nine hundred and ninety-nine to a thousand, though.'

Mamma nods.

'Neither machine amounted to anything much,' says Mr Babbage. 'Now, when I was in Paris – twelve, thirteen years ago – and you must recall, dear lady, that on the Continent they really do give scientific thinking the importance that it deserves ... I heard tell of an "arithmometer" – all of France was talking about it, or so it seemed. The designer was one Charles de Colmar. His was a machine along the lines of Leibniz's model. It could perform all the operations – although subtraction was done using complements, of course – simply by turning a handle. Oh, very pretty indeed, some people thought – something to have in your drawing room, a clever little showpiece for one's guests! But no: no, it was so much more than that. On that visit to Paris all those years ago, I realised how *essential* such a device would be. Think to yourself, dear lady – if anyone, working in any field, from science to commerce to accountancy to navigation to astronomy, required a particular mathematical figure, what would they do? Why, they would need to look it up in a handwritten chart. Now, there are plenty of those, done by human hand clergymen, schoolteachers with a bit of time to spare. But what do you think the issue might be with such a chart?'

'Errors,' I say, at once.

Mr Babbage beams at me. 'Yes, Miss Byron, just so! The charts are *riddled* with discrepancies – I have tested this hypothesis and I can assure you that it is true. The human brain, after all, is not a machine. But imagine – just imagine – a world in which these calculations are performed *automatically* – perfectly – with no errors. My dear friend Herschel very nearly died in a shipwreck in 1819; would that shipwreck have happened at all if the navigator had been able to calculate longitude and lunar distances with faultless accuracy? I think not! No; it is not an exaggeration to assert that *lives will be saved* by automatic calculation – by my Difference Engine, indeed.'

Now that I have grown more accustomed to the stop-start patterns of Mr Babbage's speech, I can see that he is an illuminating speaker. In just a few minutes, he has persuaded me – and Mamma too, I am sure – of the importance of such a machine.

'And you are in the process of building this Difference Engine?' asks Mamma.

'Indeed I am . . . that most certainly is my intention. Yes. But it'll need money. A good deal of it.'

'Have you received much funding from the government?'

'Quite a bit, yes – but not enough.'

They are both speaking quite fast; Mr Babbage refers to Robert Peel, the Home Secretary, and to the Duke of Wellington, our Prime Minister. Sums are mentioned. As they talk, I try to imagine a counting machine such as Mr Babbage says that he is trying to build. What would it look like? A steam-powered abacus floats into my head, its beads glinting with metallic promise. I want more than anything to see it for myself: this physical realisation of Mr Babbage's *ideas*.

And just as I am thinking this, Mr Babbage says abruptly: 'I've a demonstration piece at home, Lady Byron. I would dearly like to show it to you.'

'And we,' says Mamma, making sure that I am very much a part of her pronoun by indicating me with a sweep of her arm, 'would be charmed to see it.'

Dorset Street, London
June 1833

And so we are going to visit Mr Babbage, and his mythical-sounding machine.

The evening is warm; there's a feeling in the air of possibility, movement. The carriage rattles through Manchester Square; people are strolling along the pavements, beautifully dressed, full of leisurely intent. My mother's doll-like profile is perfectly still. One shoe taps a subtle tattoo on the carriage floor: a sign that she is looking forward to whatever the evening has in store.

It is not the first time that Mamma has taken me to look at machinery: I remember (dimly) our visit to the North of England where we examined the workings of the glass factory; and there were, I'm sure, other trips besides that I don't recall. Mamma derives a kind of sincere satisfaction from these excursions; she wants to understand how the machines work, and she wants me to understand how they work, and then, somehow, all will be right with the world for a while if both of these things take place.

'Now, Ada,' she says, interrupting my thoughts. 'You must be sure to ask pertinent questions.'

To this, I don't respond, giving her instead a *look* that says that I have never asked a question of anyone that was not pertinent. The carriage slows to a halt. We climb out, Mamma first, me following; then, taking my elbow, Mamma steers me along the pavement, as though I am a circus creature. Gently, but firmly, I shake my sleeve from her grip. I do not require steering. She settles for a hand between my shoulder blades instead. 'Come, Ada. Don't dawdle.'

As we approach Mr Babbage's house, I think about what it might mean to lose a beloved spouse, as I've learned he did a little over five years ago. I found my mother's reaction to the death of my father curious, and have continued to find it so, all these years – and it is almost ten years now, a fact which I decide is rather astonishing. I think of those bittersweet tears in the Hampstead library, as bright and sharp as a clatter of jewels; and the way she looked at the Villa Diodati, and the fact that our continental trip bore so many signs of a pilgrimage. But she cannot talk freely of him – never could – and while she might sometimes bring up some brief memory of him in conversation, she is just as likely to call an immediate halt to any such discussion, as though for fear of what might be said. Did she love him? I don't know; I still don't know. She can be so glacially cold sometimes that I find it hard to believe that she could ever have loved *anyone*. Not the way that I have felt love . . . I think of James Hopkins once again; my mind drifts into a kind of memorial pleasure garden, a landscape studded with kisses, and whispered sweet-nothings, and a shed at midnight, and a telltale pool of blue-black ink.

'Yes,' Mamma is saying now. 'I think we shall enjoy making Babbage's acquaintance properly. Many were offended by his criticisms of the Royal Society, but I for one am a firm believer that enterprises such as his should be fully supported. His machine is the talk of London, you know.'

Upon our arrival, a servant leads us up the stairs and into the drawing room on the first floor, and there Babbage receives us – he seems even taller, somehow, in his own setting, and no less exuberant, despite the fact that we are the only guests. He has the look, I think, of one who enjoys the act of creation: of twisting things to his whims, of *designing*.

He says with great warmth, 'It is wonderful that you have come.'

Drinks are offered, and then, without further ado, he leads us to a low table in the centre of the room. There it is: the machine that so much of London is discussing. Mamma is as collected as ever, but I find myself suddenly quite breathless with anticipation, and do my best to hide it. The demonstration piece is made of bronze and steel, perhaps two and a half feet high, and highly polished. Three columns of stacked cogwheels are interlaced with arms in a helical arrangement. The numbers from zero to nine appear above each wheel. Clever lighting lends the machine an alluring glow.

'What is the relation in size between this piece and a fully-operating model?' my mother enquires, strolling first this way and then that around the table, inspecting the machine from all angles.

'One seventh, milady,' Mr Babbage replies.

'And why is the machine so named?'

'Ah,' he says. 'Yes. The Difference Engine is named thus because of the principle on which it is founded: the *method of finite differences*. In order to produce more or less any kind of arithmetical table, you see, all that is required is a machine that can add *orders of difference* – provided, of course, that one enters the initial values. Do you . . . do you see?'

Mamma nods slowly. 'I do see,' she says. 'If one wishes to count: one, three, five, seven, and so forth, then the difference, each time, is two. It is a fixed order of difference.'

All thoughts of James Hopkins forgotten entirely, I edge a little closer to the machine. How nice that it is named for its ability to judge differences; I, Ada, have always adored those small moments in which a *difference* can be perceived – the windmills on the Continent, for example, or the taste of chocolate. So much can be measured in terms of differences, after all; it seems somehow fitting, and quite brilliant, that Mr Babbage has designed a machine to do exactly that.

'Multiplication can be done by the same process,' says Mr Babbage. 'Multiplication is a form of addition, after all.'

'Mr Babbage,' I say. 'What inspired you to use cogwheels for this machine?'

He looks at me and seems pleased to be able to answer. (*See, Mamma*, I think. *I am pertinent.*)

'Indeed, it's a perfectly apt question. The nature of the cogwheel seemed indicated from the first, although in fact each wheel has to be made by hand at great expense. What I – and others – have spent on it all so far! I can hardly begin to tell you . . . Now: each wheel has a certain quantity of "teeth", as you can see. Those teeth stand for numbers; there are ten fixed positions for each wheel.'

'Base ten,' says Mamma, nodding.

'Exactly. The wheel at the bottom represents the units. The one above, the tens; the one above that, the hundreds, you see. Though not yet thousands, I fear, not on this model. Allow me to show you.'

For a few moments he busies himself, turning a few of the wheels with gentleness and precision. 'A simple calculation, to begin with,' he mutters. Now he takes hold of the handle, and the arms of the demonstration piece begin to oscillate, dancing to their own peculiar choreography.

Click . . . click . . . click. It is strange music, this; soothing in its repetitions, but startling in its newness.

'I envisage, one day, a printer,' says Mr Babbage. 'For now, results can be read from this display. Here.'

He shows us, and we watch in silent fascination. He performs a variety of calculations for us, raising numbers to their second and third powers, and even – by some wondrous means that I cannot quite fathom – extracting the root of a quadratic equation. I watch the wheels click and whirr – they are quieter than I might have imagined, and feel a silvery thrill unfold across my palms.

'I do not understand,' says Mamma. 'What is preventing you from building the machine proper?'

Mr Babbage says: 'Dear lady, it is a rather longer story than I fear I have the patience to tell . . . I first sought funding for the Engine – well, it must be twelve years ago now. I don't think the Home Secretary, Mr Peel, saw the point of what I wanted to do: he thought the hand-printed mathematical tables were accurate enough, even though we both knew that they were prone to errors. But he referred the matter to the Royal Society. They discussed it and allowed me an initial grant. I took my plans to Europe. They were far more interested. When I returned, I asked the Duke of Wellington for more money. I built a workshop on land that adjoins this property, in the expectation that my machinist, Mr Clement, would come to reside with his family above the workshop, so that he might devote himself fully to the Difference Engine. That he was loath to do. The fellow submitted a bill for work done last year that was, frankly, extortionate. I refused to pay until he agreed to move; he then fired every man in his employment. My hope is that I shall find another machinist, but until an agreement has been made with Clement, I doubt he'll hand over the pieces of the machine that have already been crafted.'

We listen to this tale of frustration and complexity in silence. Mamma ventures a sympathetic word or two, as Mr Babbage draws his remarks to a close, and he thanks her for her understanding.

'This whole business,' he says, 'has been a fiasco.'

'Well,' says Mamma, as we journey home. 'I think I have understood the *basic principles* of his machine. Such uniformity of function. And, apart from the handle, fully automated. I am impressed. I could see, Ada, that you were too.'

I would like to demur, just for the thrill of irritating her, but I cannot in all good conscience do that. Instead, I say: 'Yes. Yes, I was.'

Mamma chatters on in her precise way, recounting the evening's events as though to describe them to one who had been absent. I let her talk. The thunderous roll of the cab wheels is quite distinct from the smooth operation of Mr Babbage's machine. It wasn't just the beauty of the thing that kept my eyes fastened to it, mapping every rotation, every ripple; its real beauty was its inhuman accuracy. Pictures appear in my head of ships crossing ice-strewn waters without fear, safe in the knowledge that their navigators are in possession of flawless numerical tables with which to steer them . . .

'It is a shame that Mr Babbage cannot build the fully-sized machine,' I say.

I am thinking again of Flyology; of the anguish I suffered when I realised that I would not be able to build my own flying machine. It is a sad thing indeed when a dream is prevented from coming to fruition.

Then I add, 'He seems the sort of man who will not allow such setbacks to deter him. I wonder . . . I do think, Mamma, that he will find a way.'

Although I shall not meet Mr Babbage again for some time, I shall not forget this first glimpse of the demonstration piece. Its motions have imprinted themselves on the fabric of my brain; as we journey home, I close my eyes, and realise that I can still see those wheels turning.

Piccadilly, London
September 1833

I am attending a dance – another one; I have gone to so many that I have lost count of them – and since there does not seem to be anyone interesting to talk to here, I have slipped away from the crowd in search of silence. I try various rooms on the ground floor of the house in Piccadilly – it belongs to a distant friend of my mother's – before settling on a deserted drawing room. The fire is unlit, and the room is cold; wishing I had a shawl, I wander around the room, looking for something to occupy my thoughts. The sound of a waltz echoes faintly from another part of the house.

The walls are hung with woven silks in delicate floral patterns of red and blue. Once, a year ago, I might not even have noticed the wall-hangings. But now, every time I see a richly-embroidered silk or piece of brocaded upholstery, the same thing happens: I don't just see the fabric itself, and the workmanship; I see the machine that was used so successfully in its working, and then, without fail, think of the designer of that machine. I imagine him as a child (for it is always a man), and try to guess at his habits, his childish games and whims.

What was it about Joseph Marie Jacquard – the peculiar balance of brilliance – that made him come up with his loom? I think he must have been a good mathematician. To envisage a system in which punched cards can inform a visual design requires a mind that understands complex calculations. But he wasn't just a mathematician; he also understood fabric, which seems the opposite of mathematical, somehow, all soft waves and gentle folds. I wonder if it was the combination of those things that provided the magical formula for his creation. Could have there been something more, besides?

And then there's Mr Babbage, who longs to have the wherewithal to make his Difference Engine a reality. On the night I saw it, I was unable to sleep for thinking about it, and now, three months later, I am thinking about it still. I would like very much to see it again. I have asked Mamma if she might write to Mr Babbage, but she has not done so. I believe that she did not *quite appreciate* what the machine represented: yes, it can count mechanically, but more than this, it shows that we can use machinery to further scientific pursuits in ways that hithertofore we have perhaps only dreamed about.

In other words: if Mr Babbage can design a machine that can perform accurate calculations by means of the finite order of differences, then what else can be designed? What else can be done?

I imagine Mr Babbage as a young boy, nudging beads on

an abacus into ever-more-intricate configurations, puzzling at their potential, testing their limits. What do they have in common, Mr Babbage and Mr Jacquard? There must be something ... something that is not explained by mere intellect, or deep knowledge ... I puzzle and puzzle over it, before I think that I begin to see. It is the ability to look *beyond* the scope of what is currently possible, as though diving into deep water and opening one's eyes, ready to take in all the wonder of the ocean floor. It is the ability to connect two ideas together – two ideas that might, on the surface, have little to do with each other, but somehow can be partnered in a way that conjures magic. It's similar, really, to what a good writer, a good poet, can do with a metaphor.

It's the letter *I* again, I realise, weaving its charms: *idea*, *inspiration*, *impression*, *imagination* ... the words light up like stars in the shadowy room. *Invention* too. And *insight*.

If all words were stricken from the dictionary but those, I wouldn't mind, for as long as we still have ideas, we will flourish.

It seems to me now that we are living in an Age of Ideas. I've heard it called a Mechanical Age, and that's no doubt true, but before the machines – and there are many – came the ideas that sparked their design. Whenever I think of any new marvel of design – the steam train, the sewing machine, the dynamo – I think also of the mind that made it. Take, for example, the Jacquard loom. When I first saw it at the Adelaide with Mary Montgomery, it imprinted itself on me with the ferocity of white-hot iron. The loom changed things for me, in a way that I wasn't quite aware of at the time, since I was fairly absorbed in my affair of the heart (or whatever it was; certainly, there were body parts involved) when we first went to the Gallery of Practical Science.

And then, as I think about all this, as befits an *I*-loving Ada, I think also of *me*. Is it so wrong, so swollen-headed and presumptuous of me, to hope that one day I might be able to design something to rival those machines?

I dream of it.

But I am under no illusions about the fact that *if* I am ever to achieve anything of the magnitude of a loom, or an engine, then I must work hard. And I must have further instruction. Understandably, perhaps, my mother has not appointed any new tutors for me lately. I correspond with Dr King, and sometimes with Arabella Lawrence and with Dr Frend, and have to content myself with their guidance from afar, but I want to learn different things. I am ready to learn them.

I tell myself that I will know my new teacher when I meet him.

I am just thinking rather fondly of this moment – hoping that it will come sooner rather than later – when I hear someone enter the room. I look around, startled, to see a tall young man with a thatch of golden hair – really absurdly golden, as though he is auditioning for the role of Apollo – smiling at me.

'Oh,' he says softly. 'I didn't realise that there was anyone in here.'

I bow my head politely. 'I'm afraid I'm hiding,' I say.

'You don't care to dance?'

'Not always. It depends on my mood, I suppose,' I say.

'Mine also.' He introduces himself. 'My name is Charles Knight,' he says, with a low bow.

'Ada Byron.'

He smiles; I realise he knows who I am, just as most people seem to know who I am. 'Would you care to return to the party? We needn't dance,' he adds.

I agree to this – after all, why not? I can't hide from potential suitors for ever – and take his arm, realising with a strange jolt that this is the first proper *touch* that I have engaged in (dancing not included) since the time of James Hopkins. I can't resist a comparison between the two. This man is older than Mr Hopkins, and taller, and more confident in himself, for I realise now that James Hopkins was not really a very confident person. He was, for example, far more intimidated by Mamma than I wanted him to be. Does this Mr Knight know everything about me? I wonder. Has he read my father's poetry? Did he ever hear the rumour – the one that Mamma sought so desperately to suppress? Does he . . .

I wish that my Ada-brain would, occasionally, turn itself off.

We arrive in time for a quadrille, and some tacit agreement passes between us that we may as well join in. As we dance, Mr Knight talks about himself. He is passionate, he tells me, about the railways. 'I am keen to invest in them,' he says. 'To me, the advent of railway travel is the most significant development of our modern era.'

This kind of talk pleases me, and as the dance progresses in its decorous way we discuss all manner of new developments. We move, after a time, from steam engines to engines of other kinds. I describe to him Mr Babbage's new machine, and he is all astonishment and interest; at the end of the dance, again by some kind of unspoken mutual agreement, we drift over to the refreshments table and continue to talk.

'To hear you speak so eloquently of the workings of this engine is most delightful,' says Mr Knight.

'I only hope that Mr Babbage will secure the required funding to be able to build it,' I say.

'Has the government given him much?'

'A good deal, I believe – some nine thousand in grants, to say nothing of the costs of the machinist.'

'Nine thousand! Why, you could build a battleship with that,' says Mr Knight.

'He has been plagued with other difficulties besides money.'

Mr Knight smiles ruefully. 'Ah, yes. It's odd, isn't it, how the most generous provision is never enough. Perhaps your mother will take an interest in the project?'

At this moment, I actually see Mamma on the other side of the ballroom. As usual, she is eating something – I never knew anyone with a more insatiable appetite than hers – and dabbing at the corner of her mouth with a napkin. 'Mamma? Oh, she is indeed *very* interested,' I say. 'It was she who took me to meet Mr Babbage, earlier this year.'

'Lady Noel Byron is well-known for her intellect,' replies Mr Knight. He smiles again, broadly, easily. We look at each other. I am quite attracted to him – it's the air of self-assurance, I think, and that Apollonian demeanour. Mr Knight goes on: 'And – who knows? Perhaps Mr Babbage will also find in her a benefactress.'

Mamma hasn't seen me yet, and I can't resist allowing the conversation to go on a little longer. It is a delicious feeling – I think, for some reason, of the Cooking with Gas demonstration I once witnessed at the Adelaide with Mary Montgomery. Those flames that danced so enticingly as they roasted the pigeon. Now I imagine twirling a lazy forefinger ever closer to those flames, daring them to scorch my skin.

'I would be most pleased to see you again, Miss Byron,' says Mr Knight.

I, Ada, have attended enough soirées in my first Season to be well able now to spot the sort of man who would steal from church altars if he thought nobody was watching. Such a man, without doubt, is Mr Knight. There is indeed a twinkle in his eye that is quite impossible to miss: glassy, leering, what Mamma described once as 'a particular gleam'. There have been other clues: his mentioning of my mother's money, several times, in a talk that has only lasted about twenty minutes; the fact that he sought me out in an empty room, pretending that it was a chance meeting.

It is time to extract myself from an encounter that I have been prolonging solely for my own amusement.

'Well,' I say. 'I—'

'*Ada.*'

It's quite incredible how much weight Mamma can get into two syllables, sometimes. I turn around, and there she is.

I am very used to being stared at by my mother at dances, and very able to translate her range of expressions. There's the mildly approving smile when I am 'behaving myself' and speaking to the right kind of person. There's the slanted left brow and pursed lips when there is some aspect of my being that is in want of improvement. And there's the other look – which manages to be both curiously blank and full to bursting-point of emotion at the same time – that is currently crossing her face. That look tells me this: Mamma does not like Mr Knight.

She extracts me, with as much vigour and flapping of hen-like wings as the Furies used to show in their days of constant vigil at Fordhook. Once we are safely out of earshot of my gold-headed interlocutor, she says: 'Ada, I expected better of you.'

'What is wrong with Mr Knight?' I say innocently. 'I realise the man has no title, but—'

'The man is a *renowned fortune hunter*. Not to be trusted.'

'Oh, Mamma, I am sorry,' I say, feigning contrition. 'I hadn't any idea.'

'That,' says Mamma, 'is a great shame. As I said, Ada, I expected better of you.'

Fordhook, Ealing
February 1834

All through the autumn and winter last year, I waited; through Brighton balls and sojourns at spa towns and cathedral concerts; smiling upon unsuitable young men with that particular gleam in their eye, and other young men, more suitable, whom I should instantly forget . . . and other young men still, who perhaps wanted to dance with me only so that they could relate the encounter at a later date – young men who would never in a hundred years truly wish to associate themselves with the *most vulgar woman in all England* . . . yes: through all of this, I *waited* for the teacher to appear. The one that I was sure would come, if only I were patient enough.

At night, I crept out onto the terrace and stared up at the stars – in the heart of London, the smog would mask them almost completely, but out in Ealing they were jewel-distinct, mapped across the heavens, twinkling with secrets – as though they contained in their constellations codes which only the brightest minds could discern. Caroline Herschel was much talked-about at gatherings – a few years ago she became the first woman to be awarded a Gold Medal by the

Royal Astronomical Society – and I was longing to acquaint myself better with astronomy. Ever since my correspondence with William Frend about the stars, I'd been deeply fascinated by the heavens. But I could see that I needed more than a telescope and a casual interest to improve my understanding.

In the end, I wrote to Dr King, whom Mamma had appointed as my moral guardian. Far better Dr King than the Furies, any day, but even so it irked me that Mamma should continue to appeal to her friends to watch over me – as though I might turn into a ravening demon at a moment's notice! I supposed the James Hopkins Affair would be brought up – not in so many words, of course; merely with the sad slanting of a knowing brow, an *I-told-you-so* expression – as evidence, for ever, of my potential to transgress. But there were notable benefits to a correspondence with Dr King – he might have been concerned with my morals, but the substance of our discussions was mathematical. Indeed, that was entirely the point: by focusing my mind on arithmetic, said Dr King, I would keep my more passionate, poetical tendencies at bay.

I wasn't sure that I agreed.

'I need a solid foundation upon which to build,' I wrote to him. 'My aim is to understand astronomy, but there are places where my knowledge of mathematics is weak.'

Dr King wrote back immediately, prescribing a course of Euclid. I was pleased to take up those propositions again, but even so, there was something missing.

I was still waiting.

*

One miserable, wet afternoon – the rain scissoring down so heavily that the view of London is nearly blotted out by it – Mrs Mary Somerville, a friend of Mamma's who has very recently returned to England from Paris, comes to take tea with us and Mary Montgomery.

Mary Somerville is older than Mamma by perhaps a decade or so, but I can see that she was once (and still is) very pretty, with dark curls all over her head, and an unusual, even eccentric, way of dressing. There's a bird-like delicacy to her that reminds me of Mamma, and – like my mother – she is a mathematician. She has recently published a book entitled *On the Connexion of the Physical Sciences*. Mamma has read it, and – after no longer than five minutes in the company of Mary Somerville – I am resolved to read it too. In her gentle Scottish accent, she talks about her work, and her self-deprecating tone cannot disguise the magnificence of her mind.

She says: 'I have not one jot of originality or genius. *Not one*. I am the first to admit it. We women simply don't possess such things.'

'But, Mary,' counters Mamma, 'you were the translator of Laplace's *Mécanique Celeste*! Without your contribution, no one who was unable to read French would have been able to immerse themselves in that immense set of books. It was an exceptional undertaking.'

'Oh, there is nothing so special about the act of translation,' says Mary Somerville.

'I don't agree,' says Mary Montgomery. 'You added to

Laplace's work your preliminary dissertation. Laplace himself said the book was unreadable – and not because it was in French. You clarified his writing; your introduction served to make the mathematics in the book more understandable to the reader. That was without doubt an act of originality.'

Mary Somerville only smiles. Is she falsely modest, I wonder, or genuinely so? She says: 'What do *you* think, Ada? Are women capable of originality?'

Answering truthfully, I say: 'I see absolutely no reason why women should not be capable of such a thing; why should a woman not think with as much originality as a man, if not more? Yes: we might not be able, for example, to lift a heavy weight, or to ride into battle. Those are physical distinctions. But there should be no such distinctions as far as the mind is concerned.'

Silence falls on our little gathering, and I am more aware than ever of the rain, and the three women in their different positions . . . Mary Montgomery's smiling unspoken approval of what I have just said . . . Mamma's perfectly-poised figure, on the edge of her chair, wanting me to impress the visitor, and not to say the wrong thing, even if she doesn't know what the 'wrong thing' might be in this context.

And then there is Mary Somerville, whose cheeks have the bloom of a young girl. She leans forward. A little tea spills unnoticed from her cup. 'Do you like puzzles, Ada?' she says.

'I love puzzles,' I say.

'Euclid?'

'Yes, indeed; I might do three or four Euclidian propositions a day. I love other kinds of puzzle too.'

'Tell me more,' says Mary Somerville.

I pause, wanting to explain myself clearly. 'I love anything that isn't clear-cut,' I say. 'A problem you have to work at, perhaps look at in a different way in order to understand. I love anything that doesn't seem to have an obvious answer. Take rainbows, for example. Why does a rainbow always appear in an arc of a circle? Why a circle, rather than another kind of curve? And why is it curved in the first place?'

'Is that the sort of thing that you think about often?'

'It's the sort of thing that I *always* think about,' I reply.

Mamma says: 'Ada's mind, for all its capabilities, flits from one thing to another rather *too* quickly, like a butterfly.'

'Butterflies,' says Mrs Somerville, 'are utterly enchanting creatures.'

So now there is another Mary in my life, and I will grow just as attached to Mrs Somerville as I have long been to Miss Montgomery. I hadn't realised that my long-anticipated teacher would be a woman, but I am so pleased that she *is* a woman; Miss Stamp was, after all, one of my most fondly-remembered instructors.

Mary Somerville is like no one I have ever met before. I visit her at her home at the Royal Hospital in Chelsea, where the army pensioners live and where her husband is a physician, and I stay for perhaps two nights each time. Mary has a son named Woronzow Greig, a young man of nearly thirty, from her first marriage. Theirs is a damp though prettily-furnished house; we often sit in the parlour, books and papers spread about us, and talk for hours, sometimes only stopping when Dr Somerville comes home, whistling under his breath as he enters the house.

The first few sessions are shy ones, in which we – teacher and student – get to know one another. I tell Mary a little about the regime of my early studies – the governesses who came and went with clockwork regularity; the tickets and punishments; the subjects I studied; the things I enjoyed, and the things I didn't.

'Mamma hopes – has always hoped – to . . . trammel my mind somewhat,' I say carefully.

'What does that mean, Ada?'

'It means that she thinks I lack rigour and organisation,' I say. I am not trying to complain about Mamma (well, perhaps I am complaining very slightly); I do, however, want to give Mary a clear picture of how Mamma feels about my abilities. 'She thinks my interests are too many, and too varied. That I am too passionate. I can't help it, though; truly, I can't.'

Mary says nothing, encouraging me to continue.

I go on, emboldened and warming to my theory: 'It is because we are not so very alike, Mamma and I. I was learning some Latin verbs a few months ago, and I realised the fundamental difference between me and Mamma. The right verb for Mamma is *cogitare* – "to think". If I had to choose only one, I mean.'

'And for you?' says Mrs Somerville.

'*Sentire*,' I reply without hesitation. ' "To feel".'

'I see,' says Mary Somerville, and I think that perhaps she does.

She tells me about her life, different to mine in many ways – her early love of nature and the outdoors, and watching things grow; her study of Latin and Greek and mathematics; the uncle that took an interest in her education. I have met the Queen, but I do not think that I have ever known a more impressive person than this woman. Astronomy, chemistry, geography, trigonometry . . . is there nothing to which she cannot turn her hand? She has published books; her translation of Laplace – known in English as *The Mechanism of the Heavens* – made her rightly famous. I have begun reading *On the Connexion of the Physical Sciences* and find myself bewitched by both its breadth and depth: there is more information contained within its covers than I could absorb in a lifetime. Lunar theory; light and sound; tides, crystals, volcanoes and electricity . . .

I am reminded of the way that Miss Stamp, with her enthusiasm and detailed knowledge, would talk to me about the world, for the book speaks to me in the warm, engaging tones of a born educator. More than anything else, I like the way in which Mrs Somerville seeks to trace the links between physical and scientific phenomena. It is as though I have discovered another kind of governess – one whose knowledge is unsurpassed. But in spite of all this, Mary

Somerville is – as she showed when she first came to tea with us – as modest as she is accomplished.

'You must understand, Ada,' she says, 'that whatever my achievements are – if we can call them that – they rely wholly on the achievements of others.'

She talks to me about William and Caroline Herschel, who discovered so much about the stars; about Michael Faraday, about Joseph Banks, botanist and explorer, and Humphry Davy, inventor of the safety lamp. I ask if she believes that we are living in a Mechanical Age.

'I've heard it called that, certainly,' says Mrs Somerville. 'And certainly, we are seeing changes the likes of which we have never seen before in this country. Why, every factory in Britain – more or less – now possesses a rotary steam engine. Industries are undergoing vast transformations; new discoveries are made every day. But it's more than mechanical, in my view. It's an age of—'

'Ideas,' I say.

She looks at me delightedly. 'Yes, Ada. Yes. Ideas.'

'Mrs Somerville,' I say. 'Do you know Mr Babbage?'

'Why, Ada, certainly I do.'

Dorset Street, London
March 1834

By the time of my second visit, about nine months after the first, to Mr Babbage's Dorset Street home, I have learned a good deal more about him.

Charles Babbage's family were originally from the Devon town of Totnes. His father was a banker and goldsmith who moved his business to London in the year that Babbage was born, where his businesses continued to thrive. On his father's death in 1827, Charles Babbage inherited the vast sum of a hundred thousand pounds. He studied at the same Cambridge college – Trinity – as my father; and although he never had to struggle for money, he did become possessed of a profound desire to contribute to some of the changes that were taking place in society.

He has four surviving children, one of whom is named Herschel (after John Herschel, who was a great friend of his at university). He is well-known for his soirées, at which all sorts of interesting people might be encountered; in spite of my occasional hints, Mamma and I have not attended any of them – not, I think, because of any reluctance or disinterest on her part, but simply due to the intricacies of our calendar of social engagements. Now, thanks to Mary Somerville, who knows perfectly well how dearly I wish to see the demonstration piece again, we are making our way to Dorset Street in a carriage after dinner.

'Why are you smiling in that secretive manner, Ada?' asks Mary Somerville.

'Oh,' I say. 'I was just thinking how infinitely I prefer the thought of one of Mr Babbage's soirées to another dull ball.'

My companion laughs gently. Mrs Somerville is, above all else, a very *reasonable* person. From her I am learning more than I ever have – from anyone – and I truly believe that I can call myself, with great pride, her protégée. I am growing very fond of her daughters, Martha and Mary – as well as Woronzow, her son – and sometimes I find myself actually running along the pathway to her house in Chelsea, while the mist rises thickly from the river that lies beyond it, so desperate am I to see them all, and to talk about a sum or equation or mathematical conundrum.

One of the reasons why I like her so much is because she is Not Mamma. She is far warmer and more personable than my mother; in fact, sometimes I find myself wanting to reach for her hand, or for her to embrace me with a mother's tenderness. These moments both surprise me and don't surprise me at all. But just as much as she is Not Mamma, nor is she anything like me. For example, she would never have done what I did with James Hopkins – she would never have acted so rashly, and with such disregard to propriety and reputation, and the expectations of others. She might have recognised her feelings, but she would have found a way to contain them. I find it so hard to contain anything.

'Balance, Ada, is the key to everything,' says Mary Somerville. '*Everything in moderation* – that, I believe, was the phrase in Ancient Greece. A dance one day, a discussion about mathematics or engineering the next, but nothing taken to excess, is a wise path.'

'Perhaps,' I say. Oh, it sounds reasonable enough, but I cannot bring myself to feel enthusiastic about an ancient axiom that proposes moderation.

'You are, after all, not necessarily likely to meet a suitable husband at Dorset Street,' says Mrs Somerville. She knows very well that this is Mamma's chief desire. I know this too, and I suppose it is unlikely to change.

But for the moment, all I want – more than anything else – is to see the model of the Difference Engine again, and I am grateful to Mrs Somerville for facilitating the encounter.

Charles Babbage is just as I remember him. 'My dear Miss Byron,' he says, looming over me and Mrs Somerville like a genial bear. 'You must meet another young lady – one who might possibly be as enchanting as you yourself.'

Somewhat taken aback by this – I am not here to enchant anyone, and am sorry that Mr Babbage thinks that I might be – I am at first relieved when he spins around to reveal, with all the dramatic flourishes for which he is famous, an automated dancer on a podium, rotating merrily for the benefit of the room. She stands about a foot high, and on one hand perches a little bird that opens and closes its beak as she rotates.

'This, Miss Byron, is my Silver Lady. Is she not a thing of beauty?'

I smile rather thinly, realising that I must look exactly like my mother, for whom thin smiles are a speciality. 'Mr Babbage, she is a wonder indeed, but there is another wonder that I would much prefer to see.'

'Oh? And what wonder is that?'

'Why, your Difference Engine – the model piece, I mean.'

Now Mr Babbage looks taken aback, but only a little. Then he looks positively delighted. It is amusing to watch the differing emotions cross his face; he reassesses me, perhaps moving me from one category in his mind to another. It has been said that in order to merit an invitation to one of these soirées one must possess beauty, intellect or good breeding. Mr Babbage might have thought that my birth is the sole justification for my presence (for certainly I am not beautiful). But now, perhaps, he is reconsidering. Minutes later, we are again in the presence of the model Difference Engine, which I notice has been moved to another part of the room, rather less on display than it was last June. Has he lost interest in his invention? I wonder. Or has he lost heart, let down by the government and unable to find the right kind of assistance?

I realise that I am actually trembling as I stretch out a hand towards it. Oh, I have *dreamed* of it: strange, to think that a construction of interlaced cogwheels could become the stuff of dreams.

'When you were a child, Mr Babbage, did you dream of designing such a machine?' I ask him, suddenly rather timid.

'I wanted to know what was inside of everything,' Mr Babbage replies, quite seriously. 'I would quite happily break anything apart in order to satisfy my curiosity as to its workings.'

'Were you the same, Ada?' says Mary Somerville, who has come to stand next to me.

'I never . . . I don't think I ever broke anything apart,' I tell them, feeling sad at the realisation, wishing that I could have broken things. I do not think that I ever wanted to – but if I had, I don't think it would have been well-received by Mamma.

'Neither did I,' says Mrs Somerville, and I feel better again. 'Observation: that was what I enjoyed, more than anything. Just standing in the garden, watching the birds, the trees. Seeing nature weave her spells.'

And suddenly I remember myself – five, six – squatting, dirt-kneed, in the vegetable garden at Kirkby Mallory, captivated by the gossamer strands of a spider's web.

'Have you made any progress since last we met?' Mrs Somerville says to Mr Babbage.

'With funding? Alas, no,' he replies, in his leonine growl of a voice. 'And besides, money is not my only problem.'

'What a pity,' says Mary Somerville. 'It would be far more

economical for the government to have tabulated calculations at their disposal.'

'As it happens, though, I have just recently begun to conceive of another machine,' says Mr Babbage, and I hear, suddenly, a streak of excitement in his voice that was absent a moment ago.

'Oh yes?' says Mary Somerville.

'It will operate on similar principles . . . I can't go into any details about it as yet, but . . .'

Charles Babbage sinks into himself, ruminating; I can almost hear the internal cogwheels whirring behind his eyes. Then he opens his eyes wide, frowns, and says: 'If I'm right – the next machine I have in mind will be able to do *more* than the Difference Engine. Yes, yes; a lot more.'

Only later, on the edge of sleep, do I realise the difference between the mind-sets of Mr Babbage and Mrs Somerville. She might advise caution and restraint; she might speak of moderation and tempered excesses . . . all well and good, I suppose, if not especially exciting. Then there's Charles Babbage's approach, and how much do I prefer it, for there was all the excitement of a child at Christmas in his expression as he uttered that single syllable, richer than plum-pudding: *more.*

Tunbridge Wells
April 1834

Tunbridge Wells, a town to the south-east of London, is Mamma's latest discovery; it has replaced Leamington Spa as her preferred destination for relaxation and the treatment of minor ailments. We are strolling down the colonnaded walkway known as the Pantiles, enjoying the spring sunlight. At the moment, we are getting along rather better, Mamma and I; I think it is because I am so much enjoying my work with Mary Somerville, and I am grateful to Mamma for her support in this regard.

'Did you know, Mamma, that they have come up with a new word: *scientist*?' I say.

'Who, Ada? Be specific.'

'William Whewell – he studied with Mr Babbage, you know – in an article about Mrs Somerville.'

I am delighted that I know something that my mother does not.

'Hmm,' she says. 'I don't know if I like it. *Scientist*: it has a harsh, almost reductive quality to it. I prefer the term "natural philosopher".'

'But someone who does art is an artist; why should someone who does science not be a scientist?' I argue. 'It makes sense.'

'Perhaps you are right,' says Mamma.

We have reached the porticoed building, known as the Bath House, that stands at the end of the Pantiles. Here we sit in the courtyard, under the canopy, and before long we are brought some spring water to drink in tall glasses. One sip is enough for me – I want to spit it out, but manage not to – but Mamma drinks it down almost greedily, with the satisfaction of one tapping the wellspring of eternal knowledge. All around us are elegantly-clad women engaged in similar activity.

Mamma sets her glass down. 'The Bath House is built on the Chalybeate spring,' she says. 'The water is rich in iron. Very good for you. You ought to drink it, Ada. Even a few sips a day will make a difference, I assure you.'

'I dislike it,' I say.

'It doesn't matter whether you like or dislike it; what is good for you isn't always what you *want.*'

Changing the subject, I say: 'Mr Babbage is thinking of designing a new machine.'

'Oh, yes?'

'The Difference Engine can only perform operations using the method of finite differences – in other words, they are all forms of addition of one kind or another. But Mr Babbage now envisages a machine that can do far more *complex* calculations . . .'

'Hmm,' says Mamma. She looks at me in a contemplative way that I struggle to understand. '*Why* is he changing his aim in this manner – wanting to build something new before even his first idea has come to fruition?'

'Because he has had a better idea,' I say, remembering my Flyology experiments, and how a steam-powered airborne passenger horse easily supplanted a pair of wings as my primary objective. 'Ideas can change, can't they, Mamma?'

'The best minds,' says Mamma firmly, 'see things through to their conclusions. I worry, frankly, that Mr Babbage's ideas and approach are fundamentally unsound.'

'They cannot be judged unsound before they have been tested—'

'They remain untested because he has shown himself unable to find the resources to construct his designs!'

We stare at each other – her eyes darker than mine, and bluer than my blue-grey, but each of us just as resolute. All around is a gentle sheep-like chorus of *oh-my-dears* and *didn't-you-knows*; with our matching frowns and lowered brows, we make for a startling contrast to the other Bath House occupants.

'You took me to visit Mr Babbage in the first place,' I say, more gently. '*You thought* it was interesting—'

'I like to see things for myself, and to judge for myself. He is not uninteresting, I admit. But I noticed, just now, a kind of nervous excitement, as you were speaking. It is most worrisome.'

'I do not consider myself to be unduly preoccupied by

Mr Babbage's designs for his machines,' I say, conscious as I am speaking that a tone has crept into my voice that I can't quite control; I sound just as excitable as Mamma is implying. 'It is not my fault that Mary Somerville is quite often a guest at his house, and that she quite often takes me with her—'

I stop myself.

'You think me unreasonable, I know,' says Mamma, looking about for an attendant to bring her another glass of water. 'It seems to me quite clear, however, that your health is directly related to the matters with which you tax your mind. That, indeed, is why I have always encouraged you to learn mathematics. Remember what happened when you wanted to design your flying machine: you were ill – incapacitated – for months, Ada!'

I sit, shoulders slumped, in mulish silence, not certain that I deserve this telling-off, and sure that she is now going to mention Dr Combe.

'Dr Combe was really most interesting in his description of your head,' she goes on. A glass is set down at her elbow and she reaches for it.

'I don't know why you felt it necessary for him to read my skull a second time,' I say. 'People do not change in a year – and certainly the shape of their heads does not change!'

She must, I realise, have been hoping for the good Dr Combe to revise his opinion of me somewhat.

'Yes,' she goes on. 'You are too easily stimulated by the things that take your interest. He advises that it is a good idea for you to spend time away from London, and I concur.

We shall take a tour, perhaps, of some northern towns, this summer. I shall arrange it.'

'And what shall we do in these northern towns?' I enquire.

'For one thing, there are factories worth visiting. Perhaps, if you are to witness machines within their actual, working environments, it will enable you to evaluate Mr Babbage's designs in a less . . . fanciful manner.'

The matter settled, she drains her glass of iron-rich water from the Chalybeate spring with relish.

Yorkshire,
July 1834

It is a blue-skied summer morning, and Mamma and are several weeks into our tour of the Industrial North. It is the second time we have taken a tour together. The last time we travelled for an extensive period of time, I was ten years old. Now, I am eighteen.

I confess that I was not especially interested in the activities that my mother proposed (perhaps because she was the proponent), but I quickly became interested in spite of myself. What machinery we have seen! I had observed the Jacquard loom before, at the Adelaide Gallery – but what a difference it made, to see it actually put to use for the purpose intended. In Coventry, we visited a silk-ribbon factory, where the imported silks were woven into ribbons that would be used to trim dresses and bonnets. Exactly the kind of sartorial detail that has never interested me, but the manufacturing of the ribbon was far more intriguing. The factory was a draughty, dusty building, whose windows, though tall, seemed to let in little light; it was filled with the sound of looms, all a little out of time with each other, like instruments in an orchestra without a conductor.

In Matlock, at another factory, Mamma drew a sketch of one of the punched cards – that innovation that permitted any picture in the world to be woven in silk – and I watched her as she did so, the way she drew her brows together in concentration as her hand gripped her pencil, the strength of her commitment to seeing and understanding.

'It's fascinating, Ada, is it not?' she said, adding the last careful line to her drawing, which was an accurate one.

If anything, however, Mamma had a greater interest in the workers themselves. She talked to them, trying to establish as much as possible about their lives. How had these looms changed their existences? What were the benefits? What were the disadvantages? How did they live? I was glad to have accompanied her to the factories, for this reason. Where I would look at a machine and consider its inventor, Mamma reflected instead on the human cost.

Then, a couple of days later, we went to stay with the Nightingales, acquaintances of Mamma's, at their house near Matlock. It was a beautiful house, with a meadow beneath it that reached all the way to the Derwent river. The Nightingales were quiet, bookish people, with two daughters, Parthenope and Florence, a few years younger than I.

At dinner on the first night, the discussion around the table centred upon the tension between the old system and the new one. My mother was saying: 'In my youth, you know, it was quite different. Living in a small village, one was able to know the conditions – the wants and needs – of the villagers quite fully and easily, simply by going out of one's own gates. One knew everyone. If a child was ill, or if someone was in need of something, one got to hear of it immediately.'

'Quite so,' said William Nightingale.

'Now, in order to understand the lives of the workers, one must go to the factories to see it all first-hand,' said Mamma. 'We have been to Matlock, and Ashby; we have seen mills and kilns and furnaces. Above all else, I have been struck by the difficulties faced by the weavers whose jobs were imperilled by the advent of the new looms. I spoke to one fellow whose hand had been badly injured by a machine, and another who was very anxious indeed about whether he was to be kept on at the factory.'

Florence – I liked the look of her, so pretty and so serious – said, 'Once, a master weaver would have worked at home with a single-handed loom. The new system brings many looms and weavers together under one factory roof. It is a significant change. You are right, Lady Noel Byron, to think of their well-being.'

'But don't forget,' said Mr Nightingale, 'that the economic advantages such machinery will bring with them are considerable – mark my words, we'll see more opportunities: *more* jobs, not fewer.'

The debate continued for a few minutes, growing more heated all the while. My mother leaned forward, as she always does when engaged deeply in conversation. 'What seems so necessary,' she said, 'is to *understand* the workers' conditions. By understanding, we know how best to help them.'

She began then to talk, as I knew she would, about education – Pestalozzi and Dr Fellenberg and her cherished agricultural schools. The Nightingale family listened with interest, and I detached myself very gently from the discussion, letting it disintegrate into unformed syllables, a kind of soft music. Here was Mamma at her best – seeing things that I did not see, asking questions that I did not ask . . . caring for the welfare of people in ways that I, quite honestly, didn't think to. Yes: this really was the better side of my mother.

We are now in Yorkshire, and nearly at the end of our tour. After this, we shall journey to Buxton, to spend the rest of the summer indulging in Mamma's favourite activity: resting, and taking the waters. But for all that we have seen, and discovered; for all the places we have visited and people to whom we have spoken, it seems that my mother had quite a different reason for undertaking the tour.

I found out what it was entirely by accident; she had left a half-written letter to Arabella Lawrence on the writing-desk at the Nightingales' house, and I couldn't help but notice that my name was mentioned in the first paragraph. My interest piqued, and my mother nowhere to be seen, I couldn't help but pick the letter up and read it.

'It has been of great interest to us both to witness the developments in the factories. I have always considered it of huge importance that Ada should observe such developments within their proper _context_ . . . in so doing, I feel I am able to protect her from surges of excitement that might prove to unbalance her temperament. Indeed, I might add that a close study of Ada's state of mind was, in fact, my primary motivation for planning this journey. For the most part, I find myself _reassured_ . . .'

I laid the letter down, feeling rather odd, not least because Mamma tends to express herself more fully in writing than she does in conversation. I hadn't any notion that while we were making our careful sketches and observations of the factories that my mother was also making her own careful observations of _me_.

Now, days later, I am still thinking about this. While I am glad that Mamma has found no particular cause for alarm – for if she had, she would no doubt be taking measures to address my perceived ailments, difficulties or shortcomings – I also feel that same strange, suffocating sense that I used to feel when the Furies lived at Fordhook. I am still being watched.

'Ada,' says Mamma. 'If you care to look out of the window, we are just now going through the grounds of Halnaby Hall.'

I stare out of the carriage window at the deer-park – lush, green, a vastness of acres – and am reminded of Kirkby Mallory. In the distance lies a Tudor mansion, with a wing on either side. This, then, is another of the Milbanke estates – not Seaham, near Durham, where Mamma spent

239

most of her childhood, but Halnaby. I have heard her speak of it.

'I remember this journey,' says Mamma. 'I'd ride my pony along it, aged eight or so. Extraordinary, really . . . to think of the passage of time . . .'

Her voice fades; I can imagine her head filling up with memories, like a pot boiling over. I think of Young Annabella – a serious, diligent little girl (and a veritable genius, if Grandama's accounts are to be believed), trotting along on her pony. That little girl could never have known that she would be married, one day, to England's most famous poet.

'Who lives there now?' I say.

'A cousin of mine.'

'When was the last time you visited?'

'Oh, before you were born.'

'With my father?'

I am, by now, so used to an almost-scientific examination of my mother's myriad expressions that I am well able to decode the face she makes. The eyes: half-closed. The cheeks: pale, with a slight flush and the indentation that suggests she is biting the inside of them. The lips: set flat. Here, again, is her secretive side – her *worse side*, for it is this woman who I am convinced drove my father away, and alienated my Aunt Augusta in the process.

'*Mamma*,' I say again, rather sternly.

She exhales through her nose, looks away, and says: 'We came here for our honeymoon. We married at Seaham, and then travelled here by coach.'

'Who was present at your wedding?'

'Oh, very few people. My parents, and B – and Byron had with him his friend John Hobhouse.'

I don't think she means to let the endearment slip, but I seize upon it. 'Did you call him "B"?'

'I . . . yes, I did.'

'What did he call you?' I ask this decisively; I feel as though I have a right to know these things. She has made her study of me, all this time; now I in turn shall make my own study. Perhaps, in some way, she understands the logic of this, for she sighs a little and then says: 'He called me Bell.'

B, and *Bell* . . . The diminutives bring them to life, somehow, in the stultifying heat of the carriage. I wait for more; there must *be* more, and sure enough, faltering a little, unsure of the order of her words, my mother says:

'We were married by Thomas Noel – the illegitimate son of Lord Wentworth, my uncle. It was the second of January; I remember it began snowing early that morning, so that the grounds were quite covered in snow by midday. I couldn't come down to breakfast that day, such were my nerves. We married at eleven o'clock in the Seaham drawing room. I wore a white muslin jacket and muslin gown, with a lace trim. No veil. My mother wept – she was always easily overcome with feeling. As we were departing John Hobhouse gave me, as a gift, Byron's complete works, bound in yellow morocco. I could hear the Seaham church bells ringing as he did so. Hobhouse wished me every happiness. I was never

241

sure how much he liked me. I told him that if I were unhappy, it would be my own fault.'

This is extraordinary: both the detail of what she has revealed, and also this last reported statement. I am reminded of our breakfast, not so long ago, in which, for some reason, Mamma started to tell me things that she had never told me before. I wonder, now, if it's the geographical location itself that presses upon her, speaks to her across the gulf of years, and asks her to tell me what it is that she is remembering. Or else, perhaps, she has decided that I am worthy of the information, and deserve to be told it.

'Mamma,' I say, with a feeling that is almost like desperation. 'Why . . . why did my father leave? Is it because you were unhappy? Or . . . was *he* unhappy?'

'I think,' she says, after a long and agonising silence, 'that we were each, in our own way, extremely unhappy. Not at first, not really, but: yes, Ada. We were.'

Silence falls again in the carriage, and for all that the day is swelteringly hot, I suddenly feel very cold.

Buxton, Derbyshire
August 1834

Our tour of the Industrial North ends in the sleepy little spa town of Buxton. Lady Gosford is here – she is a friend of Mamma's – with her two little girls, Olivia and Annabella. My cat, Mistress Puff, now a venerable old lady, is on almost permanent loan to them now. Grey-tinged, as though dipped in ash, she is irascible on occasion, her hind legs rheumatism-stiff. But she still enjoys chasing the sparrows that hop across the terrace in the morning sunshine, and mewing for milk, and I shall always remember the time when – as a lonely, book-gobbling child – I looked upon Puff as my only friend.

There is, as is often the case with spa towns, not much to do in Buxton. More out of boredom than anything else, I offer one day to tutor the little girls in mathematics. I am rather delighted both by the selflessness of this gesture, and the idea of Ada the Tutor. (Also: I have realised, rather to my embarrassment, that I do not really think about others very often.)

Lady Gosford is enchanted. 'But that is a charming idea,' she says. 'Livvy, Bella, you are lucky little girls, to have Ada to teach you.'

Mamma also smiles on my proposal, but I can't help but detect a very slight disbelief in her expression. I remember her telling me at the allotments that I did not have the temperament of a teacher; I never forget such criticisms. Then again, she herself leaves much to be desired as an instructress; every time she took charge of my education, we both suffered for it.

I do not prepare much for the first arithmetic lesson, since I don't see why I should need to. I possess all the knowledge, and shall merely be imparting it.

'We will begin with the simple things,' I tell the girls, as we make ourselves comfortable in an unoccupied corner of the hotel dining room. 'Addition, subtraction, multiplication, division; and later, some simple trigonometry.'

Their little blonde heads gleam with purpose; they smile and nod and look at me with expectation. I decide that being a teacher is a straightforward business. Puff, who is curled up on the banquette beside me, must find it a curious reversal, since she herself has been present at many lessons – hundreds – in which I was the pupil, not the teacher.

Each girl has her commonplace book, and for each I write ten sums of differing complexity. It takes them far longer than I think that it should to do the work, and at first I make a variety of impatient remarks, unable to stop myself.

'Goodness, Livvy!' I exclaim, when that dear girl asserts that seven sixes are forty-eight. 'How *can* you think such a thing?'

But I can see at once from the slump of Olivia's shoulders,

her instant dejection, how disheartening my words have been.

'The sums are hard,' says Bella, who has as much trouble holding her pencil as I used to have when holding a pen. When I propose that they construct a triangle in their books, neither girl is able to do it. It is as though they have never attempted such a thing before. Soon enough, they are both close to tears, and I am full of remorse.

'It seems that I have begun with the wrong things,' I tell them, pointing out that the fault lies with me entirely. 'Let us start again.'

The girls are young – seven and five – and I decide that I will *not* expect as much of them as Mamma expected of me, for such expectations are not fair ones. They will not be forced to lie still on a board if they do not complete their work to the highest standard; I will not bribe them with tickets for work well done, either – they should be proud of what they can achieve regardless. I remember Miss Stamp, who always allowed me the time I needed to correct myself, and try to be more like her. I change my tone of voice, making it softer and more encouraging. I simplify the sums, asking them now to count up in twos, say, or in tens. I slow down too, allowing them far more time for the sums. I might pat a sleeve in gentle support, or scribble a useful reminder on a page.

After a quarter of an hour or so, I am transformed – and so are they.

'That's very good,' I say. 'Perhaps check your work, Bella, here – and here . . .'

The time passes so quickly that I am surprised when Lady Gosford comes to claim her children.

Later on, a further realisation dawns: in order to be a teacher, I must also be a student. I don't have many of my arithmetic books with me, but I do have Pasley's *Practical Geometry Method*, and Euclid, of course, and I consult them as I prepare my notes for the next day's lesson with the girls. I have always known, if not admitted, that there are holes in my knowledge – perforations where I have flitted too fast (as Mamma would say) from one idea to another – and a more thorough approach on my part, ensuring that those holes are filled, can only be a good thing. In teaching them, I will teach myself too. All the better for my studies with Mary Somerville – for I sometimes think she is too polite to point out that I have weaknesses, as well as strengths.

In addition to this, I realise, I must be patient – not speak too quickly, nor remonstrate with them if they do not understand. I must be the kind of teacher that I myself would have appreciated – as witty and wise as Mary Montgomery; as passionate and dedicated as Miss Stamp. Yes: I, Ada, can be all those things: patient and witty and passionate and kind.

As I go to sleep, I wonder whether perhaps this is something I can do with my future.

Buxton, Derbyshire
August 1834

A few days later, I discover a harp in a dusty corner of the hotel's music room. It doesn't seem to belong to anyone, so I sit down with it for a half-hour or so, exploring the sounds that it makes, though I don't know how to use the pedals. It's an old harp, not very well cared for. But there's something about it that attracts me – a romance. I like the way the grain of the curved wood feels in my hands. The harp has *magical potential*; I'm sure of it. Beauty could be coaxed from it, like pearls from oysters, if only one knew how to play . . .

A poem comes into my head; one of my father's. It begins like this:

> *The Harp the Monarch Minstrel swept*
> *The King of men, the loved of Heaven!*
> *Which Music hallow'd while she wept*
> *O'er tones her heart of hearts had given—*
> *Redoubled be her tears, its chords are riven!*

I do not know all my father's verses perfectly, but near-enough, and I recite this one now, for the benefit of no one. I have never forgotten that he wanted me to be musical.

The web-like glitter of an *idea* holds me suddenly captive: *I, Ada, will become a harpist.*

Another passion is ignited, just so: I ask Mamma to find me a harp teacher and she obliges at once (pleased, no doubt, that I have transferred my thoughts from Babbage and his designs). Before long, I am working with a Miss Smith for an hour each morning, and then practising alone for a further hour each afternoon. I train myself to sit correctly on the low chair, positioning myself with all the elegance of a dancer; I stretch out each hand to the strings, plucking at them with a precision that reminds me so much of the way I worked so hard, once upon a time, at my shorthand. I make progress; Miss Smith is pleased, and so is Mamma. I learn scales, and then songs; after a week, I find that if I concentrate very carefully, I can sing and play at the same time: an achievement I never thought that I would master.

The semi-somnolent Buxton days acquire shape and purpose; and I realise that I am quite content. Arithmetic lessons with Bella and Livvy form a pleasant portion of each morning, before my own lesson on the harp with Miss Smith. It's an arrangement that suits everyone, and although it is hard to be *consistently* patient – with the girls, and with myself – I find that with practice I am able to be far more patient than I have ever been before.

I listen to Livvy and Bella's pretty, lisping voices as they recite their multiplication tables; I work out which sums and operations each girl finds particularly hard, and make a point of helping with those problems especially. I teach them to use a ruler properly.

'General William Pasley first wrote this book to help engineers,' I explain to them as I open that good soldier's treatise, *Practical Geometry Method*. 'Just think, Livvy and Bella – if you study hard, you could use your knowledge to build bridges, or railways . . . or even in warfare!'

Bella wrinkles her freckled nose. 'Ada, how *could* you suggest that?'

'Why would we want to do any of those things?' chimes in Livvy.

'Well,' I counter, 'why wouldn't you?'

More nose-wrinkling and feminine disgust. I can see that they are, in spite of their protestations, rather amused that I have suggested these outrageous possibilities. 'Because we're *girls*,' they chorus.

I am only teasing them, but the thought lingers, long after the lesson is over. Why should we women limit ourselves, simply because of our sex? Why should we say: this is not for us, nor this, nor this . . . when there are so many things that could be done? If Jacquard had been brought up to believe that he was not capable of designing a loom that would revolutionise the factory system; if Stephenson had never dared to dream of steam engines; if Babbage hadn't broken things apart under the benevolent eye of his mother to see how they worked . . . *then none of those inventions would exist today*. (Mamma may have warned me against spending too much time considering Mr Babbage's work, but I have just read an article about the Difference Engine in the *Edinburgh Review* by a Mr Lardner, who feels very much as I do: that the Difference Engine has much to offer everyone.)

The thought sparks oddities in my Ada-brain: all the magical potential that would have gone to waste, and all the magical potential that must, surely, be lost every day because little girls like Bella and Livvy Gosford do not believe that a bridge would be theirs to build.

One night I have a curious dream: I am playing the harp on a lonely beach covered in round white stones, a little like soup plates. The sky is purple and swollen, as though rain is about to fall. The weather doesn't deter me, though, and I play on, even as the rain comes down, soaking through my clothes. Never have I summoned such exquisite music from the strings; it is almost worthy of the angels themselves. The rain gets heavier and heavier, blanketing the beach, and then, suddenly, it stops, and the sun tiptoes out.

I become aware of an audience – someone is watching me, from just over a sand dune (although, this being a dream, it is not covered in sand but rather those round, white stones). My fingers falter; I lift my hands from the instrument and look up as the visitor draws near. He is only a shadow at first; then, as he comes closer, and a rainbow suddenly illuminates that strange, stone-strewn beach, I see who he is. He is dressed the same as in Thomas Phillips' portrait – the one that is always hidden behind the green curtain. He looks a little older, but not much.

'Father,' I say.

'Little Ada,' he says. He reaches out a hand and touches my chin – a gesture that copies precisely that of Aunt Augusta, a year or so ago, when I saw her in the street. 'Can it really be you?'

'I *am* musical, you know,' I tell him. (Of all the things to say to my father, I don't know why this is the first thing I choose, but, as I have explained, it is a dream.)

'So you are.'

'You wanted me to be musical.'

'I wanted you to be all kinds of things. And you *are* all kinds of things.'

'Why did you not want me to turn out poetical?' I say.

It is one of those dreams in which I really do know that I am dreaming. Even so, I am deeply immersed in it, wanting it never to end. But at the same time, I am very near to waking, and I know this too.

'There is more than one kind of poetical, Ada.'

'What . . . what does that mean?'

'There is more than one kind of bridge too. Remember that.'

'But I—'

'I must away, Ada. They're waiting for me on the other side of the lake.'

'Father, please . . .'

But he is fading as he walks away, lighter and more

translucent with every step, and before long he is gone, before I can say anything else. I am alone again on the flat white beach. I look for the harp; it has fallen on its side, and I kneel down next to it.

The harp is no longer a harp, I see, but a Jacquard loom.

Buxton, Derbyshire
August 1834

I rise earlier than I usually do the following morning, sharply awake for no particular reason. The hotel is quiet. I can hear a horse neighing; a man unloading coal from a wagon in the street below. Footsteps somewhere overhead suggest that the chambermaids have risen.

It's too early to go downstairs. The harp is next to my bed, occupying an entire corner of the room (I have taken possession of it while we are here, and no one seems to mind) and for a few minutes I practise the sonata that I have been learning, enjoying the way the music seems to kindle my brain into being; each note awakens another filament of thought, and then another . . . until I am fully focused, my body correctly positioned, delighted by the music that I am learning to make. But something is weighing on me – a kind of shadow at the edge of my thoughts – and suddenly – it's a suddenness that shocks me – I remember my dream. I do not often dream of my father, and the recollection is enough to quicken my heartbeat and slow my fingers to a standstill.

Abandoning the sonata, I reach for my commonplace book,

sit on the edge of the bed and scribble down all that I remember of our conversation. Oh, I know that it was not 'real'; I know that I was not speaking to some kind of cloud-swaddled angel ... but there was something in that conversation that I cannot bear to dismiss – something that sent through me a channel of pure emotion, not unlike what I experienced when I stood in the Bifrons gallery and felt his presence beside me.

I wanted you to be all kinds of things. And you are *all kinds of things* . . .

There is more than one kind of poetical . . .

There is more than one kind of bridge too.

I sit there, chewing on the end of my pencil until I feel soft-splintered wood on my tongue. What does this all mean? I think about the word 'poetical' and all that it might signify, writing a short list:

1. *Adjective pertaining to a poet, or to the poetry the poet writes*

2. *Adjective pertaining to the sort of life a poet might lead*

Is that what my father meant? Or is there something else, some other, more codified, meaning contained in his words? I have not done a lot of Greek, but I am fairly convinced that the word poet derives from the Greek verb that means 'to make'. Could my father somehow have been trying to tell me that there is more than one way that I could *make* things?

What kind of bridge is there, other than a real bridge?

(A *rainbow* flickers across my consciousness, burning with the intensity of fireworks . . .)

Is there more than one way that I could make something of myself?

But no. I am trying to find things that are not really there, like an astronomer whose view through the telescope is sadly occluded by poor workmanship, or an unforgiving smog-filled sky.

There are to be no arithmetic lessons today; the Gosfords have gone out for the day. Mamma is in her room; I linger downstairs, wanting to read for a while before lunch. As I scan the library shelves for something new to read, I notice a rather beautiful elderly lady with tightly-curled white hair. She is looking at me, as people often do; but I do not feel that skin-tingling sense of being whispered about and pointed at that I so often feel. I smile at her encouragingly, and she bows her head, draws nearer, and says in a surprisingly girlish voice how much she admired my father's poetry.

'Oh!' I say. 'Thank you. That is most gratifying to hear.'

The old lady looks at me quizzically for a moment and says: 'I am an acquaintance of dear Mrs Leigh. She speaks of you with such fondness, Ada.'

That is all she has time to say; she is swept away then by a tall man who must be her son, or son-in-law, perhaps. I remain on the couch, my book unopened, wondering who on earth Mrs Leigh might be. Then I remember: that is the name of Aunt Augusta.

'A lady came to talk to me just now,' I say to Mamma over lunch. 'She wanted to tell me how much she admired my father's poetry.'

Mamma smiles at this. 'How nice,' she says. There is a smudge of artichoke soup on her upper lip.

'She also mentioned that she knew my Aunt Augusta,' I add.

If I was hoping for a favourable reaction, I do not get one. Mamma stops smiling at the mention of the name. More: she looks anxious, as though she fears what I am about to say next.

Persisting nonetheless, I say: 'Why can I not make the acquaintance of Mrs Leigh?'

'Because . . . she is not a suitable person for you to know.'

'Is she a gambler?'

Mamma sniffs. 'She is a liar.'

I've never heard such a word on my mother's lips; truly, it has all the novelty of the word *scientist*.

Throughout the rest of our stay, I look for the elderly white-haired lady, but do not see her again. I find myself nonetheless returning, over and over, to the question of my Aunt Augusta Leigh. If she really is a liar, as Mamma claims, then it must be proved or disproved. Somehow.

Mary Montgomery, I know, would advise me to think no more of this matter. But – as much as I love Mary, and respect her advice – I don't know if I can do that. Why is it so important to discover the truth, if I can? Firstly, because I do not *know* the truth. Wanting to know should be justification enough. (After all, this is what scientists do.) I have thought, over and over, about what might have taken place between my parents, and for a long time my theories have concerned the actions of my mother. I suspect her of wrongdoing of some kind – though I cannot imagine what – that she will not admit to. Somehow – through her coldness of manner, most likely – she alienated my father and drove him away. About this, and about many other matters, she has not told me the truth – and has counselled others to reveal nothing – because she is embarrassed and ashamed; she does not want the truth to be known by anyone. Those lapses into nostalgic sorrow and affection and her refusal to speak ill of him are markers of her guilt – easier, of course, now that he is dead.

So: it is more important than ever to discover whether Aunt Augusta is *truly* a liar, or whether she is something else – another victim, perhaps, of my mother's behaviour. Remembering that encounter, long ago now, on the Strand – the plump, kindly, almost stupid expression on the woman's face – I struggle to imagine her as a liar. On the contrary, she seemed well-meaning and gentle. She said something to me, but what was it?

'I sent a prayer-book to you for your birthday – two or three years ago. Did you never get it?'

Yes; it was something like that.

Buxton, Derbyshire
August 1834

The last morning in Buxton brings a letter from Mary Somerville. My heart leaps at the sight of her writing – but it's Mamma's name, not mine, on the folded writing paper. Over honey cakes and butter-rich brioches (the hotel breakfasts are awfully good) I wait for Mamma to finish reading the letter, and then ask her what the letter contains.

'I entrusted to her a certain undertaking,' says Mamma. 'She writes to let me know that she is doing all she can.'

Almost as cryptic as my dream of my father. 'That sounds intriguing,' I say.

Mamma elucidates: 'She is giving great consideration to the matter of a suitable husband.'

'For Martha?' I ask, referring to one of Mrs Somerville's daughters, but knowing that this is most probably not the case.

'No, you little goose!' Mamma smiles at me. 'For you.'

'Oh,' I say. 'Of course.'

Something heavy lodges itself in my chest, like a cherry stone trapped between the tines of a fork. We have been so busy travelling from place to place, viewing cotton mills one day and ribbon factories the next, staying in hotels and with friends, that I had more or less forgotten something that Mamma would never forget: that I am supposed, eventually, to find a husband.

It pains me to think that Mary Somerville, the most learned woman of my acquaintance, should be giving so much thought to my matrimonial prospects; I would much rather that we talked of geology and astronomy than marriage. Besides, the whole affair seems to me to be quite futile. *No one* is suitable enough for my mother. Either they are like Mr Knight, falling into the despised category of Renowned Fortune Hunter, or else they might be respectable enough in terms of character, but devoid of title. Or else they have a title, but not the right kind of title; or else they have the right kind of title but not enough money . . . Another type of man might on paper be quite perfect – but he is always the sort who is demonstrably disinterested in me, whether because of those rumours from a year ago, or else for some other reason entirely.

And sometimes there is nothing wrong with them at all – they seem in possession of all the required attributes – but Mamma simply decides, with all the single-mindedness of an obstinate child, that she doesn't like them.

It really does seem a hopeless business, and I tell Mamma as much.

'What, then, will you do with yourself, if you do not marry?' she says.

I pause, wondering what to say. Lately, I have been thinking rather a lot about what is possible if you are a young woman. My work with Mary Somerville – of whom there is an actual bust on display at the Royal Society, although it is a place that she is not allowed to enter, because she is a woman – sparked a certain amount of this thinking. Girls are simply not educated in the same way as boys; yes, we have tutors, or governesses – or we *might*, if we have parents who encourage such things, and have the means to secure them – but we do not go to school as boys do. We cannot go to university.

This has been weighing on my mind ever since my presentation at Court; if I were a boy (hard to imagine, but one can try), I would probably be thinking of going to university now, rather than hovering at the edges of dances and waiting to meet my husband. Without doubt, I would choose Trinity College, Cambridge – a place I've never seen, and so I can only imagine a palace-like configuration of turrets and pillars and walkways and courtyards. Trinity was where my father went, and where Mr Babbage went too. Mary Somerville and I have talked about it often – how Babbage made the acquaintance there of William Whewell and John Herschel, with whom he still corresponds most fruitfully today. What an extraordinary place it must be, with so many minds meeting, so many books to be read, so many ideas to be exchanged over a hearty breakfast . . . It was at Cambridge, I know, that Babbage decided that the old system of mathematical notation needed to be abandoned in favour of the newer, and more useful, continental method. I often think: if only Mary Somerville had been able to attend such an institution, rather than rely on the goodwill of her husband to permit her to study, what wonders that lady would have achieved!

Even Mamma, I realise, who has an excellent brain, would have done well there. I admire her educational establishments a good deal, and sometimes I do not give her enough credit for her own forward thinking. She *is* capable of it.

'If I could,' I say, 'I would go to university. I know that I *cannot*' – I go on hastily, for Mamma has opened her mouth to protest at the absurdity – 'but it does seem unfair, all the same.'

She does not protest, merely smiling at the edges of her mouth. 'Yes, Ada. I do perceive that it seems unfair.'

Still wanting to answer her question – as much for me, indeed, as for her – I think on, worrying a brioche into a puddle of crumbs as I do so. I *could* propose to become a governess; or a traveller, perhaps, like Mariana Starke, whose guide-book we used for our Grand Tour. I could be a harpist – although that might be a rather hubristic thought, at this early stage in my musical career . . .

Then there's my old ambition to become a writer. I haven't written many verses lately, or any stories either, but that isn't to say that I couldn't write if I wanted to . . . I always thought that I gave up on that particular dream too quickly. My father wrote; a little part of me constantly wonders whether I should do the same. But then again, there are aspects of myself that I know I have inherited from Mamma, such as my aptitude for mathematics. I do like mathematics so much; perhaps, if one were to combine it with writing in some way . . .

'I could write books,' I say, 'like Mrs Somerville.'

'You haven't the patience,' says Mamma flatly.

'I am learning patience!' I say, feeling wounded. She has *no idea* of the patience required when trying to address the mathematical knots that two young children can tie themselves into.

'What would you write about? Little romances, perhaps, such as you used to compose?'

I don't like her tone as she says this, although I don't know if she means to be unkind. I am remembering my dream again. *You* are *all kinds of things . . . There is more than one kind of poetical . . .*

It all comes together with the beauty of two magnets of opposite poles slotting into place. For so long, I have thought about writing; from early attempts at my own little verses with Miss Lamont, to stories with Miss Stamp and the fervent rereading of Lord Byron's poems . . . then, later, the realisation, thanks to James Hopkins' tutelage, that writing is not *only* about beautiful words and the pictures those words can paint, but, as he said, about the communication of ideas. Now it transfixes me (the idea coming upon me like a whirlwind of light and harmonious sound): I must write about *ideas* – scientific ideas! In journals, most likely, or . . .

or even in books . . . It would need a special name, this kind of writing: something to capture the essence of such a craft.

A moment later, I think of it.

'Poetical science,' I say.

'Ada, there is no such term.'

'But there *could* be!' My whole body is alert now; my hand shakes as I move my glass of milk away, lest I knock it over with my gestures. 'Mamma, I must explain . . . I mean . . . it's like . . . spiders' webs and rainbows.'

She is looking at me now with concern.

'I mean the transference of one idea to another,' I say. 'I mean connecting two different ideas in the way that a spider might spin thread across a garden . . . I mean the way that a rainbow looks quite different to the human eye – which I believe to be at the centre of its entire circle – to how it would appear elsewhere . . .'

'Lower your voice, Ada, please. People are staring.'

She is right: my voice has risen, out of my control, and at least two neighbouring tables have paused their own conversations to look over at Lady Noel Byron and her daughter. I stop, and force myself to drink some milk, just for the normalcy of the action.

'I'm sorry, Mamma,' I say, expecting the conversation to end there. Privately, I resolve to continue the discussion of *poetical science* with Mary Somerville. I am sure that she will understand, even if Mamma does not.

Then Mamma says something entirely unexpected. 'You ought not to set too much store by writing books,' she says.

'Why . . . what do you mean?'

'I wrote to Mr Murray, your father's publisher – oh, a long time ago, now – and gave him very specific instructions that on no account was he ever to publish anything written by you.'

This is a shock – and also *not* a shock – because here, as I have always known, is a woman who must be in control of everything. But even so, I am stupefied. 'Mamma,' I say, struggling to keep my temper, 'why ever *shouldn't* Mr Murray publish my books?'

'I don't expect you to understand,' she says inscrutably.

We are interrupted then by a waiter who comes with assiduous grace to clear our plates, and I bury the feeling that has risen unceremoniously in my throat – the hot, hasty, agonised-anger feeling that I so often associate these days with exchanges with Mamma. Our conversation passes to other matters, such as what each of us proposes to do this morning, but this latest revelation – proof, if ever proof were required, of her controlling, calculating nature – is one that I shall not be able to forget.

Fordhook, Ealing
September 1834

I do not show it (I have learned that there is little point in doing so), but in the days that follow our return to Fordhook, I am angrier with my mother than I have ever been in my life. Even my resentment of the Fury Days can't quite compare to the thought that, all this time, Mamma has known that I could never publish a book, even if I wanted to, because she has undertaken to *prevent such a thing from happening . . .*

When I am twenty-one, perhaps, whatever preventative method she has tried to ensure might cease. Yes: surely this could be true. And there are other publishers besides Mr Murray, I know. But I am so wounded by the knowledge of what she has done – writing to Mr Murray with her bald instruction – that I feel flattened, a feather-bed unceremoniously squashed by a stone elephant. She does not think me worthy of publication. Or else she cannot bear the thought of the life I might lead if I were to be a writer – the moral deviance in which I might indulge.

Or else: she is jealous. She cannot contemplate the thought of my doing something that she has not done herself.

Our daily Ealing life resumes – visits to Ealing Grove, the theatre, lectures and so on – and I fall into the pattern of it as best I can. I am outwardly monosyllabic and inwardly verbose, so much feeling stored up in my head that I feel I might burst from it. My dreams are blurred and vicious: spiders' webs ripped apart by savage winds, books shorn of their pages, rainbows drained of their colour. I don't believe that Mamma notices that I am unhappy, for all that I am very subdued. I bide my time. All the patience I acquired over the summer is finding its purpose.

I am sitting in the library when I hear the clop of hooves that betokens Mamma's departure. I have been reading – rereading, actually – Mary Somerville's book, *On the Connexion of the Physical Sciences*. I almost want to stay here and continue, for I am convinced that if I were able to digest the book in its entirety (it is very long) I might become a little bit more like Mary Somerville in the process. But I am equally minded to do what I want to do now, while Mamma is gone, and so I set the book down, promising to come back to it shortly.

Puff comes stalking up to the table in her funny, rickety, old-cat gait. (The Gosfords have lent her back to us, something that has pleased me more than I thought it would.) Puff and I greet each other with fondness. 'Now, Puff,' I say – and feel, for a while, like a much younger version of myself as I do so. 'I *must* confide in you. Where do you suppose Mamma would hide a prayer-book – a gift that was sent to me by my Aunt Augusta, but that she never allowed me to have?'

Puff yawns, exposing a row of still-sharp teeth, although she has lost a few over the years.

Stroking her under her chin, I say, 'Of course, she might have sent it back – but then if she did, Augusta never received it, and so I doubt that possibility. She might have thrown it away . . . but no. Mamma would never throw away a prayer-book. It stands to reason, therefore, that she must have kept it.'

I pick up my ancient cat and carry her upstairs, taking care not to be spotted by any of the servants and feeling grateful that the Furies are no longer a part of our household. Mamma is, conveniently, out at Ealing Grove, where there has recently been a new intake of pupils. Her bedchamber is not far from mine, but I haven't actually gone into it much, and I enter now half-hesitant and half-bold – an explorer of some jagged ice-strewn land, desirous of finding out new things, but perhaps a little unsure of the terrain. Set down on the threshold, Puff winds herself between my ankles, pleased to be adventuring with me.

Mamma's room is vast, yet stuffed with furniture. There are beechwood chairs, dressed in yellow silk, in a row against one wall. There's a pretty ebony dressing table, stocked with glass bottles and silver brushes. An enormous bed: preposterously so – I can just imagine Mamma stranded in the centre of it, like a gnat in a lake of milk.

There are plenty of books on the writing-desk but I do

not think that the book I am searching for will be anywhere but deeply concealed. I open drawers and doors, lifting things out, sifting through piles, always careful not to make a mess or break anything. The carved inkstand on the desk reminds me of the last time I did something forbidden, and how a puddle of ink (indelible blue-black) gave me away. I do not touch the inkstand. I prostrate myself on my stomach and peer under the bed, finding nothing but a single satin slipper that may possibly have been left by the previous inhabitant of Fordhook. There is a heavy rosewood box tucked away at the back of the cupboard – locked – and this draws my attention for some time. I shake it tentatively, trying to work out what is inside. It might be jewellery, but I don't hear a rattle; just the faintest shuffle of paper, like ocean-whispers. After some time, I put the box back where I found it. I do not think that it contains a prayer-book.

I am on the point of giving up when something extraordinary happens – if I still wrote stories (here I think fondly of dear Miss Stamp), I might write such a scene, rather than believe it could possibly actually happen. I am sitting on the floor in front of Mamma's wardrobe, looking among the shoes in their boxes, when sudden movement startles me: a flash of something dark and shadowy streaks like a comet from underneath the wardrobe in the direction of the bed. Puff is roused at once from her old-cat reverie, instantly a tigress, and before I'm even quite aware of what is happening, she has trapped the mouse between her paws and is toying with it rather unpleasantly.

'Oh, Puff – don't—' I say, then stop mid-sentence.

The cat-mouse scuffle has revealed something hithertofore unnoticed: a corner of the carpet has been flipped back, and there is a broken floorboard underneath. One that I have never seen before. Slowly, carefully, I press the flat of my hand against the broken board. Nothing. Then, working at the splintered edge with my fingertips, I try to lever it upwards. It is tricky to do. I change the angle, the weight of my hand, and suddenly the broken board shifts, rises, and I am able to pull it away and set it to one side. A good deal of dust has spilled out over the floor, but no matter; a shallow space has been revealed, and there – just as though this were truly a story in a book – *is the object I have been wanting to find.*

The prayer-book is beautifully bound and engraved with my name, in the most elaborate writing I ever saw. There is a note too, hidden in the folds of packing-paper. It reads: 'To the Hon. Miss Byron, with every kind and affectionate wish, from her loving Aunt Augusta. December 1830.' In pencil, but still very neatly written, she has added: 'With Lady Byron's permission.'

The discovery chills me: so my aunt was not lying. She did send the book, just as she says she did. Of course, she might still be a liar; about this incident, however, she was telling the truth.

'Well!' I say aloud to Puff, who is still pawing at the mouse (presumably now dead) in a lazy, disinterested way. 'And what do you make of this? Why was I never given this book?'

Puff doesn't respond.

If Aunt Augusta told the truth about the prayer-book, could it be that *Mamma* was lying when she said that Aunt Augusta was a liar? I have always regarded my mother as a scrupulously honest person – sometimes to her own detriment, for tact is not one of her qualities. But it *is* possible that she might be, if not a liar, then certainly someone who is making sure that the truth is as carefully hidden as this little wrapped-up prayer-book . . .

Yes. I can certainly believe that. How many times have I asked her questions, over the years, to which she has provided no answer?

I make a point of reading the book – not cover to cover, but thoroughly enough – before, with regret, I re-wrap it and stow it in its hiding place. I leave Mamma's room covertly, again careful not to be seen, and go back to my own room, where I sit and think for so long that I start to genuinely believe that I might have altered the shape of my skull from puzzlement, and that Dr Combe – were he to do a third reading of my head – would exclaim aloud in wonder at the physical transformation.

Wimpole Street, London
September 1834

Autumn comes, and those first chill winds bring with them a downturn in my mother's health. Or so she claims. Wanting more regular access to her doctors, Mamma decides to move the household temporarily from Ealing to Wimpole Street, right in the heart of London. Knowing that Mamma is concerned about my health – which she seems to view as an extension of her own, for the most part, unable to imagine me to be well when she herself is feeling unwell – I have gone to some lengths to persuade her that I am perfectly well. But this isn't true, and I don't know if I am really able to pretend anything to the contrary.

The prayer-book preys on my thoughts: I am sure that Mamma has lied to me about many things concerning my father, and she has deprived me of getting to know his relations. She has shrouded the whole of their marriage in such a cloud of secrecy that I can only believe that she behaved very badly indeed towards him. Sometimes, I decide that she hated him, and that, perhaps, by extension, she hates me . . .

Does that not explain almost every action she has ever taken? The long absences when I was an infant . . . The lessons that I was subject to from an early age; the harsh punishments and grudging rewards; the cold smiles and closed-down conversations . . . The Furies who watched my every move . . . The love affair they put a stop to with *no thought at all* for my feelings or desires . . . The way my mother always tried to change the way my brain worked – the people she enlisted to help her do so! Miss Stamp, and Dr King, and Mr Frend . . . those constant efforts to trammel, and organise, and contain . . . writing to Mr Murray to make sure that I could never publish a book . . .

It is making me ill, and I know that it is making me ill, and yet I cannot stop thinking about it all. I feel like Pandora, who lifted the lid so innocently on a chest full of evils and watched in helpless horror as they crawled out into the world. Despite an outward calm that I force myself to present – I do not want the attention of any of her physicians – I am ablaze with inward noise, a storm cloud of ill-contained feeling. I wake with headaches that remind me of my early childhood – hard slices of pain that seem to cleave my head in half. On occasion, I open a book and try to read, then realise that I cannot see the words because they have melted into a messy triplicate. I sleep badly. The summer-soft contentedness of the Buxton hotel seems to belong to a very distant past.

London
October 1834

'How are you finding London life?' asks Mary Montgomery.

It is October now. We have just been to the Royal Institute, where we attended a lecture on chemistry. Since the weather is fine, we are walking now across St James' Park, talking of the lecture at first, and then about London life in general.

'I am glad to be in town,' I tell her. 'There is more to see, and more to do.'

'But you must look on Fordhook as home, and miss it.'

I bite my lip, withholding a surge of bitterness. I don't know that I think of anywhere as home nowadays; how can I? Sometimes I think about telling Mary how I feel – my theories about my mother, what happened between my parents, *everything* – but there is so much to tell, and for all that she is a mentor of mine, she is foremost my mother's friend. It would not be safe to tell her, and I do not think that I would feel better if I did. Sometimes I feel as though there is so much feeling walled up inside me that it wouldn't be safe for anyone around me if I were to let it out.

The worst of my theories – the one I hide inside the

smallest, darkest compartment of my soul – is that my mother is actually responsible for the death of my father. The principle upon which this is based is the scientific one of cause and effect: she treated him with coldness and sought to control him; he was unable to live with her in those circumstances; wanting to be free to write his verses, he was forced to flee the country rather than subject her to a humiliating public separation with both parties living in England; with no one to look after him but a single valet, his health suffered, as anyone's would if they were living alone abroad.

And then, as a consequence, he died . . .

No: I will not share this with Mary Montgomery. I blink, forcing the thoughts somewhere deep inside myself. Then I say: 'Mr Babbage and Mrs Somerville are both in London, and I am glad to spend more time in their company. And yours too, of course, dearest Mary.'

The leaves are every shade between umber and gold. Fire colours. The sky is a warm pinkish orange in the late afternoon. Nature's secrets are there to be discovered, if only one can find the key to open each little mother-of-pearl box. A carriage rattles by; three young men, all elongated elegance, nod to me and Mary as they pass. We are not walking quickly, and yet I suddenly find that I am breathless. Not wanting to let Mary know that anything is wrong, I press a hand to my side and hope that my energy will be renewed. But before long I have slowed to a halt. Mary urges me to sit down on a bench; I do so. My head is the weight of a planet; I let it fall into my hands, leaning my elbows on my knees.

'Ada,' says Mary Montgomery. 'You are not well.'

'I am as well as I ever have been,' I say.

'Your mother doesn't think so.'

'My mother,' I say, 'knows nothing about me. Nothing, nothing at all.'

I look sideways at Mary Montgomery, expecting her to react strongly to this statement. But instead she is looking ahead, perplexed. Then she reaches for my hand, helping me to my feet. 'There's something happening,' she says. 'Are you well enough to walk?'

Looking around, I realise that she is right – people are moving more rapidly past us than they should be, some streaming *towards* whatever is taking place beyond the park gates, and others streaming just as quickly away from it . . . I can hear shouts and screams, as though some kind of monster has risen out of the Thames.

'Ada, no. It could be dangerous,' says Mary.

'I want to see,' I protest, setting off in the same direction as the crowd. I look at the sky and realise that the colour is no mere sunset: something is on fire. Something big.

Mary calls to a tall gentleman who is coming the other way so fast that he is likely to knock someone over or trip in his haste. 'What is happening, please?'

'Fire! The Palace of Westminster is on fire,' he shouts, already vanishing into the gathering shadows.

We emerge from the park into a glut of people that seems

to be growing larger by the second, like a swarm of flies around rotting flesh. A chain of soldiers keeps them from getting too close. A rose glow – what I had mistaken for an early sunset – emanates from the top of the Palace of Westminster, where Parliament gathers. Slipping free of Mary, I move to join the crowd. Two ladies of middle age are clutching each other's arms and wailing dramatically, like a Greek chorus. Little boys with grubby faces dart to and fro, trying to get past the soldiers, uttering exclamations of wonder and glee.

A chimney-sweep is chuckling to himself. 'They'll let us sweep it now, I'll bet a guinea,' he says.

'Oh, what flames!' says someone, bursting into half-hysterical laughter.

And suddenly I am laughing too – horribly, ecstatically – and the laugh that is falling from my throat sounds nothing at all like me, Ada. I am transformed, a fire-banshee, squealing with all the ecstasy of a demon that feeds on fire. I laugh so much that my ribs ache from it, and only when Mary reaches me and digs her fingers into my arm do I realise that I am also crying.

She propels me backwards, out of the crowd. 'Ada! What are you thinking? People will notice you—'

'They won't notice anything but the fire,' I say, but I am already feeling embarrassed and guilty; I shouldn't have done that; I shouldn't have allowed her to see me do it. But oh, those flames, those extraordinary flames . . . and the vault of heat that rose from the palace roof . . . I felt something – something indescribable – as I stared at those flames: it was as though a part of me were also on fire, and I felt all the pain of it, and the ecstasy also. I was Ada no longer; I was a phoenix, reborn, reforged . . . it was as though a little valve had been opened inside of me, releasing something that had been trapped for the longest time.

If my father had been there, surely, surely he would have laughed, just as I did, at the sight of it.

My lips move automatically, reciting another of his poems, one fit for the occasion:

> 'The palaces of crowned kings – the huts,
> The habitations of all things which dwell,
> Were burnt for beacons; cities were consum'd,
> And men were gather'd round their blazing homes
> To look once more into each other's face.'

Dorset Street, London
November 1834

Mr Babbage is holding another of his Saturday-evening soirées. I am attending with Mary Somerville; Mamma is not present (her health, she says, will not allow it). There is the usual mix of people, including a young journalist named Mr Dickens whom I have never met before. Mr Dickens writes political sketches and has covered many aspects of the recent electoral campaigns. I enjoy talking to him – he has rather piercing brown eyes, and gives the impression of deep thought. Our discussion becomes political in nature.

'What do you think of our new Prime Minister?' I ask him.

'Mr Peel is a *fine old English gentleman*,' he replies, in wry tones that suggest he might think quite the reverse.

Mr Babbage interjects. 'Know him fairly well. He gave me my first lot of funding. Doubt if he'll give me any more.'

'Oh, but he must,' I say. 'He has to understand what you are hoping to do.'

'Miss Byron,' says Mr Babbage. 'Sometimes I fear that *I* don't understand what I am trying to do.'

I know Mr Babbage well enough now to understand that these sudden dips and peaks in his spirits are to be expected. I say: 'Tell me about the new machine you are thinking of designing.'

He brightens at once. 'As you know, I was more or less exhausted by everything to do with the wretched Difference Engine – been feeling that way for some time, what with all the disagreements with Clement, my machinist, and the government and everything else.'

I nod sagely. I have always wondered whether Mr Babbage's manner goes against him, sometimes. He isn't the most tactful of men, and he doesn't always explain himself well. But now isn't the time to say such a thing – and, indeed, I couldn't possibly. I wait for him to continue.

'Then, in July, I started scribbling. Thinking, as you know, of a machine that could tabulate all functions – using every operation – and that could take the results of a calculation and *utilise those results* for further calculations. You see?'

'Yes . . . yes,' I say.

'The image that comes to me is of a serpent eating its own tail,' says Mr Babbage. 'Or an engine laying down its own railway tracks, perhaps. Come. I shall show you.'

Mr Dickens is deeply engrossed in conversation with someone else. With great, purposeful strides, Babbage leads me to the room next door. I've never seen such a sea of paper as now lies before us – great rectangular sheets littering every surface, each covered in a dense language of sketches and shapes and notations. I move closer to the sea of paper; my hand moves independently of my body, reaching out to touch the edge of one of the sheets. Yes: I can see that this machine represents something very different indeed to its predecessor. He has written labels here and there: leaning even closer, I see the word 'mill', and also the word 'store' – on the face of it, strange terms indeed, but even as I am thinking this, something at the back of my mind begins ticking over . . . for surely they remind me of something?

'The machine will be powered by steam,' says Mr Babbage. 'I've found a new machinist. A Mr Jarvis. He will, I hope, be of great assistance to me. And less troublesome than Mr Clement. At the moment, Miss Byron, there is a good deal that I *do not see* . . . But I have a vision of some kind of device – something you could insert, somehow, into the machine to instruct the engine to perform whatever function is required. I can't quite conceive of *how*, but I do think that . . . yes, it *might* be possible.'

'What will you call this machine?' I say.

'I mean to call it the Analytical Engine.'

There's a lump in my throat; clearing it with a small cough, I say: 'May I . . . may I borrow some of these plans? I'd like to study them, if I may.'

Mr Babbage looks surprised but not displeased. 'Why,

280

certainly, Miss Byron. I have duplicates of many of them. Take . . . let's see, now – yes. Take this paper, and this one. I believe they will give you as accurate a picture as anything could of what I have in mind.'

When we leave the Dorset Street house, I am clutching a folder, stuffed with papers and tied with string. 'Oh, Mrs Somerville, I could *weep* with excitement,' I say. ''To be given Mr Babbage's plans for his new machine . . . why, I feel very honoured indeed.'

'And so you should,' says Mrs Somerville. 'He thinks very highly of you. And so do I.'

'Really, it is the most delicious problem,' I say, as the carriage transports us down the dim gas-lit street. 'Mr Babbage knows *what* he wants to achieve, but not *how*; he believes in himself, and in all that might be possible – and that . . . that is probably enough. I once had a governess who told me how important it is to believe in yourself. Oh, I am sure that he will manage it one day. It's the . . . *magical potential* of the thing that's so exciting, isn't it?'

I am babbling now; not making very much sense.

'Ada,' says Mrs Somerville, 'I noticed earlier that you ate no dinner.'

'I couldn't,' I say. 'I just don't feel hungry these days.'

'Perhaps, but the body needs food. You are becoming very thin.'

This comes as a surprise, and then not a surprise. I have noticed that my hip-bones stick out more than they used to;

my wrists are bonier, and my face is more gaunt. I *have* noticed; I just haven't cared.

'You will forgive me, Ada, if I give you some advice,' says Mary Somerville. 'As one who is concerned for your well-being, I wonder if you should not give me those plans for safe-keeping. I shall return them to Mr Babbage.'

'But why?' I say.

'Because I think this is all too much for you,' says Mary Somerville. 'You would do well to leave these intellectual pursuits for now, and do earthlier things instead.'

'Such as what?'

'Such as needlework.'

'Oh, I cannot think of needlework now,' I say, but I make an effort with my voice, trying to speak at a more regular pace. I do not want Mrs Somerville to report anything untoward to Mamma. I thank my companion for her consideration, and by the time we part ways, I believe that I have convinced her that my equilibrium is fully restored.

But as I climb the stairs to my bedroom, the folder under my arm, I am shaking.

Wimpole Street, London
November 1834

'Good news, Ada,' says Mamma, approaching with a letter in her hand. She has the rosy, excited expression that she usually reserves for mutton chops, or syllabub. 'Mary Somerville has written.'

'Does Mr Babbage make progress with the building of the new machine?'

'There is no mention of Mr Babbage,' says Mamma. 'I wish you would abandon your fervid interest in it. I have seen you studying the plans – yes, don't pretend that you haven't been, Ada.'

A wave of heat rises in me at once. I wish she wouldn't do that – notice everything. It makes me feel as trapped as a prisoner in Mr Bentham's *panopticon*.

'I must tell you that you are mistaken in your excitement about it,' Mamma goes on. 'I am convinced, as I've told you before, that Mr Babbage's ideas are fundamentally unsound. And now: do you not wish to hear what Mrs Somerville has to say?'

'Very well,' I say, resigned, wondering inwardly how she

could possibly have decided that Mr Babbage's ideas are unsound.

A dramatic in-breath. 'Mary's son Woronzow has identified a suitable candidate for marriage!' Squinting down at the letter, my mother reads aloud: ' "*Lord King is an old acquaintance of mine from our Trinity days. He will inherit large estates in both Surrey and Somerset. A tall, genial young man, some eleven or twelve years Ada's senior, he is quite clearly in want of a wife.*" '

Tall, genial. Is he a giraffe? I am already resolved to hate him. I am very fond of Woronzow, and consider him to have excellent judgement, but he is doing this for Mamma, and not for me. This Lord King will no doubt please the mother and not the daughter; I do not see how he can possibly appeal to both of us. Also, if he is so clearly in want of a wife, why does he not already have one? There must be something wrong with him. I amuse myself by thinking about what this might be.

'There are other points in his favour too,' Mamma goes on, 'apart from wealth and title, both of which are a *sine qua non*. Firstly, he has lived abroad for some time, and thus will most likely be quite unaware of the . . . Events of Last Year.'

Mamma has always such difficulty referring to the affair with James Hopkins that her awkwardness about it has infected my own memories of it, and I am now as acutely embarrassed about the shed and everything that went on there as she is herself.

'What else?' I say. An ache starts behind my eyes, the

kind of hollow burning sensation with which I am only too familiar these days.

'She ... Now, where did ... ah. Here it is. *"The most amusing part of all this is that Lord King cherishes an affection for all things Byronic that borders on a delightful obsession. Not only does he possess a charming portrait of himself done up to look as much like Lord Byron as possible (which he commissioned while working for Lord Nugent in Corfu); he has also named the fields of his Surrey estate, Ockham Park, after Lord Byron's poems. I have spoken to Woronzow at length and we both agree: it is impossible to imagine a suitor who could be a better match for our precious Ada than William King."* '

My mother lays the letter down and beams at me. 'Well?' she says.

I am momentarily without the faculty of speech. Then I say: 'There is no possible way that I will be prevailed upon to marry this man.'

'Ada, but why not?'

'For a start, he sounds like a collector. Fields named after my father's poems – a portrait in the Byronic style – he ... he sounds like the kind of man who would lie in wait for Harriet Siddons outside Drury Lane with an autograph-book!'

'Oh, don't be absurd—'

'He wouldn't be marrying *me*; he'd be marrying an Idea.' The longer I think about it, the more furious I feel – that Woronzow, an intelligent man, and Mary, the woman whose intellect I revere more than anyone's – could have come up with this. 'He would build a glass case for me, and prod me, and show me off, and watch me for all traits Byronic – those very traits which *you* have always discouraged in me – and assess me for moral deviance, *just as you have always done.*'

Mamma is staring at me, face drained of its rosiness. 'I have never – oh, Ada, be reasonable . . .'

But I do not feel reasonable, because this is not a reasonable proposition. I stamp my foot, on the verge of tears. 'You never wanted me to turn out like my father, but now that a suitor has appeared who worships him you are all enthusiasm! It is baffling, Mamma. Oh, I have never understood your attitude towards him – never! Nostalgic one moment, and buttoned-up like an oyster the next . . . he must have found you as maddening as I do. Why, I have an aunt you've never let me meet – who sent me a prayer-book that you wouldn't let me have . . .'

She looks quite astonished by this.

I go on, reaching blindly for words: 'And . . . and cousins besides. Do *they* hate you too? As much as he must have done? For he went an awfully long way to get away from you, didn't he?'

'Don't . . . don't speak to me like that, Ada,' says Mamma. She is very pale now; she looks angry, but there's something else in her face that I am struggling to read.

'I have always been convinced of it: you drove my father away,' I say, very quietly, knowing at the same time that I have surely gone too far.

We stand facing each other. I am taller than she is, now. I never noticed that before.

I say, more quietly but with all the conviction that I can summon: 'I will not meet Lord King, and let that be the end of it.'

Then I walk past her and out of the room, heart thundering against my ribs so loudly that I'm sure she can hear it, and leave her standing there, robbed of speech, the letter dangling helplessly from her fingers.

Chelsea, London
November 1834

For the first time in the history of our acquaintance, I do not want to visit Mary Somerville: not after this news of a possible husband. But I cannot undo the arrangement we have made without seeming rude, and so, feeling a despondence that I do not usually associate with our time together, I arrive at her house in Chelsea just as it is growing dark.

'Oh, Ada, did your mother tell you?' says Mrs Somerville, greeting me at the door.

'She told me,' I say, rather woodenly.

'It *is* very exciting news,' says Mary, looking at my face. 'No, Ada, it is. You need a husband. Someone who will look after you.'

'As though I am incapable of looking after myself!' I burst out.

'It is not that you are *in*capable,' says Mary Somerville. 'Don't be so melodramatic. You and Lord King are an excellent match; I am convinced of it.'

To my relief, however, we move on to other matters. I have brought with me Mr Babbage's plans. 'I want to consult with you about these diagrams,' I say to Mrs Somerville. We are sitting side by side at the small parlour table. 'Mr Babbage has written some notes here, and here, in the margin, and I would like to ask you about them.'

Mrs Somerville calls for a servant to attend to the lights, and when more lamps are lit in the damp little room and the fire built up into a diminutive furnace, I show her the notes. 'Look,' I say. 'Babbage has identified two parts of the new machine, which he calls the "mill" and the "store". These terms fascinate me. He is clearly referring to the cloth industry, is he not?'

Mary Somerville frowns. 'Ye-es,' she says. 'Yes, I think he must be. But I don't quite see . . . It is a little fanciful, is it not?'

'I don't think he is being fanciful,' I say. 'It is just a metaphor – a comparison. He is using one system to describe another – quite a useful thing to do, since the new system – the one he is designing – does not yet exist.'

'I suppose so,' says Mary, squinting at the page. 'The mill is where the actual work is done.'

'That's right. The computations, if you will,' I say, speaking rather slowly, though my heart seems to be beating unnaturally fast. 'The store, meanwhile, is where the materials are kept. Babbage is proposing to separate the actions of the machine in order to facilitate its working.'

'I don't know that he is even sure what he is about, you know,' interjects Mrs Somerville. She still seems doubtful.

'And this large barrel here, he refers to as the "drum",' I say, pointing to the centre of one of the diagrams.

'Yes: this is the bit he is struggling with. It would turn very much as a drum in a music box would, but in order to be able to control so many operations it would have to be a barrel of incredible size.'

Together, we puzzle over the designs, teacher and pupil, while the darkness grows beyond the window and mists gather outside that are so thick that I know I would not be able to see my own hand in front of me, if I were to venture outside. But inside it's as warm as a fur-lined cloak – so much so that I find myself feeling dozy, dreamy, almost drifting off to sleep sometimes. Mary gets up once to fetch a book from a shelf, and then again to put more coal on the fire. I prop my head on my hands, feeling the ridge of my cheekbone, and allow my eyes to close . . .

At first, I see those round white stones on the dream-beach where I met my father. They are less like soup plates now. Their edges are ridged. They darken; now they are neither plates, nor stones, but wheels. Cogwheels, interlaced, and set in a circular shape around a central barrel – a drum – that continuously turns, slowly but with great regularity. It is the Analytical Engine at work – I know this, even though I cannot see every part of the machine clearly. It is like a gigantic music box: the sound that comes from it is harp music initially, before it turns into the kind of jaunty brass-band tune that one might hear at the seaside. I walk closer, and see that something is coming out of the machine – it looks like paper, but it is thicker; perhaps canvas, or . . . no. It is woven silk, in one of the most exquisitely coloured compositions that I have ever seen: calculations, and equations are written upon it, and, at the centre, in letters the colours of the rainbow, one word: *imagination*. This is not a machine that will simply calculate figures; it will be able to create too . . .

'Ada! Ada, my goodness – Ada!'

Mary Somerville seizes me by the shoulders just as my head falls forward; her touch startles me, pulling me out of my reverie. Suddenly I am back in the small, damp room, aware of the fire grumbling in the grate, the scratch of the upholstered chair against my legs.

'The loom,' I whisper. *'It is like Mr Jacquard's loom.'*

'No, don't talk,' says Mary, fussing her hands about my face, my hair. 'Come – come and lie down.' She manoeuvres me over to the chaise longue; I protest, but she won't hear any of it. 'We'll wait for Somerville. He'll be back soon.'

'Mr Babbage,' I say hoarsely. 'I must speak to him. I saw . . . I saw something, Mary . . . his machine, the Analytical Engine . . . it could be used for music, you know, and – oh, even the creation of pictures and words and poems . . . magical potential . . . they are not just numbers, you see . . .'

'Not numbers? Ada, what are you talking about? I can't understand you.'

'They are not just numbers,' I say again. 'The numbers represent – oh, anything, anything at all . . . but he must use his knowledge of the *loom*. That is how it will work.' I dissolve into a fit of weak coughing.

'You are not making any sense, my dear,' says Mary Somerville. 'Try not to talk now, until Somerville arrives.'

'Oh, Mary, I *saw* it . . .'

But she has gone from the room.

'Her eyes were fairly staring out of her head,' I hear her saying to Dr Somerville, out in the hall, when at last he arrives. 'I've never seen anything like it. She's really not herself; she must go home at once, and I am going to write to Lady Noel Byron to recommend an immediate stop to her studies. No; she is not herself at all.'

Not myself: it's the last thing I think about; that I, Ada – according to Mary, at least – have ceased to become Ada.

If not my Ada-self, with my Ada-brain, who am I?

When Dr Somerville enters the room, with Mary fluttering at his side, I sit up and ask him exactly that.

I lie in bed for a week, two weeks, four. I am quite unable to do anything else.

Mamma stays by my bedside most days, although we do not say much to each other. Sometimes I feign sleep, not wanting, or not able, to talk to her. She reaches for my hand occasionally, and I allow her to hold it, wishing that I had not said as much as I did to her, the last time that we actually spoke. I hear her draw in her breath, with the sharpness of one who has just had some kind of unpleasant realisation. I wonder if she is going to speak, but she never does.

My nineteenth birthday comes unnoticed, and Christmas

too, and the New Year thereafter. We return to Ealing, and I barely register this change of scenery, although Nanny Briggs will tell me afterward that Mamma felt that the country air would suit me better, and she was probably right.

I prefer my bedroom at Fordhook to the low-ceilinged Wimpole Street chamber. I think that I do breathe more easily. Doctors come and go; I hear them muttering instructions to Nanny Briggs, and to Mamma. I hear occasional snippets: *nervous exhaustion ... mustn't trouble herself further with intellectual pursuits, not for a long time . . .*

I hear Mamma say: 'The fault, if there is any fault, must be mine.'

Sometimes I dream: the shapes of Babbage's engines form in my head with all the transparency of ghosts; I see scenes from my childhood, and from recent years. . . pebbly beaches, and spa towns with their iron-rich waters . . . carriage journeys and roadside inns . . . conversations with Mamma over a hundred brioche-laden breakfasts . . . and dance-cards, and unsuitable suitors who care for nothing but my fortune . . . People whispering in corners of crowded rooms.

'That's Ada Byron, my dear. Oh, but she has grown so pale and ill.'
'Whatever can the matter be?'

I think of my father. Strains of his verses come to me with all the suddenness of rainbows that burst out unpredicted from cloudy skyscapes. I see him: slightly lame, loose-trousered, shouldering his caged squirrel or scrawling a letter at his desk. I think of him on his deathbed too, sending me his blessings.

Sometimes I cry, and they are not the harsh, hollow tears that I wept when I watched the Palace of Westminster burning – more a muted dribble of tears that leave patches of moisture on my sheets to surprise me, later, as I sleep. For I do sleep; I sleep more than I have ever slept in all my life.

Sometimes I do not dream at all.

Fordhook, Ealing
March 1835

Spring has not quite come to Fordhook, but it feels as though it might. Each morning I awaken to new strains of birdsong, and although the little buds are not yet sprouting all over the garden, I know that they will. There's almost the smell of new earth, new beginnings; quite soon, over in the allotments, they will be turning the soil, taking out the hard bits of flint, readying the ground.

I, Ada, am feeling better every day. And every day I regret my outburst to my mother a little more deeply. Do I really think that my father hated her – and that his sister did too – just because I sometimes hate her for all the ways in which she strives to control me? But it is *wrong* to hate her – even a little, even sometimes – when she only thinks of my well-being. Oh, I think about it so much that it twists and tangles up like yarn in my mind, and I can't separate the strands. And after a while the person I hate most is myself.

If only, I think . . . If only she'd told me *more*. I wouldn't have been so deeply in the dark; I wouldn't have had to scrabble together the little snippets that people gave me, struggle to assemble a puzzle whose picture was permanently obscured . . . I think of all the people I questioned, over the years: Miss Lamont, Miss Stamp, Signor Isola, Harriet Siddons, Mary Montgomery, James Hopkins . . . People who either knew very little or who did not feel qualified to speak freely on the subject of my father, or of my parents' marriage. And then there were all my questions to Mamma herself – perhaps nine-tenths squashed like unwanted beetles under a grinding heel, with only one-tenth answered, and begrudgingly at that. Why couldn't she have answered more than just one-tenth?

But there's not much chance of that now. Mamma is delighted that I am better, of course, but there exists between us now a barrier. Perhaps it has always been there, unnoticed. I am not sure.

But I now find myself horribly concerned that I have broken something in our relationship, something that cannot be fixed.

Mamma finds me in the garden one morning after breakfast.

'I am going back to Tunbridge Wells, Ada, for a short while,' she says. 'I think it best that you remain here, so that the doctors can continue to attend you.'

'Of course.'

She doesn't even want me to accompany her, I think; that's how badly I have hurt her.

'There is to be a ball at Weston House, in Warwickshire, in May,' says Mamma. 'Lord King will be there. I have written to Lady Phillips, who will be hosting the ball, saying that you hope also – health permitting – to be present.'

'I don't . . . Mamma, I have said that I do not want to meet this man.'

'I know, Ada. I heard what you said. I heard everything that you said.'

This last is uttered with such a sad cadence that I feel another twist of guilt.

'Mamma,' I say. 'I don't hate you. I have never hated you.'

She doesn't respond to this. Instead, she winces sourly, as though she has bitten the inside of her cheek. With eyes half-closed, she mutters: 'I have left something for you on your writing-desk. But . . . but wait until I have departed, please, until you look at it.'

I do wait, although I can barely manage it, impatiently checking the progress of the carriage from the drawing-room windows until it has vanished from sight. Then I more or less run upstairs, aflame with curiosity – even though I know from past experiences that she has most likely left me something that is either educational or improving, something designed to make a difference to my mind or my character.

But there's a chance – the smallest, slimmest chance – that this time she has left me something else.

And I'm right.

On my desk lies a rectangular box – made of rosewood, I believe, with tortoiseshell inlays. I have seen it before, I realise, on my hunt for the prayer-book. It looks as though it might contain jewellery, or else sewing materials, but when I lift the lid (it is unlocked, though there is a keyhole), I find neither jewels nor needles. Instead, there are letters, several stacks of them, tied with coral-coloured ribbon. One, right at the top, is loose, and addressed to me. I carry the box and its contents over to my bed and climb onto the counterpane. I lift out the stacked letters and place them carefully to one side.

Then I open the one that has my name on it.

Dear Ada,

I must confess that I was most deeply aggrieved by the way that you spoke to me on that Friday afternoon – the day that you fell ill. That you could have believed me to have been so hated by my husband – your father – and by his relations too, was so hurtful that at first I resolved simply never to speak of the matter to you again. But, on reflection, I perceived that you had come to your own conclusions – as wrong as they were – because you had not had any other means of knowing the truth. That truth is now something that I will try to share with you. It is a prospect that I have avoided all these years, and certainly I did not feel able to tell you in person. It is easier for me to write this down, and I hope that it will also be easier for you to read it. I hope too, that once you have finished, you will understand a little better.

I shall start at the beginning. I met Lord Byron in March 1812, at Lady Melbourne's. Childe Harold *had just been published, to great fanfare and acclaim. As you know, Byron was famous – more so, perhaps, than anyone of his ilk at the time. When I told you, Ada, that I was intrigued by him, that was quite accurate. Only the previous month he had made a speech in the House of Lords, in which he voiced his passionate opposition to a punitive new bill that proposed the death penalty for some poor stocking-makers who had smashed some looms in Nottinghamshire. Clearly, then, he must have had a strong desire to do good – as much as I myself did. But my cousin Lady Caroline Lamb had called him 'mad, bad and dangerous to know' – it was on everyone's lips at one time or another – and indeed I did perceive an arrogance, a lofty pretension and a tendency to sneer at all and sundry. How, then, could these different tendencies be reconciled? It was intriguing, and I found myself wanting to learn more.*

Each time I met Byron, I found something new to interest and enchant me; he was, I suspected, the type who suffered from changeable moods and fits of temper; I also thought that he was rather proud. But beneath those fits of temper was concealed a shyness, and I was convinced, as I have said, that he was a good person. I began to realise that I was in love with him. Other suitors – and there were plenty – I dismissed with haste.

In September of 1812, Byron proposed – not in person, but through my aunt, Lady Melbourne. And here, Ada, I made a dreadful mistake, for I refused him. Yes, I thought myself in love, but I had certain reservations, not the least *of which being that I was aware (for he had written so) that he thought me <u>perfect</u>. I couldn't bear to witness his disenchantment on learning that I was far from perfection. I refused, again through my aunt, and offered friendship instead.*

Now, here is something that I did not know at the time. Lady Melbourne was not only my chaperone but also a close correspondent with Byron himself. The interest she showed in my burgeoning affection for Lord Byron was due in part to her own wish to put a stop to the affair that was taking place between Byron and her daughter-in-law, Lady Caroline, who was married to her son William. It pains me to remember my innocence – the evenings I spent in Caroline's company, not knowing how infatuated she was with the man I was so naively discussing. (You met her once, at the theatre – you were quite young, perhaps nine or ten.) The affair was, it goes without saying, the height of unsuitability, and would have caused a scandal had it gone on much longer. A woman with a curious lack of moral restraint, Lady Caroline would – apparently – dress up in the uniform of post-boy in order to gain access to his rooms, and slashed her wrist with scissors in an attempt to regain his affections. But of all this I knew nothing.

I thought often of Lord Byron. Almost half a year after the proposal, I saw him again at a ball. I was relieved to meet him and hoped very much that we would now be able to forge for ourselves a friendship. He was unattached (an affair, again of which I knew nothing, with Lady Oxford,

300

who was married, had recently ended) and was spending a good deal of time with his half-sister Augusta, who had come to stay with him.

In August of 1813, I took it upon myself to write to him myself, rather than use my aunt as a go-between. I asked only that we could be friends. We wrote to each other often. And what letters they were! Whatever my pretences were – to both Byron and to my own self – the reality was that I was even more in love than ever after only a few months. I was very young, Ada, and very naïve. I did not know how I might elicit from him a second proposal of marriage, having rashly rejected the first. In the end, I did something out of character and invited him, in April 1814, to stay with my family at Seaham. No answer came. I waited in an agony of emotion. Finally, in a rare fury, I wrote to him, saying that he and I were in no way compatible as characters. This, for some strange reason, worked wonders. Byron proposed. At last! My friends and family approved whole-heartedly of the match, although it is true that some had reservations. I also received a letter from Byron's half-sister Augusta, offering her congratulations.

When I saw him – when he finally arrived at Seaham – I had not seen him for over a year. I observed that his manner was distinctly odd; I took it for shyness. It was a difficult two-week visit, but by the end of it I was hopeful for the future, and excited to become his wife.

We were married three months later at Seaham. I have told you a little of the simple ceremony. I did not tell you how

Byron behaved as soon as we were alone together in the carriage on the way to Halnaby, where we would spend our honeymoon.

'You ought to have married another,' he said, between bouts of fitful, toneless singing.

He later pretended that this was a joke, but I did not think it a good one.

At Halnaby, he insisted on sleeping alone. (Forgive me, Ada, if this is a picture too rich in detail, but now I have begun to tell the story, I feel I should not omit such detail.) On one occasion, I did join him, and he cried out, in the middle of the night, that he was surely in Hell. I had never known a person so changeable: sweet-natured one moment, frighteningly morose the next. He alluded to 'evils' in his past; several times, he told me that we should never have married. My maid saw that I was unhappy, and urged me to return to my parents. I could do no such thing. My loyalty was now to my husband. And besides, there were times – plenty of times – when we were quite content together. I was determined to make a success of the marriage. And, Ada, I loved him.

Our visit to Six Mile Bottom was very much at my own instigation: I wanted to get to know the half-sister of whom my 'B' was so fond. But as soon as we had reached the house, not far from Newmarket, I realised I had made yet another mistake. The pendulum of his moods had swung back again – inexorable as ever – and he was at his most contemptuous, his most disdainful. I felt that I both bored and antagonised *him; nothing I could say pleased him, and at the same time I felt that I was being all the things that would irritate him most – righteous, didactic, all the things that you, Ada, dislike too – and yet was unable to stop myself.*

Byron made it quite clear that he preferred the company of his sister. I was desperately unhappy. Not long after, I realised that I was pregnant.

You have asked me about your birth, and I believe – for you are as observant and sensitive a young person as I could ever have hoped for – that you have noticed that I am often sad on your birthday. Well, perhaps when I tell you of the circumstances of that birth you will understand why. By the time of my confinement, your father was most grievously in debt – he could seldom control his spending. His health was not good (he was taking regular doses of both laudanum and calomel, neither of which agreed with him) and his moods were most terrifying in their mutability. One night, I sat up in bed, alert to the sound of shots being fired! Tiptoeing down to investigate, I found my husband smashing soda bottles with a poker. When you were born, his first question was whether or not you had been born dead. I began to convince myself that Byron was mad; that he was not responsible for his actions. But responsible or not, he was beginning to cause me to fear for my life – and for yours too. And so, I left him, on the morning of the 15ᵗʰ of January. You were six weeks old.

At the time, I still believed that he __was__ mad, and that – with care, and in time – he could be nursed back to health.

*I wanted so much for this to be the case, for the alternative –
a separation, and all the outcry that such a thing would
entail – was worse. But the doctor found no evidence to
suggest madness. And then I learned something about my
husband that I had not known previously. Not only had
there been several affairs during the short course of our
marriage – with theatre actresses, mainly; but Lady Caroline
Lamb also told me – not without a certain amount of
malicious glee – that Byron's affections towards his sister,
Augusta, might well be more than mere fraternal feeling . . .*

*I hesitate, Ada, as I write this now, for I can hardly bear
for you to think the worst of him, even as I seek to set things
out for you as plainly as I can. Could it possibly be true?
Byron often told me he had committed some kind of grievous
act, but I had never known to what matter this alluded.
Could the private jokes and close connection that he and
Augusta shared mean something more than the bond of
siblinghood? There were rumours too that he meant to have
you kidnapped, and brought up by Augusta. Those rumours
terrified me.*

*I have always been a woman of somewhat rigid ideas;
that is one thing that I understand quite clearly about myself.
I had married Byron – for better or worse – and marriage
is a bond that is not to be severed. And yet, Ada, in the face
of everything that I now feared to be true, I made a decision.
There would be a proper separation – a difficult thing, yes,
but, as far as I knew, the right thing for all concerned. The
lawyer I saw, and to whom I revealed much more than*

I allowed my parents to know, agreed with me. I resolved to say nothing in public – to hold my head high – and to survive the scandal of our separation.

And there was a scandal indeed.

Now do you see why I reacted so strongly to the events of two years ago? I have lived through it. Idle whispers leave long traces. The public, though fickle, seldom forgets. I sought to distance myself – and you – from the attention that Byron seemed to attract with every move he made. As for myself, I would try to do some good in the world; I would give you the best education that I could procure, and hope that neither of us would be tarnished by an association to England's more famous – and most notorious – poet.

You may ask why I have continued to love and to speak well of him, as I have done, all these years. Firstly, Ada, I have done so for you: you were the product of a union that was not as successful as I had hoped that it would be, but that was not ever your fault. Secondly, he had good qualities too, so many of them – and it was those qualities – his talent, his humour, his vivacity – that I longed to preserve in my memory. It is possible to love someone who has caused one pain. And when he died – when I was no longer afraid of fresh scandal, or that he might arrange to have you kidnapped, or slander me – it was easier still to remember only the good things. As for Augusta, I promised Byron that I would do my best to protect her and her reputation. That I have tried to do, although the thought of you getting to know her, as you asked to do, was more than I could bear.

I know that at times you have found me cold, unforgiving, and overly controlling. If I were to make a list of my own characteristics, good and bad, I would not hesitate to list such attributes. But you must know how deeply I love you, Ada. Everything I have done has been for your own protection.

Your very loving,

Mamma

It is dark by the time I close the lid for the last time, and set the rosewood box on my bookcase, out of sight, where I will guard it until she comes home. The other letters I will leave until later. They will serve as corroboration, I know that; but in a way, I don't require any proof. What she's told me is enough, because my mother is not a liar, and what it will have cost her to set down this history in such detail for me to read is unimaginable. There's a bloody dent in my lower lip; I must have been constantly biting it as I was reading, without being aware of it. I am also very cold.

Fully clothed, I climb into bed, my mind – as always – full of *pictures*. The lean, lame poet, on his face a sneer that my mother interprets as a facade. Mamma at her writing-desk, noting down her thoughts and impressions of Lord Byron; composing verses that she hopes will please him; writing letters that betray her growing desire. A cry of anguish (remorse?) in a marriage bed. The pretty, plump face of Augusta Leigh. The sound of soda bottles shattering as my mother lies awake, so close to the time of her confinement. A bitter-white morning; Mamma stealing out, frost crunching beneath her boots, with me wrapped in a blanket in her arms.

Why did she never tell me all this? But even as I'm framing the question, I know the answer.

The last thing I think before I go to sleep is how much I do love my mother.

And if she really wishes for me to meet Lord King, then I will do as she asks, and meet him.

Epilogue
(17 months later)

London
August 1836

When I return to the steps of the Royal Academy, my husband is waiting for me. 'Little Bird,' he says.

'Oh, Crow,' I say, folding myself into his embrace.

They are funny names we have chosen for ourselves: I never thought of myself as a bird – indeed, I used to think that the Furies had a flustered, chickeny aspect to them, and I had little to say about the Furies that was in any way complimentary. But now I am Little Bird, and I like it: it makes me feel warm, and settled; curiously domestic. And William *is* a crow: a long-legged, dark-feathered, beak-nosed raven, with the sweetest temperament I ever knew.

'Where did you go?' he asks, kissing the top of my head.

'For a walk. Did you see? There was a rainbow—'

'I did see it, and I thought of you.'

My husband takes my arm and helps me up the steps. Ever since our son was born, three months ago, I have found stairs terribly difficult. (I found pregnancy difficult as well, and the birth too – but I dote on my son. We asked Mamma

308

to name our firstborn child, and she did. The name she chose? *Byron*.)

'I am all excitement to see the finished portrait,' says William. 'Do you like it?'

'Well enough,' I say evasively. 'You may make up your own mind when you see it. I am curious to know your opinion.'

If I had not known all that I did know – all that Mamma told me in that long, heartfelt letter that must have cost her so much to write – I think I would have endeavoured to sabotage my first meeting, at the Weston House ball, with Lord King. Certainly, it crossed my mind. When I came downstairs at the Phillips' elegant mansion wearing a dress that I had myself sewn – and my skills in that department leave much to be desired – Lady Phillips looked at me somewhat dubiously.

'Of course, she is known for not taking much care over her appearance,' I heard her saying later on to one of her daughters; I had no doubt that it was I to whom she was referring.

That slighting remark had a very odd effect on me. I realised, suddenly, what I was doing: consciously or not, I was undermining my mother's every effort to ensure that I made a good match. I was trying to punish her, but really I was only punishing myself. I no longer wished to punish either of us. Chastened, I rushed back to my rooms and found something much more attractive to wear. I also attempted to tidy my hair. The looking glass showed an Ada who was, at the very least, trying.

'You will have to do,' said Ada-in-the-Glass.

When I returned, Lord King had arrived. I felt shy; as shy as I had done when I first met James Hopkins in the entrance hall at Fordhook. I had no intention other than to see what this young man, who had studied with Woronzow at Cambridge, had to say for himself; I knew he was a collector of Byronic things, and I resolved – as much as I could – not to hold this against him, for I had not been best pleased by the idea of becoming a collectible item. I did not think I would fall in love with him almost within the first few minutes.

But I did.

We stand side by side in front of the *Portrait of Lady King*, commissioned by Mamma to mark her delight in our marriage, and painted before my pregnancy was showing.

'Well,' I say to Lord King, much as Mamma said to me, not two hours ago. 'And what do you think?'

My beloved Crow takes his time before replying. I wonder, as I watch him in his own silent appraisal of Painted Ada, what he sees, and what he is thinking. Is he perhaps remembering how I first appeared to him, at Lady Phillips' ball? At that moment, he was looking, perhaps, for something that would remind him of the poet he had long idolised. There I stood, rather awkward and inwardly scowling, in the drawing room of Weston House. Did he see something

Byronic in me (perchance my father's air of awkwardness that so often came across as disdain)? In a way, it does not matter what he saw; and even if he did see something Byronic, I am convinced that what he really saw was Ada herself. We danced a quadrille, and then another. He was a great deal taller than me, and yet the discrepancy in our heights did not affect the quality of our dancing in any way. As we danced, we talked; I had never heard anyone speak with such passion for a place as Lord King spoke about his estate in Porlock. He described the way the wooded hills rose up from the coastal path with the look of a small, enchanted child.

'I must show it to you,' he said, suddenly almost shy at the realisation of what he had said. But I was thrilled by such a wish on his part, and echoed it with my own willingness to accept the invitation.

I am glad – I am so very glad – that I did.

'Darling,' my husband now ventures, having concluded his appraisal. 'What, er . . . what has the artist done with your jaw? I *like* it, but it's not a true reflection of you.'

'I knew you would notice.'

I am about to explain the provenance of my too-large jaw when I see Mamma advancing, alight with pride. For her, this is the pinnacle – the highest possible Ada-achievement there ever could be. I hang, Painted Ada, in the Royal Academy, painted by a woman who is renowned for her skilful portraits. My jaw has been enhanced by Mrs Carpenter's painterly skill; I am Byronic – which will be pleasing to my husband, who loves all things Byronic so well. Or rather: I am just Byronic *enough*. I am no longer a Byron in name; now, I bear my husband's name; and it is an old title, just the right kind, just as Mamma wanted.

'Come, William, my dear,' she says. (She adores my husband, which suits me very well, for he has an ease of manner which permeates our own mother-daughter relationship too, nowadays.) 'I want you to meet Lady Gosford.'

She leads him away. I am left with the portrait. It feels odd, indulgent – embarrassing, even – to continue to stare at this version of myself, especially when I have frankly admitted that I do not like it. I never cared much for looking in mirrors, either; I think perhaps I dislike the idea of myself being fixed, permanent, immutable – as the portrait suggests that I am. I also think that I dislike the portrait because I, Ada, have never truly known what it is that I really want to be. All my life (for as long as I can remember), I have flirted with identities – assumed them as I once threw an old shawl around my head and pretended to look more like my father than I did, in the gallery at Bifrons. I have delved into music, pondered verses, longed to write books, been desperate to invent and design . . . I have been a student, and also (briefly) a teacher. Now I have a new identity, of wife and mother.

The question I really want to ask, and have been asking myself all afternoon, is this: is it over?

Am I fixed in my Ada-ness now, just as Mrs Carpenter says I am?

*

312

The people come and go. Mamma, of course, cannot be tempted away; she is enjoying herself too much. William drifts here and there, finding a watercolour of Lynmouth Harbour (very close to his Somerset estate in Porlock) that fills him with homesickness. The afternoon wears on. I grow tired, and start to wonder whether we can reasonably leave.

I notice Mr Turner standing beside his picture of Venice, holding forth with such vehemence and verbosity that I long to hear what he is saying. Mary Somerville – clad in an extraordinary orange gown of some oriental design – comes to say hello, clasping my hands in her own and saying how very, very glad she is that I made a full recovery.

'Why, you seem a different person altogether, my dear,' she says, almost conspiratorially. 'Oh, that awful, gloomy afternoon is one that I'll never be able to forget. You frightened me, Ada! Chattering of goodness knows what, and with *such* an expression on your face.'

'I am sorry to have scared you,' I say, meaning it.

I don't say it to her, but I think afterward (as I have thought on occasion, since the time when I fell ill) that I have studied many patterns in my life – in music and mathematics especially – but I never gave much thought to the patterns in my own life. The habit I had, that Mamma compared to the flight of a butterfly, was a bad habit. Or rather, it was a habit I couldn't control. It felt so wonderful, at the time, to flit and fly between passions, but (as I once commented to Miss Stamp) the wing's up-swing had, perforce, to swing down again, and each down-swing was worse than the one before.

When Mary Somerville counselled me to find balance, she was right, though I didn't want to hear it.

And the person who was most right of all – as much as I am loath to admit it – was my mother. She may not have done the right things, always, in her attempts to help me, but she certainly did them for the right reasons.

I do see that now.

Just as I am turning away from Mrs Carpenter's portrait, and quite ready to depart, one last person greets me. He looks the same as ever; a little greyer, perhaps, at the temples, but no less leonine.

'Lady King.'

'Mr Babbage!' I can scarcely contain my delight.

'I came,' he says, 'very much hoping that you would be here today. How is your son?'

'He is remarkable.' I am about to enter into a long list of the infant Byron's accomplishments – I really do want to, but I don't. 'Tell, me, sir – what progress has there been with your Analytical Engine?'

'Oh, you don't want to speak of that here, surely.'

But I get the impression that these words are a pleasantry. 'Surrounded by these works of exceptional skill and dexterity,' I say, taking his arm, 'I can think of no better place. Tell me, did you come up with a solution for the problem of the over-large drum? I still have your diagrams, you know. In fact, you must come to stay with us at Ockham Park, or else at Porlock. You'll like William's house overlooking the Bristol

314

Channel – so secluded and high up; you'll be able to do all sorts of wonderful work . . .'

We stroll through the gallery, hearing nothing now of the babble of the crowds, the excited exclamations as friends and acquaintances meet and greet; in the distance, I am amused to see Mamma and William, strolling in a similar fashion, their heads inclined at angles towards each other. My mother looks perfectly content, and so does my husband, and I am glad of this.

'I have, just recently, made quite an interesting breakthrough as far as the Analytical Engine is concerned,' says Mr Babbage. 'It has to do with – of all things . . .'

'The Jacquard loom?' I say, suddenly remembering again that strange sequence of visions I had in Mary Somerville's Chelsea parlour.

A look passes between us. He is older than me, and no relation of mine, and really, I do not know him terribly well, and yet in that moment, I am sure, Mr Babbage and I are thinking *exactly the same thing*.

'Yes!' he says. 'The loom! The punched cards, you know, instead of the drum . . .'

'It *will* work,' I say. 'I'm sure of it.'

'There are further investigations to be done—'

'Of course, but what fascinating investigations they will be.'

He begins to speak, relating to me his newest ideas, his voice low but distinct against the echoing voices, and I listen, offering a nod here, a thoughtful interjection there. It is a conversation, a true one. Mr Babbage *will* develop this extraordinary machine of his – I have never been more certain of anything in all my life – and I, Ada, will do everything in my power to be of assistance.

On we go through the Royal Academy, past lush-leaved landscapes and stern-browed bronzes, until the portrait of Ada is forgotten, and far behind us.

Afterword

Family life and health

Ada's story did not end there. Her marriage to William was a happy one, especially at the start. The couple had two more children, Anne Isabella (after Lady Noel Byron) in 1837 and Ralph Gordon in 1839. The births were difficult, and although Ada doted on her sons, Byron especially, she found her relationship with her daughter harder to manage. Ada had a difficult mother-in-law too: Lady Hester King, by all accounts an unpleasant woman, exploited a loophole in William's father's will in order to deprive him of property that was rightfully his. In order for Ada to be differentiated from her mother-in-law (they were both known as Lady King), Annabella petitioned for a change of title, and so William and Ada became the Earl and Countess of Lovelace in 1838.

In 1841, Ada discovered something that shocked her to the core: her father's incestuous relationship with his half-sister Augusta had resulted in a child, Medora. This young woman was currently in Paris, and Annabella – ever-drawn to those things that reminded her of Byron – had taken her under her wing. Ada travelled to Paris at once and instantly liked the charming, dark-haired Medora, who bore a close resemblance to Ada herself. Unfortunately for both Ada and Annabella, Medora was a manipulative liar; after two uncomfortable years of Medora's presence in England, both were relieved when she was dispatched back to France with a stipend from Annabella.

Ada and William's often-diverging interests (he became increasingly preoccupied with architectural expansions of his properties, while she continued to devote herself to music and mathematics) meant that they drifted apart to some extent. Ada attracted a certain criticism for her fondness for riding in Hyde Park in the company of married men (a scandalous thing to do at the time), and it is likely that she had an affair with a man named John Crosse from about 1844 onwards, although their correspondence was destroyed. In the late 1840s, it seems that Ada became interested in horse-racing, and lost vast sums of money, possibly in her attempt to find a mathematical way to game the system. In spite of whatever difficulties the couple faced, William remained supportive of Ada and was proud of her work with Charles Babbage.

Ada's health, as had been the case in her childhood, was never good. She has been retrospectively diagnosed with conditions ranging from manic depression to anorexia to an allergy to alcohol; several sources have mentioned her 'staring' facial expression which does suggest some underlying medical cause. No explanation has ever been found for the long illness, once thought to be complications arising from measles, that left her bedridden in 1829.

Ada became very ill with cholera not long after her daughter was born, and she often subjected herself to strenuous dieting. There remained a clear correlation between the intensity of Ada's academic work and her periods of sickness that needed to be carefully monitored. Towards the end of her life, she took large quantities of laudanum and opium in order to manage her pain.

The Analytical Engine

Ada's keen desire for intellectual development remained with her throughout her life. She set up two schools in 1838 that followed the same model as her mother's (her relationship with Annabella had, by this time, grown easier) and she also continued to correspond with Mary Somerville.

When Mary moved abroad in 1838, a new tutor entered Ada's life in the form of the mathematician Augustus de Morgan. A wise and patient teacher, de Morgan encouraged Ada to consolidate those basic skills that she had not yet developed before moving on to the harder concepts she wished to learn. Spurred on by her fortnightly studies with de Morgan, Ada wrote to Babbage in 1841, offering to help him with the ongoing development of his Analytical Engine.

In 1842, she did something that would prove to be quite extraordinary, and whose repercussions are still felt today.

The Italian engineer Luigi Menabrea had written an article in French about Babbage's as-yet-unbuilt Analytical Engine. Ada, who spoke French fluently, was commissioned by a friend of Babbage to translate the account into English. Her translation was an excellent one, but she did more than simply translate the article: she added various 'Notes' (labelled 'A' to 'G') at the end of it, which were longer than the article itself. In these, she carefully explained the difference in function between the Difference and Analytical Engines: 'while the Difference Engine can merely *tabulate*, and is incapable of *developing*, the Analytical Engine can either *tabulate or develope* [sic]'. Speculating that the Engine could be used, for example, to compose 'elaborate and scientific pieces of music', Ada unmistakably foresaw, and tried to express, how the needs of a changing world could be served by the limitless functions of Babbage's invention – far beyond what Babbage himself had imagined. This contribution was a credit to the working of a highly unusual mind. In addition to this, Ada constructed in 'Note G' a chart that demonstrated how the Engine could theoretically process a sequence of fifty Bernoulli numbers – a sequence of rational numbers that plays an important role in many mathematical computations; it is this chart that is recognised as the world's first example of a machine algorithm – the same kind that is used in computing today. She also noted that the Analytical Engine was not capable of thinking for itself – something that Alan Turing, the founder of modern-day computing, would describe as 'Lady Lovelace's Objection' (he disagreed with her on this point). The notes were not signed, merely attributed modestly to 'A.A.L.', but after the publication of the article in 1843 the identity of the author became widely known.

In demonstrating her deep and intuitive understanding of the potential of the Analytical Engine, Ada was also showing how greatly she wanted Babbage's plans to be understood, and valued, by others. Unfortunately, Babbage did not always present his ideas in the most useful or engaging way. An interview with Prime Minister Robert Peel in 1842 in which Babbage had sought more money for the Analytical Engine had gone disastrously badly. Ada, who had a better understanding of the niceties of social interaction, and knowing that Babbage's personality was not, perhaps, ideally suited to promoting his inventions, wrote to him and effectively offered to take on the role of a modern-day agent or publicist. Babbage refused; perhaps he simply disliked the idea of her taking on such a role, or else perhaps he did not fully understand the import of what Ada had contributed in her 'Notes'. In spite of his refusal, their relationship continued on good terms, and he referred to her in a letter as his 'Enchantress of Number'. It is very tempting to speculate about what might have happened in the history of computer science had Babbage accepted Ada's offer.

Death and Legacy

In 1851, Ada began showing signs of uterine cancer. The disease rapidly worsened, and although she tried to remain positive in outlook, she became more and more frail and was in a great deal of pain. Soon she was bed-bound. Charles Dickens visited her at least once, and read to her the deathbed scene from his novel *Dombey and Son*.

On the 27th of November 1852, Ada died. She was thirty-six – the same age that Byron had been at his own death. At her request, she was buried with her father near his old home, Newstead Abbey – a place she had visited for the first and only time in 1850.

Annabella, who would live until the age of sixty-seven, continuing her philanthropic work, made a memorial for her daughter at Kirkby Mallory, on which a sonnet of Ada's, entitled 'The Rainbow', is inscribed. Ada, whose fame in her own short life had been due to her famous father, died with no knowledge of how she would later come to be remembered. Her vital role in the development of computer science has only become recognised relatively recently, after Babbage's own contributions were rediscovered in the 1970s.

Ada is now, and increasingly, given the credit that she always deserved. She has been commemorated in books and television programmes of all kinds and for all ages, both factual and fictionalised. There is a computing language, ADA, named after her. And the second Tuesday of October is a day in which the achievements of women in Science, Technology, Engineering and Mathematics are celebrated yearly. It is known as Ada Lovelace Day.

Author's Note

Once, long ago, I went to a lecture on classical art in a university library. I remember almost nothing about it – only one thing, in fact: being handed by the lecturer a small pottery triangle called a *sherd* – a fragment of some antiquated amphora. It had a pattern on it, I think, or else part of a picture. With the sherd was a slip of paper with printed instructions; one instruction was this: 'Imagine out from your sherd'. I don't think I fully understood, at the time, the invitation to take a single piece of a picture and try to *imagine out* from it, to construct in my mind the rest of the picture, the whole artefact – and not just what it looked like, but what it was used for, and who made it, and who used it – from just one tiny fragment. But although I forgot everything else about that day, there was something about that phrase, and its invitation to *imagine out*, that I never forgot, and, oddly, in the writing of this book, I have thought about that strange little line many times.

From letters and maps; from old books and new ones; from pictures and diagrams and newspapers and poems, I have tried to take what is known, or what has been written, about the girl who was born Ada Byron and died the Countess of Lovelace and *imagine out* from there. As far as I can tell, there should be some kind of middle plane between fiction and non-fiction where books like this one must sit; no matter how deep my research, or how wide my reading on topics such as the history of the allotment movement in England, or the educational principles of Pestalozzi, there would always be questions that could only be answered by *imagining* (which also feels to me quite appropriate, given Ada's own imagination) what might have happened.

Sometimes, therefore, I have added scenes or details that *might* have taken place, but most probably didn't – for example, there really was a Roman shield on display at the public library in Geneva, but we can't be sure whether Ada and Annabella visited it; and although the Houses of Parliament did burn down in October 1834, there is no evidence that Ada watched it happen. It is doubtful, though not impossible, that Lord Byron ever visited Kirkby Mallory Hall, but I loved the idea of his favourite tree so much that I decided it ought to have a place in the story. Not much is known about Ada's affair with her shorthand tutor – indeed, we can't know with certainty whether the young man *was* in fact her shorthand tutor; we do know, however, that the shorthand tutor's contract was terminated rather abruptly, which does suggest that something untoward went on. That tutor's name was William Turner, but due to the high frequency of Williams in *I, Ada* already, and the fact that so little survives about this entire chapter of Ada's life, I have rechristened him James Hopkins. Ada's 'Numbers' poem that she shares with Miss Stamp before their Grand Tour is fictionalised.

Lastly, I do not think that Lady Byron would ever have written to her daughter a letter such as the one at the end of the book, in which she explains so much of what took place in her marriage; but if she had ever decided to write such a letter, the details it relates are, I hope, accurate ones. The other letters in *I, Ada* (with the exception of the note in the prayer-book sent by Augusta) are, likewise, products of my imagination.

Acknowledgements

I want to thank my editor, Chloe Sackur, for suggesting to me that I write this book and for being so encouraging at every point of the process. I also want to thank Louise Lamont, my agent, for her endless enthusiasm and thoughtful contributions. As always, huge thanks to the fantastic team at Andersen Press – Klaus Flugge, Paul Black, Charlie Sheppard, Sarah Kimmelman, Rob Farrimond, Jack Noel, and also to Sue Cook for the copyedit. My dear friend Paddy Thomas – we have spent over a year talking about Ada Lovelace and I still don't think we have finished our discussion. I am in awe of your knowledge and generosity. Thank you to Nick Turner and the boys and girls in Creative Writing Club for listening to some chapters as they were written. Thank you also to Jennifer Johnson, Imogen Russell Williams and Laura Lankester for reading early extracts, and to Birdie Johnson for her help. I am grateful to the many authors, historians, researchers and writers whose books I consulted while writing *I, Ada*, and especially to Miranda Seymour for taking the time to answer my very specific questions, and offering advice. Thanks are also due to the staff of the British Library in King's Cross and the Weston Library in Oxford; to the Society of Authors for their wonderful support; to Lord Lytton and Katy Loffman at Paper Lion for allowing me to quote from Ada's work; to my family and friends; and to Calum and Jonathan, for everything.

JULIA GRAY

Nora has lied about many things. But has she told her most dangerous lie of all?

There's a new art assistant at Nora's school, and he's crossed a line. Nora decides to teach him a lesson he won't forget. But not everything goes quite to plan, and Nora finds an escape with her new friend – chaotic, unpredictable and jealous Bel. As events start to spin wildly out of control, Nora must decide where her loyalties lie – and what deceits she can get away with.

'Intense, psychological, gripping;
The Talented Mr Ripley for YA'
Anna McKerrow

'A gripping, smoothly executed
psychodrama . . . I genuinely could
not stop reading this: a treat for
teens and above' *Literary Review*

9781783446919